DO NO HARM

ALSO AVAILABLE BY DAWN EASTMAN

Dr. Katie LeClair Mysteries

Unnatural Causes

Family Fortune Mysteries

Pall in the Family

Be Careful What You Witch For

A Fright to the Death

An Unhappy Medium

DO NO HARM

A Dr. Katie LeClair Mystery

Dawn Eastman

CROOKED
LANE

NEW YORK

Published in the United States by Crooked Lane Books, an imprint of The Quick Brown Fox & Company LLC.

Crooked Lane Books and its logo are trademarks of The Quick Brown Fox & Company LLC.

Library of Congress Catalog-in-Publication data available upon request.

ISBN (hardcover): 978-1-68331-787-6
ISBN (ePub): 978-1-68331-788-3
ISBN (ePDF): 978-1-68331-789-0

Cover design by Melanie Sun
Book design by Jennifer Canzone

Printed in the United States.

www.crookedlanebooks.com

Crooked Lane Books
34 West 27th St., 10th Floor
New York, NY 10001

First Edition: December 2018

10 9 8 7 6 5 4 3 2 1

For Anna

1

Not yet, but soon. He felt it like a shimmer in the air.

He stood by the window, peering out from behind the drawn curtains, flicking ash from his cigarette into an empty cat food tin resting on the table nearby. His nose wrinkled at the smell. Should have rinsed it out first. Another in a long list of should haves.

The cat, possibly attracted by the odor, skulked into the room. It weaved through his ankles, leaving long white hairs behind on his jeans, and meowed imperiously. He leaned down to pet it and it skittered away. The cat had moved in during his ten-year absence from his childhood home, and it saw *him* as the intruder.

He stood and fumbled for the lamp. Clicking it off, he squinted into the dim evening light. Darkness arrived earlier than when he'd first returned home a month ago. Then, it had seemed that summer would linger forever, and that he had his whole life ahead of him once again.

He clicked a beaded bracelet through the fingers of his

left hand, bringing the cigarette to his lips with his right. Drawing deeply, he listened to the quiet crackle of the tobacco as it burned. He'd promised himself all those days, weeks, years in prison that he would appreciate the little things when he got out. Like a peaceful smoke in his own house, a clear blue sky, and the freedom to go anywhere. But on this evening, as the light faded and the streetlights flickered on (except for the one near his house—broken three weeks ago and still not repaired), he watched with the twitchy anxiety of prey waiting to be found.

He heard his mother's heavy tread in the kitchen and quickly stubbed out the cigarette.

"Eugene," she said quietly. A slight quiver in her voice gave away her concern, and he tensed with guilt. "Are they out there again?"

He shook his head. "Not yet."

She took several more steps into the room. "We have to do something. You have to go to the police."

He spun from the window, feeling anger replace the self-loathing. It felt better, more powerful, even if it was directed at the only person who had ever been kind to him.

"I'm not going to the police." He clenched his fists and turned back to the window. "Do you think they care?"

He'd dutifully reported the first acts of vandalism. GO AWAY spray-painted in red on the garage door had been hard to deny. After the officers had taken his statement, they'd said they'd look into it. Nothing had changed. He'd quietly painted over the letters and waited. Next was a classic: a bag of dog shit on the porch. Then, a rock thrown through the front window. Finally, a snarky map slipped under a dead bird on the hood of his pickup truck. The map had dark red arrows showing all the ways out of Baxter, Michigan.

Just as he drew breath to apologize for snapping at his mother, he heard it. A scraping sound outside. Someone sneaking along the side of the house. Before he had time to think, he ran outside to confront the intruder.

2

D r. Katie LeClair was running late. As usual. She stepped out of room one—a baby with colic whose mother was at the end of her rope—and glanced morosely at the line of plastic green flags that greeted her. Each one signified a patient who was ready to be seen and had probably been waiting longer than Katie would have liked.

She'd been working with Emmett Hawkins and his son, Nick, at the Baxter Family Medicine office since the previous summer when she'd finished her residency. Baxter was about twenty minutes west of Ann Arbor, and Katie had spent some time at the clinic during her training. She loved the way Emmett practiced an old-fashioned kind of medicine. The pace was slower and the pay was lower than Katie could have found in a bigger city, but she thought it was the perfect fit for her.

She moved to the next room and pulled the chart from the plastic bin affixed to the door. The file was thin. Katie flipped it open, hoping it wasn't a new patient wanting a physical. That would push her into the rescheduling zone and she hated to do that.

She released a sigh when she saw it was only a suture removal. She read the brief intake information. *Eugene Lowe: 30 years old, 5' 10", 140 pounds, blood pressure 124/82.* The patient had been to the ER a week earlier. She noted Matt Gregor's signature at the bottom of the ER note.

She knocked and entered the room. The clinic building was old and the decor had not been updated in years. Someone had decorated in the eighties or nineties, which meant all the rooms had wallpaper borders running along the edge of the ceiling. Her patient had been put in the "kid" room, which had a brightly colored train border. The man sat hunched in the patient chair. He held a bracelet of light-pink beads in his hand and ran it through his fingers like a rosary. His dark hair was thinning on top, which didn't help disguise the large ears that stuck out from the sides of his head. He wore big round eyeglasses that covered the top third of his face. Thick black eyebrows almost met in the middle, and Steri-Strips covering a long cut over his left temple accessorized the lenses. Yellow-and-purple bruising betrayed a healing black eye.

Holding out her hand, she said, "Hello, I'm Dr. LeClair."

He reached up and took her hand lightly, not meeting her eyes. "Eugene Lowe."

Katie sat in the wheeled stool by the low counter. She opened the file and pretended to read its meager contents. Something about his demeanor and the healing bruises had set off alarm bells. She wanted to question him, but he seemed skittish, as if he would bolt any minute. "It looks like you need to get rid of some stitches." Katie flipped the file closed and turned back toward him. "Have you had any problems with the wound?"

He shook his head and studied his shoes. The beads clicked through his fingers.

"This won't hurt nearly as much as getting them put in. It just feels like a slight pinch."

He nodded.

Katie sighed inwardly. He wasn't much of a talker, and it made her feel like a camp counselor trying to jolly the shy kid into having fun. But she didn't need to get his whole story today. That was one of the things she loved about family medicine. There was time to get to know the patient.

She stood and gestured at the exam table. "Do you want to lie down on the exam table, or sit there?"

"I won't faint on you," he said. "I'll sit here."

Kate pulled the metal tray on wheels over to where he sat. She used sterile gauze and saline to wet the Steri-Strips and loosen the scab.

"What happened?" she asked. She pulled up on the knot of a suture and slipped the scissors underneath.

"I ran into a door."

Katie glanced quickly at his face. No one ran into a door and got this kind of injury.

"I haven't seen you here before. Did you just move to town?" Katie tugged a suture free and placed it on the tray.

"You could say that," he said. "I grew up here, but I just got back recently." He'd stopped clicking the beads and held his hands clasped tightly together—was he worried about the stitches or about her questions?

Katie had removed the first two sutures and tried to distract him by keeping him talking.

"Where were you living?"

"Jackson Prison."

Her hands hesitated, and he glanced up at her.

"They didn't tell you?"

"No," Katie said. She moved on to the next suture, not meeting his eyes. His guarded manner began to make sense.

He laughed bitterly. "You must be the only person in town who doesn't know."

"I'm new here myself, so sometimes I'm out of the loop on the gossip." That was an understatement. She felt like she was always playing catch-up. Katie pulled the last stitch free and set down her instruments.

She put a regular bandage over the cut and slid the tray away. "You may have a bit of a scar there. It should fade in time."

"Most things do," he said. He began fidgeting with the bracelet once more.

Katie placed a hand lightly on his shoulder. "Mr. Lowe, I'm not sure what kind of health care you received in prison, but if you'd like to come back for a physical or if you need anything else, I'd be glad to see you."

The beads stilled again. Eugene Lowe looked Katie in the eye and held out his hand. "Thank you." This time his grip was firm and warm.

* * *

Katie moved to the next exam room in line and pulled out the file. She smiled. Miss Betty Simms was one of her favorites.

She knocked once and opened the door. Miss Simms was in the paisley-border room, Katie's least favorite. Katie was surprised to see Mrs. Peabody sitting in the guest chair while Miss Simms sat on the exam table.

"Hello," Katie said. She extended her hand to Miss Simms. She was a small woman with silver hair pulled up into a bun and the rounded physique of someone who enjoyed sweets. "It's good to see you up and about."

Mrs. Peabody made an indistinct noise, and Katie turned and shook her hand as well. Tall and thin, Mrs. Peabody wore her hair short and spiky with a pink streak on the right side. Both women were in their eighties. They wore velour tracksuits and brightly colored running shoes. Mrs. Peabody's tracksuit was the exact pink of her hair streak.

"I'm surprised to see you together today," Katie said. Usually the ladies made appointments at the same time but took separate exam rooms so they could fill Katie in more thoroughly on their concerns for each other.

"Well, I didn't need to be seen today," said Mrs. Peabody. "But I wanted to be sure Miss Simms didn't try to convince you she's totally recovered." She lowered her voice, as if it would make a difference in the tiny room. "You know how she is."

"Agnes, I'm sitting right here and I can hear you," Miss Simms said. "Honestly . . ." She shook her head and rolled her eyes at Katie. Katie suppressed a grin, feeling like she was in a room with a teenager and her mother rather than two retired teachers.

Two weeks earlier, the ladies had been driving their Vespas just outside of town to enjoy the fall colors when

Miss Simms had hit a rock and tumbled off the scooter. Fortunately, she had been going only about ten miles an hour at the time and had escaped the accident with a few scrapes and a sprained wrist. Considering her age, Katie was grateful the accident hadn't been worse.

"How are you doing?" Katie asked.

Miss Simms sniffed and sat a bit straighter on the table. "I'm doing much better now." She held her wrist out for Katie to examine.

The swelling was gone, as was most of the bruising. She had good movement in the joint.

"Are you still wearing the brace?" Katie asked.

"Yes," said Miss Simms.

"No," said Mrs. Peabody.

Katie stepped away from Miss Simms so she could look at both women at the same time. "Which is it?"

Miss Simms sighed. "It gets in the way. My knitting production is down and we're heading into the holidays." She shot a glance at Mrs. Peabody. "*And* I don't think it helps."

Mrs. Peabody gestured at Miss Simms as if she were Exhibit A in a court case. "I told her to keep it on until you say it's okay, but will she listen? No."

"I think if you're to the point where it gets in the way and you don't have pain, you can probably stop wearing it." Katie addressed herself to Miss Simms. "We don't want the joint to get stiff or for you to lose strength in that hand."

Miss Simms smiled and shot an I-told-you-so look at Mrs. Peabody. Mrs. Peabody crossed her arms and looked away.

Miss Simms leaned closer to Katie. "Dr. LeClair, I hope you don't mind me asking, but did I see Eugene Lowe in the waiting room earlier?"

Katie thought that if anyone else had asked her that question, she would have said, "I don't know, did you?" But that would have been like kicking a puppy.

"It was," Katie said. "Do you know him?"

Both women nodded vehemently. "We both taught him in our classes," Mrs. Peabody said.

"I think it was just before I retired, maybe a year or two," Miss Simms said. "And then, of course, there was all that trouble with him during his senior year."

Mrs. Peabody nodded. "He was such a sweet boy. I couldn't believe it when he went to prison."

"He told me he's just been released," Katie said. "Why was he in prison?"

"Oh, my dear, of course you wouldn't know," said Miss Simms. "We forget that not everyone has been here forever. He was convicted of murder."

3

"Murder?" Katie said. Katie knew very well that murderers could hide in plain sight. That lesson had been brought home six weeks before when a patient's presumed suicide had turned out to be murder. But when Eugene had said he had been in prison, she'd assumed tax fraud, or maybe he was a hacker or an identity thief. Murder had not entered her mind.

"Yes, dear," said Miss Simms. "We were all just as shocked as you. It was around this time of year."

"Halloween," said Mrs. Peabody.

Miss Simms nodded. "It must have been twelve or so years ago. He was found standing over the body of a dead girl."

A quiet tap sounded at the door. Katie's signal to wrap things up. There were some patients that could take up the whole clinic time if you let them. Katie and her nurse, Angie, had a little code to move things along if necessary. She glanced at her watch.

"I'd really like to hear more about this," Katie said. "Can I stop by this week sometime?"

"Oh, yes. That would be lovely," said Miss Simms.

Mrs. Peabody nodded. "You know we have tea every day at five. You should stop by then."

"I'll do that," said Katie. She handed the clinic paperwork to Miss Simms along with a sheet on post-sprain care. "Be sure to take it slowly with your wrist and let me know if you have any trouble."

Mrs. Peabody snatched the instructions from Miss Simms and tucked them into her large straw tote bag. "I'll keep an eye on her, Doctor." She leveled a beady-eyed stare at Miss Simms, who pretended not to notice.

*   *   *

The rest of the clinic proceeded in a blur of coughs, colds, aches, and injuries. Katie finally made it back to her office at six o'clock and slumped into her desk chair. She tugged Eugene's chart out from the bottom of the stack and took out the ER discharge note. Matt was on the schedule to work that day as well, and since she hadn't seen him all afternoon, she assumed he'd been just as busy as she had. Midautumn was always a crazy time with all the back-to-school viruses, yard work injuries, and early influenza cases.

When Matt Gregor had first begun working with the practice, Katie had worried that it would negatively affect their new relationship. But, so far, they had been so busy it was almost as if they didn't work together at all. Matt spent part of his time in his father's internal medicine practice and did locum tenens shifts to fill the extra hours. It was like being a temp doctor. Physicians could fill in at clinics, ERs, or hospitals where they were short-staffed due to illness, vacations, or unfilled positions. Matt claimed to love the freedom and variety of his arrangement. He was filling in in Katie's office while her other partner, Nick Hawkins, was away dealing with personal issues.

Just over a month ago, Katie had solved a murder involving one of her patients and uncovered her partner's addiction to pain medicine. Nick had jeopardized the practice, and Katie was still not sure if she could forgive him for that, or for the stress he had inflicted on his father, Katie's mentor, Emmett Hawkins.

Katie got up, grabbed the ER note, and went in search of Matt.

She found him in the next hall over just coming out of a patient room. He was tall with dark hair that fell onto his forehead. His strong features and intense brown eyes made him classically handsome. But Katie loved his warm smile and the scar on his chin from a bike accident as a boy. Katie continued to be amazed at the way her pulse increased whenever she caught sight of him. He broke into a dazzling smile when he saw her.

"That's my last one," he said, and crooked his thumb at the door. "Are you finished?"

Katie nodded and followed him to his office. All of Nick's things were still there, waiting, but at least the desk had been cleared so Matt could work.

He dumped his stack of charts on the corner of the desk, peeked out the door, and pulled her into an embrace, which led to a long kiss that only ended when they heard footsteps in the hall. They broke apart and assumed casual poses.

Angie Moon, the office manager and nurse, peered

around the door frame. She was a small woman with straight dark hair and thick bangs. A little older than Katie, Angie had helped Katie get used to the rhythms and routines of the clinic. She knew absolutely everything that happened in the clinic. By the way Angie's eyes sparkled, Katie suspected she and Matt weren't fooling her with their feigned businesslike appearance.

"I'm off; see you both tomorrow," she said.

"Thanks, Angie," they said in unison.

Katie took a step back and held out Eugene's ER discharge paper to Matt. He looked at her curiously and took it.

"Yeah, I remember him. Skinny with big ears?"

"That's him. I took his sutures out today," Katie said. "Nice work, by the way; it looks like he won't have much of a scar."

"Good. He had quite a laceration."

"That's what I wanted to ask you about. Did he tell you what happened?"

Matt glanced at the ceiling, thinking. "I think he said he fell while running, although it didn't seem like that's what happened. He had the beginnings of a black eye, but no scrapes on his hands or knees like you might expect with a fall."

Katie nodded. "Hmm. He told me he walked into a door."

Matt shook his head. "Not unless it was a really sharp door."

"Did you know he just got out of prison?"

"I heard something about that." Matt tugged on his ear and focused on his pile of charts. "But I'd think he'd be better off now. He doesn't look like the kind of guy that would survive prison very well."

Katie pressed her lips together. "Maybe. Unless he has more enemies on this side of the prison gates. I can't put my finger on it, but there's something off about him."

"Ten years in prison might do that to a person." Matt pulled his jacket from the back of his desk chair and slung an arm over Katie's shoulder. "Are you interested in dinner at Riley's?"

Katie shook her head. "I have my Gabrielle dinner tonight."

"Oh, right. Forgot," Matt said. He gave her shoulder a squeeze and pulled his jacket on. "Maybe tomorrow?"

"Sounds good."

4

Katie pulled into her driveway a half hour later and vowed never to schedule a dinner with Gabrielle on a Tuesday. At least not one where Katie was supposed to cook. Gabrielle was due in fifteen minutes and Katie needed to get ready.

Gabrielle Maldova was Katie's best friend. They'd met during residency on the obstetrics rotation. Katie had been a family medicine intern and Gabrielle had been one year ahead doing her OB/GYN residency. They'd bonded during late nights and long days. When their schedules got so crazy that they hardly ever saw each other, they'd instituted monthly dinners. The problem was that they were both competitive, and a contest had cropped up. They alternated hosting the dinners, and every six months they voted on the best one. The winner got the trophy—a plastic model of the gastrointestinal system permanently "borrowed" from a drug rep.

This month was Katie's turn. She took a moment to shift

from work mode to home mode. Climbing out of her car, she looked at her house and let out a sigh of satisfaction. She'd fallen in love with her house on first sight. It had a big front porch, lots of trees in the yard, and enough room for her and Caleb. And more work than the former apartment dweller had expected. She'd moved in at the beginning of the summer and still felt as if she would never be settled. At least she'd finally purchased real furniture and not the student-housing cast-offs she'd used in her first months. But it was hers and she loved it.

Katie opened the back door that led into the kitchen and set the Riley's takeout bag and her purse on the counter. She went into the dining room to see if there was any quick tidying to do and gasped when she saw the room.

"Hey, sis!" Caleb said from the head of the table, which was covered in papers, pens, and various computing devices. Caleb was in the end phase of designing a gaming app that he planned to launch on Halloween. Katie had grown used to the idea of eating her meals from a small, cleared space on the otherwise occupied dining room table.

"Hi, Caleb," Katie said, tentatively. She walked slowly into the room. It was okay. This could all be cleared away. "You remember I'm having Gabrielle over for dinner tonight?"

Caleb groaned. "I forgot. I asked the gang over to test out the new app. I'm having trouble with midgame crashes. It will only be three or four guys. I think they're bringing pizza and beer if you want to join us."

Katie narrowed her eyes. "You're kidding."

Caleb smiled. "Yup. I'll get out of your way in ten minutes."

Katie gestured at the table. "Will all your stuff get out of the way, too?"

"You're so picky," he said.

Katie waited.

"Yes, I'll clear it up," he muttered.

Katie shook her head and stomped back into the kitchen. Brothers. Caleb knew the best way to get her blood pressure up to stroke level, and he reveled in it. But she didn't know what she would do without him. She and Caleb had had an itinerant childhood. Their mother had died when Katie was thirteen and Caleb was nine. Their father had found solace not in his children, but in bottles of whatever alcohol he could lay his hands on. The siblings had been shuttled around Michigan from one relative to another until Katie went off to college. Caleb had joined her when he graduated from high school, and they had been together ever since.

Katie occasionally wondered what would happen when either of them married, but she quickly changed the subject with herself.

She pulled the food containers out of the bag and got to work while tamping down a twinge of guilt. She'd tell Gabrielle it was takeout after they finished eating. Probably. Maybe. Unless Gabrielle didn't notice.

* * *

The doorbell rang at exactly seven o'clock. Katie said her friend was OCD about promptness, but Gabrielle claimed she just liked to exercise *some* control over her time since she had zero control at work. She had a point. Babies were not known for their attention to the needs of others. And the preferred time to be born was still the middle of the night.

"I got it!" Caleb yelled into the kitchen.

Katie was pretty sure Caleb harbored a tiny crush on Gabrielle. Just about anyone who met her did. Katie gathered her supplies for the special cocktail she had planned and placed them on a tray. At least this part was "home-cooked." She carried it into the living room and set it down on the new coffee table.

Gabrielle looked stunning as usual in skinny jeans, high-heeled boots, and a slouchy sweater. She had long dark hair and beautiful olive skin and always seemed to pick the perfect color to set off her complexion. She came forward for a hug, and Katie was enveloped in her spicy perfume.

"The place looks great!" Gabrielle turned in the room, taking in the new furniture. "I knew that coffee table would fit perfectly."

"Come, sit," Katie said. "I have a new drink to mix up." She gestured at the sofa. She raised her voice and called into the other room. "Caleb, do you want to join us for a drink?"

"Whatcha making?" Caleb wandered in from the dining room and peered at the tray. "Looks kinda girly."

Caleb had joined Matt in his love of whisky and now refused anything that might actually taste good.

"I'm not twisting your arm," Katie said.

"Well, maybe just a little." Caleb sat at the opposite end of the sofa from Gabrielle.

Katie rolled her eyes. There was a precise ratio of ingredients; didn't he know she couldn't just make a little? She carefully measured the vanilla vodka, Irish cream, and pumpkin-flavored liqueur into the shaker.

She poured out two glasses, plus "a little" for Caleb, and added cinnamon and nutmeg.

Gabrielle took a sip. "My weakness. Pumpkin spice. This is awesome."

Caleb finished his in one swallow and pushed his glass toward Katie. "Is there any more in there?"

She poured out the rest for him. "Not too girly for you?"

"Oh, it's very girly, but you women seem to know what you're doing when it comes to cocktails."

The three clinked glasses and sipped contentedly.

"What's up with you, Caleb?" Gabrielle asked. "Is your app ready for downloading yet?"

"Almost. Just putting the final touches on it and trying to debug the code. I don't want any of those nasty reviews saying it wasn't worth the two dollars because it crashed or it was too easy."

"You'll get some of those no matter what you do," Katie said.

"Yeah, but if I can catch a few errors before it goes live, then I won't have to sweat an update immediately."

He pulled out his phone and checked the time. "I'd better head out. I'm meeting with some of the beta testers in Ann Arbor." He pushed his half-empty drink toward Katie, who shrugged and divvied it up between her glass and Gabrielle's.

After the kitchen door banged shut behind him, Gabrielle said, "I have news."

"I could tell you had something to say."

She nodded and grinned. "I think I'm in love."

This happened about once every six months. Gabrielle dated frequently, and every once in a while she'd meet a guy who was "the one."

She held up a hand. "I know what you're going to say. You're thinking that you've heard this before, but this time I really mean it."

"I'm very happy for you." Katie smiled and leaned back in her chair. "Tell me everything."

"His name is Russell Hunt, and he teaches sociology at the university," Gabrielle said. Katie knew she meant University of Michigan. They had both become used to the pervasive idea in Ann Arbor that no other university existed. "He's a little older, gorgeous, smart, and he's *never* on call. It's so nice to not have to coordinate call schedules just to plan a date."

Katie nodded grimly. Matt was on call a lot through all of his locum tenens work. Between that and Katie's call schedule, there was usually one day a week that they were both off. And it wasn't always on a weekend.

Gabrielle continued to fill her in on the details while they shared another martini. They'd met when she had delivered his sister's baby. Russell had come to the hospital to visit and happened to meet Gabrielle while he was there. He'd spent several days convincing his sister to give him her phone number. She was worried Gabrielle would be mad, but clearly that hadn't been the case.

"It's really nice to be with someone who doesn't want to talk medicine," said Gabrielle. "That orthopedic surgeon only ever wanted to talk about new surgical techniques and the latest arthroscope. When I go out, I want to get away from work."

"Me too. The job is all-consuming as it is; I don't want to talk about it on a date."

"How do you and Matt avoid it? You guys even work in the same place now."

Katie shrugged. "I don't know, actually. The fact that he's a doctor is the least interesting thing about him, so medicine hardly ever comes up. Or, if it does, it's not all science-y."

Gabrielle smiled over the rim of her glass. "I knew you two would be perfect together."

"Yes, yes, you called it. I give you all the credit." Katie flapped her hand at Gabrielle to brush away the self-satisfied smirk.

Gabrielle sat back on the couch, pleased to have won her point.

"Are you hungry?" Katie gathered the glasses and alcohol back onto the tray.

"Starved. And something smells amazing."

She followed Katie into the dining room. Katie held up a hand when Gabrielle tried to follow her into the kitchen.

"Have a seat and I'll bring everything out," Katie said.

Katie went in the kitchen and sliced the pork tenderloin that had been resting on the counter. She poured the apple-and-brandy sauce over it and garnished it with apples. She took the bacon- and maple syrup–coated Brussels sprouts out of the oven and tipped them into a bowl. After delivering those to the table, she grabbed the garlic-mashed potatoes and joined Gabrielle.

"Okay, this looks fantastic," Gabrielle said. "I thought I was a shoe-in for the trophy this time."

Katie glanced at the side table that held the plastic model to avoid meeting Gabrielle's gaze. "There's still time. We don't vote until January."

Gabrielle stood up. "I just need to grab something from the kitchen."

Katie stood as well. "I'll get it. What do you need?"

"The truth," said Gabrielle. She stepped past Katie and went into the kitchen.

Katie's shoulders slumped and she followed.

Gabrielle pulled the Riley's bag out of the trash and held it up. "I knew it!"

"I was going to tell you when we were finished," Katie said.

Gabrielle narrowed her eyes. "Really? I'm not sure I would have."

"Gabrielle! That's cheating!"

"What do you call this?" Gabrielle waved the bag around again. "I go to Riley's, too, you know. Did you think I wouldn't recognize their new fall special?"

Katie grinned at her. "I kinda hoped you wouldn't."

Gabrielle laughed. "Maybe our contest has gotten a little too intense for you." She crossed her arms. "Should we call it off?"

Katie shook her head vehemently. "*I* don't want to call it off, unless *you* do."

"Nope. Let's just add a full disclosure clause. If you have to order out, you divulge up front."

"All right," Katie said.

They shook hands on the new bylaw and went back into the dining room to enjoy Katie's fake homemade dinner.

They filled their plates and grew quiet as they enjoyed the food.

After a few minutes, Gabrielle said, "I was going to wait until after dinner, but there's something else I have to tell you."

Katie looked up and saw Gabrielle's serious expression.

"What is it?" Katie set her fork down and leaned across the table to touch Gabrielle's hand.

"Have you heard about the student who went missing over the weekend?"

Katie shook her head. She never watched the local news and hadn't been on any news sites since last week. "No, what happened? Did you know the student?"

Gabrielle swallowed. "We both do. It was Taylor Knox."

Katie sat back in her chair. She felt briefly dizzy and knew it was just the moment of shock.

Gabrielle volunteered in the student clinic on campus, and Taylor was one of her patients. Taylor was premed and wanted to be a family medicine doctor. Gabrielle had introduced her to Katie, and Taylor had spent two weeks in Katie's clinic over the summer as part of a job-shadowing program.

Katie and Taylor had clicked immediately, and she had loved feeling like a mentor to the younger woman. Taylor was full of idealism and energy and wanted to work with Doctors Without Borders, the Peace Corps, and the Indian Health Service. Pretty much any underserved area was going to be Taylor's mission. Katie knew some of that idealism would be stomped out of her during her training, but if

24

Taylor met even one of her goals, she would make a huge difference.

"I . . . I can't believe it," Katie said. "When you say 'missing,' you mean they suspect foul play? She didn't just go off with some friends for a few days?"

Gabrielle shook her head. "I don't think so. I only know this part because of Russell, but her phone has been shut off, her computer is gone, and her roommates haven't heard from her since last week."

Katie pushed her plate away. She had lost her appetite. "I don't understand what Russell has to do with it."

"He's one of her professors. She was taking one of his upper-level sociology courses." Gabrielle hesitated. "He's been questioned by the police. They've been retracing her steps, and his class was one of the last places she was seen."

"What day did she disappear?"

"I think she was last seen on Sunday. Her roommates say she never came back from studying at the library."

Katie cleared her throat. "I saw her on Sunday afternoon."

"What? Where?"

"Here, in Baxter." Katie put her head in her hands. She couldn't believe this.

"What happened, Katie?"

"I thought it was a little strange at the time, but I was on call and we got interrupted. I had to go admit a patient." Katie stopped, recognizing that she wasn't telling the story very well. "Taylor texted me around five o'clock and asked if I had a few minutes to talk to her. I told her she could meet me at my office."

"And she never showed up?"

Katie took a sip of water. "We met in the garden near the hospital. I don't know why, but I know she always liked it there."

Gabrielle waited for Katie to continue.

"She asked me if I thought there was ever a reason to let someone get away with a crime."

"What kind of a crime?"

"She didn't say. She said she was struggling with what to do with some information she had. I told her I thought it would depend on the crime. I figured one of her roommates was smoking weed or something. I said that if the crime was not ongoing and no one had gotten hurt, maybe it was best left alone."

"How did that go?" Gabrielle asked. They both knew that Taylor had a strong desire for justice and fairness.

"Not so good." Katie shook her head. "Because next she said it was a serious crime and someone had already taken the blame. Again, I thought it was likely some minor thing. You know how she can be sometimes."

"Well, I don't know her as well as you do, but yes, she does like her causes."

Katie took a shaky breath.

"So, after I got the call from the hospital asking me to come in, I told her she should do whatever felt right. That if she couldn't live with what she knew, she should either confront the person or go to the police."

"And you didn't hear from her again?"

Katie shook her head. "I left her there in the garden and went to deal with my patient. What if my advice put her in danger?"

"I don't know, Katie. I doubt she would have dropped it

if you'd asked her to. We don't even know that she *is* in danger. Russell said the police are just trying to track her movements."

Katie bit her lip and looked away.

"Did he know anything about what was worrying her?" Katie asked.

"No. He said she acted like her usual self. She stopped to talk to him after class. He'd assigned this project where they have to research an old criminal case that got a lot of media attention. She was really into it, but she'd chosen a local case and wanted to be sure she was allowed to include interviews as well as just media articles."

"She has so much energy, she always made me feel like an old lady," Katie said. "I'm not surprised she wanted to interview people. I think her favorite part of seeing patients with me was hearing their stories."

Gabrielle smiled. "She's an original, that's for sure. But Russell saw her on Friday. If she disappeared on Sunday, I'm sure he wouldn't have any information that would help the police."

They sat quietly, neither one wanting to think the worst. Then both of them realized at the same moment that Russell *did* have some important information.

"What was the local case she was working on?" Katie asked, her voice low.

Gabrielle put her fork down, pushed her plate away, and took a sip of her drink. "Something about a girl that was killed around Halloween time. I think Russell said it was ten or so years ago. Apparently, Taylor thought the guy who was convicted had been innocent."

Katie sat very still. It couldn't be, could it?

"I saw a new patient this week. He just got out of prison. For murder. Well, technically manslaughter, but still."

"What? Wow. That's pretty crazy. Was he scary?" Gabrielle said. "Wait, you don't think it was the same guy?"

"I don't know. And no, he's not scary. He's nice and not threatening at all," Katie said. "It would be very strange if Taylor was researching his case."

"So, he was from Baxter, went to prison for murder, and then returned here? Why wouldn't he just go and get a fresh start somewhere else?"

Katie lifted a shoulder. "His family is here, I think. I got the impression he liked Baxter. But I was only removing stitches and he wasn't a big talker."

"So, who did he kill?"

"A student at U of M. It was twelve or thirteen years ago around Halloween."

* * *

After Gabrielle left, Katie decided to wash the dishes by hand. There was something about the warm sudsy water and the quiet clinking of plates and cutlery that calmed her. They hadn't had a dishwasher in the tiny house where Katie grew up. Her mother would wash the dishes while Katie sat at the counter and did her homework.

"What does 'peculiar' mean?" Katie would ask.

"That's a tough one; maybe you should look it up," her mom would reply.

"What's six times eight?"

"Do you know any other math facts that would help you figure it out?"

Fourth-grade Katie had sighed. She was convinced her mother had never been to school since she didn't know the answers to any of her homework questions. It was only when Katie was much older that she realized the gift of self-sufficiency her mother had given her. By then her mom was gone, and Katie had never gotten a chance to thank her.

But the fresh smell of dishwashing liquid and the sound of running water helped her think through the tough questions.

And she was facing a tough question. *Had* she sent Taylor off to confront a criminal? Had she gone to talk to Eugene? Katie had been distracted by the call from the hospital and left without really talking it through. She pictured Taylor standing in the middle of the garden, one hand raised in a wave as Katie hurried down the path to the hospital. Where had she gone after that?

Katie needed to find out.

5

He'd promised himself he wouldn't. After all he'd been through, he didn't want to be back here. Watching.

But, because of all he had been through, he'd reverted back to the one place he felt safe. Even if he couldn't be with Alicia, he could be near her. All that time in prison, keeping his head down, learning how to play the game, trying to avoid danger, he had thought of her.

Warm golden light poured out of Alicia's windows, and Eugene fought the urge to stand in that light. He knew it wouldn't be as warm as it looked. It never was. He stayed toward the back of her yard but not in it, crouching behind the large shrubs that separated her yard from the neighbor's. The old habits died hard. When the restraining order was in place, he'd had to stay at least one hundred yards away. But he didn't want to be caught in her yard anyway. How would he explain it?

He thought back to the last time he'd been restricted by the order. It had almost killed him to be denied access to his best friend. But that night, so many years ago, he had no longer cared if he got caught. He'd gone to the party and watched Alicia from across the room. She seemed happy. Laughing with her friends. They were all dressed in the same costume. A coven of blonde witches.

When she spotted him, she had made her way quickly through the crowd. He'd thought she would be happy to see him, but she wasn't. She was mad that he'd broken the restraining order. She said she didn't want to get him into any more trouble. He'd left in a huff, storming across the campus to his car. He'd walked past dozens of students in every kind of costume. Pirates, witches, a few dressed as Austin Powers, and of course the superheroes.

He'd parked way over by the athletic complex. It was at least a twenty-minute walk, but by the time he was near his car, he had calmed down and come up with a great idea. He would convince her to come home with him. He knew Alicia's parents were worried about her. If he brought her home, he could be the hero and they would remove the restraining order. It could all go back to the way it had been. He'd headed back to campus and decided to cut through the Law Quad. Then he saw her. But he had promised himself not to think about that.

Now, almost twelve years later, he was watching Alicia again. If he were honest, he would admit that this hadn't been a spur-of-the-moment decision. He'd been planning it since he got out. He'd watched the neighbor's house to figure out their schedule. And he'd watched Alicia's house from a distance. All of his patience paid off when he saw the neighbors leave, he assumed for dinner, and he knew he'd have some time to crouch in their yard undetected.

He thought of the other girl who reminded him of

Alicia. Why was she dredging up the past? He didn't want to be reminded of that awful time. He just wanted to move forward if the rest of the world would let him.

He took the bracelet out of his pocket and let it sit in the palm of his hand. He lit a cigarette, got comfortable, and waited. Half an hour later, he was rewarded.

He saw her in an upstairs bedroom walking back and forth past the window. She was holding the baby on her shoulder, and he thought he could almost hear the lullaby she was singing. After five weeks, he finally felt like he was home.

He lost himself in memories of Alicia. From the moment she moved in next door when they were both twelve, they had been best friends. Then, in high school, things had changed. She wasn't the same Alicia at school as she was at home. He stood to push the memories of that time away. He dropped the cigarette and ground it out under his boot.

Just as he turned to walk back home, he realized his mistake. He'd let his guard down while reminiscing.

The first fist to the gut knocked the wind out of him. He bent over and wheezed. The push on his back only prompted what he already wanted to do. He fell to the ground and clutched the bracelet tightly in his fist. He curled into a ball and waited for it to be over.

6

Wednesday morning, Katie was surprised to see Eugene Lowe on her patient list again. She felt wary after her conversation with Gabrielle the night before. He couldn't have anything to do with Taylor going missing, could he? Katie wondered again if Taylor had interviewed Eugene. But Katie hadn't sensed any threat from him, and why would he want to hurt a stranger? Of course, he'd been convicted of doing just that, and Katie had only met him once. It made her uncomfortable. She'd always thought of herself as a good judge of character, but her recent brush with murder had made her question herself. She didn't like it, but there it was. Fortunately, a doctor's job was straightforward: treat the patient regardless of who he was. He wasn't booked for a physical. She flipped open the chart and saw the reason for his visit: contusions and rib pain. Katie frowned. Why hadn't he gone to the ER? It sounded like a car accident. Katie took a deep breath. The only way to find out was to open the door, which she did after a brief knock.

Eugene hunched in his seat and looked up through his fringe of dark hair as she entered. He looked terrible. Red, swollen cuts and scrapes disfigured his face. He held himself in a protective way that made Katie worry about a rib fracture.

"Mr. Lowe, what happened?" She stepped forward and crouched near him to look in his eyes.

"I fell off a ladder trying to put up some Halloween decorations," he said. His voice was low and hoarse.

Katie didn't believe him. He certainly could have hurt his ribs falling off a ladder, but it was unlikely he would get his face as swollen and bruised as it was.

She pressed her lips together, stood, and gestured to the exam table.

"Can you climb up?" She asked. "I'll need to examine you and be sure nothing is broken."

He nodded and moved stiffly to the table. She pulled out the metal step and helped him onto the cushion.

He had a bruise on his left cheekbone, a small cut above his right eye, and a split lip. She pulled the otoscope off the wall and asked him to tilt his head so she could look in his ears. Both eardrums were intact and there was no bleeding.

She pressed along his collarbone and didn't elicit any tenderness.

"I'll need you to lie back if you can," she said. "I want to examine your ribs. Does it hurt to breathe?"

He nodded and moved slowly into a faceup position on the table. Katie pulled the metal shelf out for him to rest his legs.

She asked him to pull his shirt up. She noted more

bruising on his abdomen and along his rib cage. Although it was tender, she didn't think anything was broken.

She helped him to a sitting position again and watched him carefully. He wouldn't meet her eye.

"I don't think anything is broken, but you definitely have some severe contusions. When did this happen?"

"Last night, around eight or so."

"You were putting up decorations in the dark?" Katie crossed her arms and looked him in the eye.

He squirmed a bit and didn't answer.

Katie moved to the wheeled stool by the small desk. "It looks to me like you fell onto someone's fists and maybe the toe of their boots."

Eugene sighed. He looked up at the ceiling and then finally looked at Katie.

"Ever since I got home, they've been harassing me. First, it was just notes left on my car, or egging the house. They painted things on my garage. But recently it's gotten worse."

"Who is doing this?"

Eugene lifted a shoulder and winced. "They wear masks. I don't know who they are, but they don't want me in town."

"Where did this most recent attack take place?"

"A few blocks from my house." Eugene looked away and became interested in his fingernails. "I went for a walk."

Katie sensed another lie but let it go.

"Did you see who attacked you this time?"

He shook his head. "I don't know."

"Have you told the police about this?"

He nodded yes. "At first, they came and took a statement.

But nothing changed. It's not like an ex-con is their top priority."

"Mr. Lowe, I'm sure if Chief Carlson knew you had been attacked, he would have a plan to protect you."

Eugene remained silent.

"Do you mind if I talk to them?"

"I'd rather you didn't," he said. "I'll call them again myself."

"Okay. Do you need something for the pain?"

He shook his head and held his hands up. "I don't like to take pills."

"Even if you don't want to take it during the day, you could take some at bedtime so you can sleep. It's going to be a week or more before your ribs feel normal when you breathe."

Eugene shrugged, winced, and then nodded.

Katie scribbled a prescription and held it out to him.

Eugene took the paper and slipped it into his jeans pocket.

"I also want you to go to the radiology department at the hospital and get an X-ray." Katie handed him a radiology requisition. "I want to be sure I haven't missed a rib fracture, and your cheek is too swollen for me to be sure you don't have a fracture there. And I'll need to run some blood tests and take a urine sample. Your kidneys took a beating; I want to be sure there wasn't any more serious damage."

He nodded glumly and took the lab slip and X-ray request.

"I'd like to see you again early next week to be sure everything is healing okay. And call me if things get worse."

"Thanks, Doc." Eugene slid off the table and followed Katie out of the room.

* * *

After a busy morning clinic that left time for only a protein bar before the first afternoon patient arrived, Katie was glad to see that her last two appointments had canceled. She'd struggled to stay focused on her patients and hoped they hadn't noticed her distraction. Gabrielle had texted just after lunch to say, RUSSELL SAYS THE CASE TAYLOR WAS RESEARCHING INVOLVED EUGENE LOWE. IS THAT YOUR GUY?

Katie managed to leave clinic just after four o'clock.

She jumped in her car and headed to the downtown area of Baxter—this consisted of three blocks on Main Street where three restaurants and multiple shops were located.

The police station was tucked between an antiques store and a yarn shop. Its bright-yellow door blended with the rest of the cheerful facades in the shopping area. Katie parked down the block and marched to the station.

A young receptionist was on the phone when Katie burst through the door. The girl held up a finger to indicate that Katie should wait.

"Uh-huh. Uh-huh. No way!" The girl twirled her hair and smiled in a way that told Katie this wasn't police business.

Katie narrowed her eyes. She stepped closer to the desk and looked at her watch.

"Yup. Okay." The girl licked her lips and eyed Katie warily. "Listen, I gotta go."

Katie could hear a voice still talking as the girl set the phone in its cradle.

"Can I help you?" Her tone was frosty, but Katie didn't want to call her on it. In about thirty seconds, she would regret her attitude. Katie and John Carlson were good friends. Katie wasn't going to rat her out, but she wasn't above letting the girl think it was possible.

"I need to see Chief Carlson."

"Name?"

"Katie LeClair."

The receptionist pushed a button and spoke quietly into the phone. Before she had replaced the receiver, John Carlson was walking down the hall toward Katie. He tugged on his shirtfront, its buttons straining, and hiked up his pants as he walked. As he approached, he raised a hand in greeting.

"Hey, Doc!"

"Hi, John."

The girl smiled sheepishly as Katie walked back to Carlson's office.

"New receptionist?"

"Yeah, Marcy had bunion surgery and she has to be off her feet for a week. That's her daughter." Carlson made a face. "Not quite the same work ethic."

Carlson pushed the door open and ushered Katie into his office. As usual, it was filled with the organized clutter of a person with too much paperwork. Several piles languished on his desk, and there were Bankers Boxes piled in the corner. A sad-looking fern wilted on the windowsill.

John Carlson had one picture of his wife, Linda, on his

desk and three of his dog, Bubba. Katie wondered how Linda felt about the ratio.

"What can I do for you, Doc?" He gestured to the visitor seat and lowered himself into his desk chair.

"I wanted to ask you about the missing college student from Ann Arbor." Katie moved the molded plastic chair a little closer to the desk and set her bag on the floor as she sat.

Carlson's eyebrows inched upward. "I can't talk to you about an ongoing case, Doc."

"Are you involved?" Katie asked. "She spent two weeks working with me over the summer. I was really impressed with her." Katie stopped and swallowed hard. "I just want to help if I can."

Carlson leaned forward. "The Ann Arbor police are coordinating with police departments all around the area. I didn't know you knew her. If it seems like we need any more background information, I'll be sure to let you know."

"Do you think she's still alive?" Katie asked. "I know she wouldn't just run off. She's very responsible and she was close with her family."

"We're exploring all possibilities." Carlson kept his voice even and his face blank.

Katie sighed. Part of her had known he wouldn't tell her anything. She'd just felt so helpless. And when she'd heard that Taylor had been researching Eugene's case, she'd suddenly felt like she needed to *do* something. She didn't really believe that Eugene was involved, but she didn't know him at all. What if she had been patching up a kidnapper? Or worse?

Carlson lowered his voice. "Katie, we want to find her just as much as you want her found. We're going over her last movements and hoping someone will report seeing her."

"That's why I'm here," Katie said.

"You've seen her?" Carlson pulled his phone closer, as if he was about to send a car to Taylor's location.

"I saw her late Sunday afternoon here in Baxter."

Carlson released the phone. "Why are you just coming to us now?"

"I didn't know until last night that she was even missing. And then I realized I might have been the last person to see her before she disappeared."

"I'll need you to give a statement and tell us exactly what she said and where you were. The Ann Arbor guys have been focused on the school and her friends there. If she was here Sunday evening, that will change everything."

Katie told him about her meeting in the hospital garden and the odd questions Taylor had been asking. He took notes even though he was recording everything she said.

"Since I met with her, I've heard that she had been researching an old crime. Do you think that had anything to do with her disappearance? I feel so guilty that I basically told her to confront the person. I didn't know she'd been looking into an old crime."

Carlson sat back in his chair, his forehead crinkling in a frown. "How did you hear about that? If Sean has been talking to his wife again . . ."

Katie's receptionist, Debra, was married to one of the officers who worked with Carlson. Debra was Baxter's information superhighway.

She held her hands up. "No, I didn't hear it from Debra. It was . . . another source."

"Now you sound like my wife," Carlson said. "She never reveals her sources either."

Linda Carlson wrote and published the *Baxter Gazette*. Katie was sure that had led to some tense dinner conversations over the years.

Katie was about to ask about Eugene and whether Carlson knew he was still being harassed, but decided against it. She needed more information before mentioning Eugene and his recent injuries. Plus, he had explicitly asked her not to tell the police. But did that mean he was guilty of something?

Katie remained silent and waited.

Carlson ran a hand over the few hairs left on his head. "Yes, we're looking into that angle as well. But that's all I'm going to say." He held his hands up to fend off further questions. "And you can't blame yourself. It might not have anything to do with whatever project she was working on. We're still hoping she'll turn up claiming she needed a break from school." He smiled kindly, but Katie didn't think he believed Taylor had just taken a mental health break.

"Thank you." Recognizing she had gotten as much intel as she could, Katie stood to leave. "How's Bubba? I need to come visit him soon."

This elicited a genuine smile from Carlson, as Katie had known it would. She'd "saved" Bubba after he was hit by a car, and John Carlson never got tired of thanking her. Katie wasn't sure she had really done that much, but Carlson's version involved Katie wresting the black Lab from the jaws of death, carrying him to safety, and providing urgent medical treatment. Only some of that was true.

"In the dog house at the moment. He got into the garbage this morning and scattered it all over the new carpet."

"Oh, no! Are you sure it was safe to leave him alone with Linda?"

Carlson laughed. "You think I'm the one who's soft? She just cleaned it up and promised to take him to the dog park to run off some energy. As far as Bubba is concerned, that was a win-win for him."

7

Back on the sidewalk outside the police station, Katie glanced at her watch—a few minutes to five. She'd be just in time for tea.

She walked the half block to her car and climbed inside. She pulled out of her parking spot and turned off Main Street into the residential area. Like most neighborhoods near downtown, this was a mix of craftsman bungalows, small Victorians, and colonials. Katie pulled up in front of Miss Simms's house. As she got out of her car, she glanced at the house next door. It was a pretty colonial, but shuttered now. One owner was dead, the other away indefinitely. Katie sighed and pushed those memories aside.

Miss Simms's place was an adorable light-blue bungalow surrounded by trees and shrubs and decorated with containers of chrysanthemums. Multiple pumpkins guarded the porch. Katie climbed the steps to the front door and rang the bell. She waited a moment and was about to ring again when she heard muffled noises from inside. The lace curtains in the front window twitched. Katie heard the rattle of locks being turned and the door opened.

"Dr. LeClair! So glad you could join us." Miss Simms held the door wide and ushered her inside.

Mrs. Peabody stood in the hallway and nodded sedately at Katie.

"Come back to the kitchen and I'll get you a fresh scone," said Miss Simms.

Katie felt her stomach rumble and remembered she'd only grabbed a protein bar for lunch.

"That sounds wonderful, thank you." She followed the ladies to the kitchen.

The cheerful room caught the afternoon sun, which was fading to the deep golden light of midautumn. The yellow curtains, oak table, and shiny copper pans hanging over the stove gave the room a warm and cozy feel. Katie felt herself relax. It was like visiting her grandmother's house when she was a kid.

Miss Simms placed a teacup and saucer in front of Katie and poured from a little brown pot that wore a pumpkin-shaped tea cozy. The delicious aroma of pumpkin spice and cinnamon in the scones wafted upward as Miss Simms set a plate of them on the table.

Mrs. Peabody sipped her tea and watched Miss Simms bustle about.

"This looks wonderful," said Katie.

"I do like a little pumpkin spice in the fall," said Miss Simms.

"It seems you aren't alone if all the ads in town are any indication," said Mrs. Peabody. "The movie theater was advertising pumpkin spice popcorn! I think that's going too far." She sniffed and took a large bite of her scone.

"People do seem to like it," Miss Simms agreed. "I think it's the cinnamon smell." She lowered her voice and leaned toward Katie. "I once read a study that showed men get"— she glanced around the kitchen and whispered—"sexually aroused when they smell cinnamon."

Mrs. Peabody snorted. And then both women giggled like teenagers.

Katie smiled at them and thought of Gabrielle. Would they still be laughing together when they were old? Katie hoped so.

Recognizing the signs that this could devolve into all sorts of topics that wouldn't further her cause, she decided it was time to redirect the conversation. Knowing Taylor had been investigating Eugene's case, Katie wanted to learn as much about him as she could. Maybe she could help find Taylor. Maybe she could fix the mess she'd made.

"Miss Simms, Mrs. Peabody, I was hoping you could tell me more about Eugene Lowe."

They stopped giggling immediately, and Miss Simms used the corner of her apron to wipe her eyes.

Mrs. Peabody shook her head sadly. "That was a terrible drama."

"Oh my, yes," Miss Simms agreed. "We never would have believed that Eugene could do such a thing."

Katie waited.

"We should probably start at the beginning, Betty," Mrs. Peabody said.

"Yes, I think you're right. Eugene was a very bright

child. I taught him in fourth grade and Mrs. Peabody had him in sixth." Miss Simms took a sip of tea. "He was a bit awkward with the other kids, and I know they used to tease him about one thing or another." She lowered her voice and leaned toward Katie. "His ears didn't help matters. I think they were always adult-sized, and even after he grew into them, they were on the large side."

"Dumbo," said Mrs. Peabody.

Miss Simms nodded. "Children can be so cruel."

Mrs. Peabody picked up the tale. "By sixth grade, he had become gawky and probably too eager for friends. The other kids could sniff out his desperation, and they punished him for it."

Katie's delicious bite of scone had become dry in her mouth, and she struggled to swallow it as she thought of the young Eugene. She had several patients who struggled with bullying and subsequent self-esteem issues. She always hated these stories.

"But then, the most amazing thing happened," Mrs. Peabody said. "Alicia Stewart's grandmother passed away, and she and her parents moved from their small cottage to the larger house, which happened to be right next door to Eugene. The two of them began an unlikely friendship, and because she was one of the most popular girls in the class, Eugene was allowed into the group."

Miss Simms continued the story. "Well, once they got to know him better, they all realized he was a decent kid, and I think Alicia's move probably changed his life—at least his young life."

"So, what happened?" Katie asked, her tea forgotten.

"High school," said Mrs. Peabody.

"Hormones," said Miss Simms.

Katie nodded to encourage them.

"We only heard this secondhand from our colleagues at the high school, and of course after what happened later, everyone had an opinion . . ." Mrs. Peabody began.

"What she's trying to say is that things took a turn," Miss Simms said.

"Yes," Mrs. Peabody said. "Alicia and Eugene stayed close through high school. Alicia's father was very strict and wouldn't allow his daughter to date until she was a senior. The parents apparently didn't see a threat in Eugene, and so the two kids spent a lot of time together."

Katie sensed that she wasn't going to like the rest of this story.

"At some point, Alicia's mother caught Eugene sneaking out of their house when no one was at home," Miss Simms said. "She thought he had stolen something and called the police, and both parents insisted that Eugene should be questioned. They spun the friendship as more of a one-sided romance and claimed he was dangerous."

"Didn't Alicia stand up for him?" Katie asked.

"Yes, she did, but her father was convinced that Eugene had influenced her in some nefarious way," Miss Simms said.

"In the end, they actually searched his room—his mother gave them permission, as she was sure that would clear up the misunderstanding," Mrs. Peabody said.

"Of course that only made things worse." Miss Simms stopped to shake her head. "They found a drawer full of women's underthings."

"They were Alicia's." Mrs. Peabody sipped her tea and looked out the window.

"The parents banned Alicia from spending any time with him and even applied for a restraining order," Miss Simms said. "Which was hard to do, since they were next-door neighbors."

"Wow," said Katie. "What happened to Eugene?"

"Fortunately, this all happened in the summer, but by the time they started their senior year, people could tell something had happened." Miss Simms stood and brought another plate of scones to the table. She pushed it toward Katie and waited until she took one. Satisfied, she continued. "Alicia fought with her parents all through the fall, and finally she ran away."

"I think I heard about this," Katie said. While investigating her patient's murder earlier in the fall, Katie had read an old *Baxter Gazette* that reported a "missing" Baxter girl. "She went to Ann Arbor and then returned a week or so later?"

"Returned is one way to look at it," said Mrs. Peabody. "The friend she was staying with was killed on the night of Halloween, and Eugene was found with the body."

Miss Simms stood and took her cup to the sink. "Oh, no," she said, looking out the window. "It's Delores."

"Delores?" Katie said.

"Delores Munch," said Mrs. Peabody, her mouth puckered as if she'd bit into a lemon. "She lives behind Betty, and she's the biggest busybody in town."

"I know that name," Katie said.

"She sees Emmett Hawkins. Maybe you've run across her name at the clinic," said Mrs. Peabody.

Miss Simms quickly cleared the table of scones and tea things. Mrs. Peabody hopped up to help her.

"Can I help?" Katie asked. "What are you doing?"

"She knows we're here because she can see your car in the driveway," whispered Miss Simms. "She'll bully her way in here, and if she sees we're having tea, I'll never get rid of her."

Just then, an imperious knock came at the back door.

"Quick, come through here," said Mrs. Peabody. She pulled Katie into the living room.

The knock came again, louder.

Miss Simms opened the door and greeted Delores. "Hello, Delores. I'm a bit busy right now," she said in a monotone. "Do you need something?"

A voice floated in through the open door. Miss Simms must have been blocking entry.

"I just brought some cookies over for you," said Delores. "I was baking for the church sale, and these didn't turn out as pretty as I'd like. They taste good, and I know how you like your sweets."

"How . . . kind," said Miss Simms.

Mrs. Peabody held her finger to her lips and rolled her eyes at Katie. It was like being in junior high all over again.

"Yes, well, I like to watch my figure, so I couldn't keep them," said Delores. "Do you have a guest?"

"Guest?"

"I saw the car in the driveway."

Katie could tell that Miss Simms was still blocking the door, as Delores's voice sounded distant.

"Actually, I do, and she was just leaving," said Miss Simms. "I really shouldn't keep her waiting. Bye, now."

The door clicked shut. Katie heard Miss Simms pull open her cupboard and dump something in the trash. She came into the living room brushing crumbs from her hands.

Mrs. Peabody held back her laughter as long as she could, but it burst forth as soon as she saw Miss Simms.

"She's so irritating!" said Miss Simms. "Did you hear her? 'I have to watch my figure, but you can have all of these cast-off cookies.'" Miss Simms glowered and clenched her fists.

Katie smiled at the ladies but didn't know quite what to make of this new side of Miss Simms.

"I'm sorry you had to see that, Dr. LeClair," said Miss Simms. She smoothed her skirt and adjusted her cardigan. "I try to be charitable to most people, but Delores Munch isn't one of them."

"Old enemies?" Katie asked.

"Sometimes it's hard living in a small town," said Miss Simms. "But you'll have to go now. She'll be watching from her kitchen, and if you don't head out soon, she'll be back over here."

Both ladies pushed Katie in the direction of the front door.

"Oh, okay," said Katie. She grabbed her bag off the table by the door and stepped onto the porch. "Thank you for the tea and scones."

"You're very welcome, dear," said Miss Simms.

"We'll have to do this again soon," said Mrs. Peabody.

The door closed, and Katie heard the sharp click of the lock.

8

Riley's Grill sported its weekday calm when Katie walked in. Wednesdays were not a big night out in Baxter. The restaurant was one large room with high ceilings and exposed ductwork. The glass front wall gave diners a view of the quaint downtown area of Baxter. The contrast between the retro outside and the shiny inside always felt very cosmopolitan to Katie. On a Friday or Saturday night, it would be almost impossible to hear the person sitting across the table.

Katie preferred this version. She spotted Matt sipping a drink at the bar and climbed onto the stool next to him. After ordering white wine, she glanced at his glass and repressed a shudder. Whisky. Straight. How did he drink that stuff?

She had suspected at first that it was some kind of tough-guy prop, or a nod to the Rat Pack (Matt was a big Sinatra fan), but she had come to realize he actually *liked* it. He'd tried to convince her once to taste some with a bit of water

in it "to bring out the flavor," as if that was what was holding her back. She didn't need to bring out the flavor of dirt
and smoke. They'd reached a truce. He wouldn't comment
on her love for white wine and sweet mixed drinks, and she
would not make faces at his whisky.

"You hungry?" he asked after she'd taken a sip of her
drink.

"Sort of," she said. "I only had a protein bar between
patients around one o'clock. But then I stopped by Miss
Simms's place, and she forced me to eat pumpkin scones."

"Forced you?"

"Well, she put one right in front of me. I had no choice."

Matt laughed. "I see. Let's get a table and fill up on bread."

He stood and held out his hand to help her down from
the stool. Not that she needed it, but there was something
about his old-fashioned gallantry that made her feel safe
and cared for. She'd spent enough of her professional life
proving she was just as capable as any man; she didn't feel
the need to prove anything in her private life. And who
wouldn't want to feel respected and cherished? That was
Matt's superpower. He filled a space in her life that she'd
never known existed until he came along.

They carried their drinks to a table in the corner by the
front window. The waiter brought menus and the coveted
basket of bread. They caught each other up on the day
in clinic between bites of soft stretchy bread and melted
butter.

"I feel like we may need to refer some of the pain clinic
patients to Ann Arbor," Matt said. "Some of them need
more specialized care than we can provide."

Katie nodded, held one finger up, and finished chewing. "I've tried to talk to Emmett about that, but I think he feels like he wants to keep the patients here for when Nick comes back."

"Any news on when that might be?" Matt focused on buttering his bread.

Katie shook her head. "It will be at least six months, I think." She set her bread down on her plate. "I'll have to push Emmett a bit more. You're right, we can't limp along for six months or more running a pain clinic with no certified pain physician." Katie didn't voice her biggest worry, which was that maybe Nick wouldn't come back at all. He was in treatment for his own chronic pain condition and subsequent addiction to opioids. His desperation had almost run the practice out of business.

"Better you than me," Matt said, and gave her a crooked smile.

The waiter came by at that moment to take their order, and they moved on to happier subjects.

"I don't know if I thanked you for helping Caleb out on his new app," Katie said.

"Only about five times." Matt grinned. "You don't have to thank me. The app sounds great, and I love doing beta tests for that sort of thing."

When they met, Matt and Caleb had hit it off immediately over a shared love for video games. Although Katie was pleased that the two men in her life got along, it also meant that she had to share them both.

Matt leaned forward, elbows on the table. "Katie, there's something I need to tell you."

Katie didn't like the sound of that. Her old boyfriend, Justin, had ended a five-year relationship in a restaurant with that line. She knew it was ridiculous but couldn't help the clenching in her stomach. She really liked Matt, and even though they'd only been dating for a month or so, she felt comfortable with him in a way she had given up on ever finding again.

Katie took a deep breath, "Okay, shoot."

Matt leaned back, concern in his eyes. "You look like you think I might actually shoot you. It's not *that* bad."

Katie smiled and consciously relaxed her shoulders.

"It's about Eugene Lowe," Matt said.

Katie really did relax at that. What could he possibly have to say about Eugene Lowe that warranted such a serious tone?

"The night that Heather died, when Eugene was found with her body . . ."

Heather? Was that the name of the victim? Did Matt know her?

She waited, impatiently, but with the bland expression she used to encourage patients to share uncomfortable details.

"I was at the party," Matt said.

"What party?" Katie asked.

Matt held her gaze. "How much do you know about Eugene's case?"

"Almost nothing. He only told me he'd been in prison, and another patient told me it had been for murder. Did you know the girl who died?"

Matt nodded. "Actually, we dated very briefly in college."

Matt held up his hand at Katie's expression. "It was casual and had been over for a long time when she died, but we'd stayed friends. That's why I was at the party."

Katie took a swig of her wine. It was ridiculous to feel jealous of someone he'd known more than a decade ago. (And who was now dead.) She shoved the feeling into a little box and took a deep breath. "So, tell me about this party."

"It was a big Halloween bash that was put on every year by the student activities group. I think the university tried to commandeer Halloween in the hopes that the frat houses would be less destructive, but all it did was create a huge blowout every year."

"So you were at the party because of Heather?"

"I'd run into her earlier that week, and she talked it up so much, I promised I'd go. It was supposed to be a costume party, but not everyone dressed up. It was kind of a 'go big or go home' kind of thing. If you wore a costume, it had to be really good." Matt paused and glanced out the window. "Anyway, I don't remember much about that night—it was twelve or thirteen years ago. I saw Heather early in the evening, and then she wandered off into the crowd. I found a group of my friends, and we hung around rating the costumes and drinking beer. I never saw her again." Matt finished his drink in one long swallow.

"I'm really sorry, Matt." Katie reached forward and touched his hand. "It's always hard to lose someone your own age. And in such a violent way."

"Well, I have a feeling that, now that Eugene is out of prison, the whole story will reenter the gossip mill. As you know, small towns have long memories."

"So, did you know Eugene?"

Matt shook his head. "I'd never met him prior to last week at the ER. I knew his name sounded familiar but couldn't place it until I heard the nurses saying he'd just gotten out of prison."

"How did Heather die?"

"According to what I heard at the time, she left the party alone and cut through the Law Quad on her way home. There was construction and landscaping going on at the time. There were piles of building materials covered in tarps. The story was that they fought, he pushed her, and she hit her head on a brick. It looked like an accident, which is why he got manslaughter instead of murder. I don't know if he even knew her, but they must have argued about something and then she was dead. The truth is, I didn't follow the story that closely. There was so much in the papers about her ex-boyfriends and the fact that she was walking alone at night. Like she was to blame for what happened. And honestly, I didn't want to know those things. She had been a funny, vibrant person, and after her death she was only remembered as a victim. And used as a cautionary tale."

Katie chastised herself for the flash of jealousy. A young woman had been killed with her whole life ahead of her. Katie shivered a bit wondering if Eugene Lowe had enough anger under the surface to become violent. Or was he innocent, as Taylor thought?

And what about Taylor? Where *was* she, and was her project to blame for her disappearance? Katie didn't know, and she felt helpless. She'd already talked to Matt about Taylor and didn't want to spend any more time discussing young lives in danger.

Their food arrived, and they made an effort to talk about more pleasant things. Murder and violence tended to put a damper on an evening. Matt regaled her with stories about his evenings in the ER—either losing quarters to the nurses playing poker all evening or spending the entire night treating chest pain and stitching up lacerations. Emergency room shifts in Baxter Community Hospital were almost never slow and steady. It was either a ghost town or a war zone. By the time they ordered dessert, Katie had put Eugene, Heather, and Taylor out of her mind.

9

John Carlson kept his face blank but clenched his fists. From his seat behind his desk, he watched Nathan Nielsen pace, threaten, and yell.

"You have to do something about this," Nathan said. "He's a known killer and he's stalking my wife."

"Sit down, please, Mr. Nielsen." Carlson tried to keep the growl out of his voice. "Has he threatened your wife? Have you seen him on your property or anywhere near your wife?"

Nathan sat in the visitor chair but was so angry that he seemed to be emitting waves of heat and energy. The room felt very small.

"No, he hasn't threatened her," Nathan mumbled. "And I haven't seen him close to the house."

Carlson pulled a thin file to the middle of his desk and opened it. "Mr. Lowe made his own complaints a few weeks ago. Spray paint on his garage, threatening notes, and vandalism to his property." Carlson looked up from the file. "Know anything about that?"

Nathan looked away and shook his head. He gave a short bark of laughter. "I come in here asking you to protect my wife from a known murderer and you accuse me of teenage pranks?"

"I didn't accuse, just asked if you knew anything." Carlson let the silence lengthen. "I've also heard that Mr. Lowe has had some injuries lately. It seems he's the one who needs protection."

Nathan pressed his lips together and blew air out of his nose like an enraged bull. "So, I need to wait until Alicia has been injured before I can get a restraining order?"

"It's not as simple as that." Carlson folded his hands on his desk and leaned forward. "Why isn't Alicia here to make a complaint? Does *she* feel threatened?"

"She doesn't want to make trouble for him because he just got out of prison." Nathan spoke into his lap.

"You probably haven't had to deal with something like this, but it takes evidence of a real threat to get a restraining order. I'll have to talk to her before I can proceed with any action against Mr. Lowe," Carlson said. Then, just to see what reaction he would get, he said, "Should I stop by the house? Or do you want to ask her to come in to the station?"

"Not yet. I'll talk to her and get her to stop by."

Carlson sat back and lowered his voice. "Does she even know you're here?"

"No," said Nathan. "I hoped to take care of this without upsetting her, but if the complaint has to come from her, then I'll convince her."

Carlson stood and held out his hand. "I think we're done for now. If Alicia wants to make a complaint, I'll be happy to talk to her."

Nathan stood and, ignoring Carlson's hand, yanked his jacket off the back of the chair.

When he reached for the door, Carlson stopped him with a word.

"Nathan, call me if you think someone is trespassing or threatening. In the meantime, I hope Eugene doesn't have any more accidents. I'll talk to him informally and let him know you have concerns; it's the best I can do at this point. You and Alicia should just go about your lives."

Nathan opened the door and stalked out.

10

After Matt dropped her off, Katie hadn't been able to settle. She'd washed the dishes, tried to read a thriller, and flipped through channels on the TV. By midnight, she'd decided to go to bed. That had only given her more space to think and worry. About Taylor, and whether she was alive. And about Eugene. Was he dangerous? Should she be more careful around him, or did he need her help rather that her fear? And about whether she should be doing more for either of them. Therefore, it was no surprise that, by mid-morning and after three cups of her favorite French roast coffee, she was yawning and struggling to concentrate.

Katie decided she had to do something and her first step should be to gather information. Both about Taylor and her activities before she disappeared and about Eugene. Since she had no authority to go around interviewing people, she decided to start with people she knew.

She pressed GABRIELLE on her phone and waited.

"Hey you," Gabrielle said.

"Hi," Katie said. "I think it's time I meet this new man of yours. Want to go for drinks tonight?"

"Sure! I've been wanting to get my two most important people together."

Katie tried, and failed, not to be irritated that she was being lumped in with some guy Gabrielle had known for a few weeks. Then she reminded herself she was only meeting Russell to pump him for information and the guilt canceled out the irritation. She smiled—because someone had said it made your voice sound warmer—and said she'd see them that evening.

"Bring Matt if he's not working," Gabrielle said.

"Of course he'll be there." Katie had no idea if he could make it, but she wanted to sound as if she'd been planning this for a while, not just the last five minutes.

They said good-bye with Gabrielle sounding much more excited than Katie felt.

After she ended the call with Gabrielle, she thought about who else might be able to fill her in on Baxter happenings from ten or fifteen years ago.

Katie glanced into the hallway and saw that there were no patients waiting to be seen. She walked to the front reception area to see if she could catch Debra alone. Debra Gallagher was Katie's main source of Baxter news. Between her husband Sean, who was a police officer, and her own job as receptionist at the only family medicine practice in Baxter, she knew everything about everybody. And any gaps in her intel were filled in by her friend Lois at the Clip n' Curl.

Debra didn't have a molecule of discretion in her body. Not only would she share any gossip she heard, but she also shared every thought or concern that crossed her mind. As Caleb would say, her life was an unencrypted hard drive. Katie was a much more private person, and it had taken her a while to get used to Debra's cavalier approach to private information. She still felt guilty every time she took advantage of Debra's forthcoming nature to gather the latest scoop.

She pushed open the door that led from the patient rooms to the front waiting area. It was empty. Where was Debra? Then she heard muffled mumbling from under the desk. She peeked over the edge.

"Debra?"

The muttering stopped and Debra emerged, just barely missing smacking her head on the underside of the desk. She was short and curvy with bouncy blonde curls. Her best feature was her dimpled smile.

"Oh, hi, Dr. LeClair. Have you heard anything about Taylor?" Debra had also bonded with Taylor during her brief tenure at the office. But Debra bonded with everyone.

Katie shook her head. "Still no word. What are you doing under there?"

"The cords were all tangled and I accidentally pulled the plug out of the wall. The computer shut down, the printer shut down, everything was plugged into the same box. I thought we'd lost power for a minute." She grinned, then assumed a more somber expression.

Katie scanned the waiting room again. All clear for now.

"Debra," Katie began, "I was wondering if you remember anything about Eugene Lowe and his troubles from years ago."

"I was so surprised to see him when he came for his

appointment!" Debra wheeled around her workstation while she talked, rebooting the computer and checking on the printer. "I'd heard he was out of prison and back living with his mom, but for some reason I never expected him to come *here*. I don't know why—I guess because he sort of became famous for a while, and you don't expect famous people to be real people, you know?"

Katie nodded and hoped Debra would get to the story of *how* Eugene had become famous before another patient came through the door. "What do you remember from that time?"

Debra stopped her chair in front of Katie and rested her chin on her hand. "Well, Eugene was a year or so behind me in school, so I didn't know him well. I know he and Alicia Stewart were friends and that there was some sort of drama during their senior year. Her father banned her from seeing him and made all sorts of threats against Eugene." She twirled her hair around a finger, which was her thinking pose. "It was a big deal at the time because they lived right next door to each other. I think it was especially traumatic for Eugene because she was really one of his only friends. But then Alicia ran off. In fact, her father accused Eugene of kidnapping her or scaring her away. I do remember that. It was right around this time of year and I ran into Eugene at the grocery store. He looked like he hadn't slept in months. It was as if his entire world had collapsed. The next thing I knew, he'd been arrested for killing some girl in Ann Arbor."

"Someone told me he was found with the body," Katie said. "Was there any more evidence against him?"

Debra shook her head. "I don't remember exactly. Sean

and I were planning our wedding at that point and I was focused on that. You might talk to Linda Carlson. I know my parents said she was refusing to reprint any of the news stories from Ann Arbor and went to visit Eugene in prison. She always claimed he had been set up, or at the very least was in the wrong place at the wrong time, but she didn't think that was enough to convict him—all circumstantial is what she said."

"Thanks, Debra," Katie said. "I'll have to make a stop at the newspaper office."

Katie turned to go back to her office.

"Hey, did Taylor ever get in touch with you?" Debra asked.

Katie turned slowly back to face Debra. "Taylor?"

"She called last week and I gave her your cell phone number. I forgot all about it over the weekend. She didn't leave a message." Debra blinked the tears away. "I just wondered if you talked to her before . . . she went missing."

Katie was about to press for more information when a mom and her three kids bustled in the door. She came to the desk, slightly out of breath.

The woman wore an oversized T-shirt and leggings. The two older children swarmed the toy area, pulling every toy out of the box. The youngest looked flushed and had obviously been crying.

Debra spun in her chair and rubbed her fingertips under her eyes.

"Sorry, I'm a few minutes late," the mom said.

"No problem," Debra said. "I'll get you checked in."

11

He borrowed his mother's car. It seemed the prudent thing to do after the last time. His old green Chevy pickup had rusted so badly while he was away that it was even easier to pick out of a lineup than he was—even with the ears. But the truck was loyal and he valued that above everything else. It was one of the things he'd learned in prison—who to trust (no one), who's got your back (anyone who owes you). On the outside, it was less clear. So many things could shift and slide.

He sat in the car parked a couple of houses down from where Alicia lived. He wanted to smoke, but didn't. He didn't want the hassle of an argument. His mother hated cigarettes.

Because it was daytime, he slouched in the seat and hoped there wasn't a nosy neighbor watching him as he stared at the house. He knew she usually came home around this time. She picked up her little girl at day care and came home an hour or so before the husband arrived. Who could have predicted that Alicia would marry Nathan Nielsen? She'd hated him in high school. But maybe that was just because Nathan had been such an ass to Eugene himself. Maybe, after everything that had happened, she didn't care about how Nathan had treated him.

He saw Alicia's car coming down the street toward him and congratulated himself again on using his mother's nondescript Ford sedan. Alicia would know his truck anywhere. They'd had such good times driving in that truck, singing at the top of their lungs to the Proclaimers (Alicia in a retro/ironic way, but Eugene had meant every word) and talking about the future.

Reality crashed into his thoughts as Alicia pulled into her driveway and got out of the car. She walked to the other side and reached in to unbuckle the baby. He wished he could get close enough to see the baby. She was probably beautiful like her mother.

He had been waiting for this moment for weeks. Slowly working up the courage to talk to her. He hadn't planned on this sense of paralysis. What if she rejected him? What if she didn't want to be friends anymore? Could he take the disappointment?

As he sat debating with himself, another car pulled in.

Nathan. Home early. Eugene knew better than to hang around. He started up the sedan and drove slowly away from Alicia's house.

12

After work, Katie and Matt drove to Ann Arbor to meet Gabrielle and Russell. Katie had been thrilled when Matt said he didn't have to work and that he'd love to meet Gabrielle's new "friend."

They walked into the dimly lit bar, and Katie squinted around the room. It was a typical just-off-campus bar. Dark, with lots of wood and small black tables. There was an enthusiastic game of darts in progress in a room separated from the tables by a half wall. The requisite large blue M hung over the bar, but there were no other nods to the university. Instead, license plates, street signs, and hubcaps had been nailed haphazardly on the walls. Katie spotted Gabrielle sitting at a table in the corner with a very attractive dark-haired man. His hair was on the longer side, like Matt's, but where Matt had the slightest curl that fell across his forehead, Russell Hunt's was stick straight.

Katie led the way to the table, with Matt right behind her.

Gabrielle stood as they approached and gave Katie a quick hug. "Katie, Matt, this is Russell."

They shook hands all around and said their hellos while grabbing seats. Before they had a chance to say anything more, the waitress was at the table for their drink order.

Whisky for Matt, of course. Katie ordered a pinot noir.

"You look really familiar; have we met before?" Matt asked Russell.

"I don't think so," Russell said. "Did you go to undergrad here?"

Matt nodded.

"Maybe you took one of my classes?"

"Doubt it. I was on a pretty tight premed track."

Russell shrugged and smiled at Gabrielle.

Katie asked Russell about his classes to distract him from Matt's continued staring.

"Gabrielle says you teach sociology," Katie said. "She was telling me about a project your students are working on. Something about true crime?"

"Yes, I've assigned that project for a couple of years now." Russell leaned back in his chair. He had that look of someone about to launch into a lecture. Probably an occupational hazard for a professor. "I like to have the students look at a criminal case through the lens of the media and then to try to get alternate views to demonstrate how media bias can skew public perception."

"That's very interesting," Katie said. "I'll bet you learn a lot yourself reading those papers."

"Definitely." Russell chuckled. "I learn a lot just sitting

in the classroom and listening to them debate and defend their positions. It's usually a pretty lively class."

The waitress arrived with the drinks, and Gabrielle took the opportunity to interrupt.

"I'm sure Russell doesn't want to talk about work all evening," Gabrielle said. She slid her hand around Russell's arm and gave Katie a pointed look.

"Oh, I don't mind," he said. "I love my work. I can't imagine doing anything else."

"You're a lucky man," Matt said. He lifted his glass in a toast, and Russell did the same.

"Don't you enjoy your work, Matt?" Russell asked.

"I do, most of the time," Matt said. "I'm not sure I love it the way you seem to. But it is rewarding to help people."

Katie looked at Matt. He'd alluded to this before. It made Katie wonder if *she* loved her work. She thought she did. She certainly had worked hard enough to get to this point. You didn't do that unless it was your calling, right?

"I understand," Russell said. "Sometimes I'll have a student that just really gets into the class and the projects, and it's rewarding to see that happening. To see a young person reshape their ideas about the world."

"Did you think Taylor Knox was that kind of student?" Katie asked.

Gabrielle raised a warning eyebrow at Katie. Katie pretended not to notice and focused on her drink.

"Taylor?" Russell looked momentarily confused.

"Katie also knew Taylor," Gabrielle said. "I introduced them because she wanted to be a family medicine doctor. They spent some time together over the summer."

"Oh, you're *that* doctor!" Russell said. "She talked about you. She really liked you." He took a gulp of his drink—something mixed with soda. "I really hope she's okay."

A heavy silence fell over the table as they all thought of Taylor Knox, who had been missing for four days. Katie thought Russell would ignore the question about Taylor, but he sighed and nodded.

"Taylor was exactly that kind of student," he said. "She took this project seriously and threw herself into the spirit of it. In fact, she was almost too invested. I didn't know how to stop her."

"Why would you want to stop her?" Matt asked.

Katie tilted her head and waited for Russell's answer. She would have asked the same question if Matt hadn't beat her to it. Regardless of what Russell said, she sensed he definitely *had* wanted to stop Taylor.

Russell shook his head and stirred his drink, avoiding eye contact. "Not stop her exactly. Just, I don't know, it was like she'd lost sight of the reason for the project and got herself wrapped up in trying to prove her subject's innocence."

"Gabrielle said she was working on Eugene Lowe's case, is that right?" Katie said, and ignored Gabrielle's glare.

"Yes, that's right. He was accused of killing a young woman ten or fifteen years ago. They never found a motive and there was a lot of talk at the time that maybe the police jumped to conclusions, but he went to prison just the same."

Gabrielle stood up. "I need to use the restroom. Katie, want to help me find it?"

Katie did *not* want to help her find it, especially because there was a large neon arrow at the back of the bar indicating the location of the restrooms. But she couldn't ignore Gabrielle's pointed looks any longer.

"Sure," Katie said.

As soon as they turned the corner into the hallway where the restrooms were located, Gabrielle turned and faced Katie.

"I know what you're doing," she said.

Katie held her hands up and tried to look innocent.

"Stop interrogating Russell. This is supposed to be a fun night out, not an investigation."

Katie figured she'd gotten as much out of Russell as she could anyway. She held her hands up in surrender. "Okay, no more questions."

They returned to the table, and Gabrielle steered the conversation toward Michigan's chances of going to the Rose Bowl. It didn't matter that they were barely halfway through the season. In Ann Arbor, the discussion was ongoing.

Russell spent ten minutes pontificating on the defense and the offense and the coach's errors so far this season. It seemed sociology wasn't the only thing he liked to lecture about.

After they had exhausted the football talk, Matt stood. "I'll get us another round."

"Looks like the dart board has opened up—anyone up for a friendly game?" Gabrielle said.

No game was ever friendly with Gabrielle, but Katie felt she owed her.

"I have to warn you, I've won some tournaments in darts," Russell said. He dropped an arm over Gabrielle's shoulders.

"Maybe you can teach me a few things," Matt said.

Katie jumped up to help Matt bring the drinks to the dart board.

She stood next to him and leaned closer, lowering her voice even though Russell and Gabrielle were halfway across the room. "How good are you at darts?"

Matt turned to her with a broad grin. "It's how I covered my bar tab all through med school."

Katie's shoulders relaxed. She knew Gabrielle could barely hit the target, let alone rack up a high score. There was something too self-satisfied about Russell and it rubbed her the wrong way.

This game was not going to be friendly.

13

Still gloating at the thought of Russell's face when Matt hit a bull's-eye three times in a row, Katie arrived at clinic on Friday morning and was met by both Debra and Angie in the back hallway.

"We have a bit of an issue," said Angie.

"You're overbooked and you have a walk-in," Debra said.

"Emmett is scheduled to see the emergencies today," Katie said. "Doesn't he have space in his schedule?"

Debra shook her head. Angie said, "She's refusing to see him. She'll only see you and she's very upset."

"Okay, who is it?" Katie asked. She turned to Debra. "Can I squeeze her in?"

"It's Gretchen Lowe. Eugene's mom," said Angie.

"You don't really have time . . ." said Debra.

"Is she sick?" Katie asked.

"No," Angie and Debra said together.

"I'll see her," Katie said. "Put her in the conference room and I'll see what I can do for her."

Debra bustled back out to the front and Angie followed. Katie knew Angie would be giving her "the doctor had an emergency and is running late" speech all morning. And she wouldn't be happy about it.

Katie went to her office and hung up her jacket. She put her stethoscope around her neck and glanced at the stack of phone messages. She closed her eyes, took a deep breath, and marched into the hallway.

Gretchen Lowe was a small woman, made even more so by her hunched posture. It was as if she were collapsing in on herself. Her dark hair was streaked with gray. Katie could see the resemblance to Eugene in her fine, pointy features and dark eyes.

"Mrs. Lowe?" Katie closed the door behind her and held out her hand. "I'm Dr. LeClair. How can I help?"

"I'm so sorry to burst in on you like this, Doctor," Gretchen Lowe said. "I didn't know where else to go. The police have been no help so far. They say he's a grown man. We have to wait twenty-four or forty-eight or five hundred and two hours . . ." Her eyes welled up and a tear escaped. She brushed it roughly away. "He said he really liked you. That you treated him with respect and kindness. He hasn't had that experience much in his life. I'm grateful to you."

Katie tried to piece together the emergency and decided she'd have to guide Gretchen through the story. She handed her a tissue and pulled up a chair.

"Tell me what's happened," Katie said, "Has Eugene been hurt again?"

The distraught woman shook her head and sniffled loudly. "I don't know. He's gone!"

"Gone?"

"Yes, I woke up this morning and he was gone."

"Was he planning a trip?"

"No, he would have told me." She waved her tissue around and then dabbed at the new tears. "He would have said good-bye," she said. "After everything we've been through, he wouldn't just leave me wondering what happened to him."

Katie ran through a list of responses in her head. The first of which was, "What am *I* supposed to do?" She rejected that one as being unfeeling, but she thought it was a good point.

"Okay, let's talk this through slowly," Katie said. She reached out and put her hand over Gretchen's tightly clenched ones. "When did you see him last?"

Gretchen took a deep breath and seemed to calm a bit. Possibly just the idea of doing something, anything, made her feel more in control.

"I saw him last night at dinnertime," she said. "He'd borrowed my car to run an errand and he came back in the late afternoon. I thought something was bothering him even then. He was quiet and kind of spacey. I had to ask him questions twice before he'd even notice I was talking."

Katie immediately thought drugs, but she hadn't heard any history of that.

"Was he a drug user, Mrs. Lowe?"

Gretchen caught her breath. "I didn't think of that. Do you think he could be using drugs? Did you get that sense from him when he was here to see you?"

"No, I didn't," Katie said. "I got the impression he was glad to be home except for the . . . accidents he'd been having."

"Accidents! Is that what he told you?" Gretchen looked at Katie, and she sensed the anger underneath the worry. "There was never any accident. They were harassing him. They didn't want him to come back and they were trying to make him afraid of his own hometown."

"Mrs. Lowe, do you know who 'they' are?"

She shook her head. "I have no idea. I don't think Eugene knows either. The cowards only come at night, and they're very careful to never be seen."

"Eugene didn't even see the men who assaulted him?"

"He says not, but I don't know." She looked at Katie through red, swollen eyes. "He didn't do it, you know. He never touched that girl and he went to prison for it, and now he's still in a kind of prison."

Katie sensed the conviction in what Gretchen said. But was that just a mother's bias? Did she actually know anything about that night? Katie wondered what Eugene's excuse had been when they found him with Heather's body.

"Okay, let me see what I can do," Katie said. "I think you should report this to the police. They may not act immediately, but at the very least there will be a record of it and people can be on the lookout for him."

"Okay, if you think it will help," she said. She pulled a tissue out of the box and blew her nose loudly.

"I have a friend in the police department, and I'll talk to him and be sure he does whatever he can to help find Eugene," Katie said.

Katie didn't say what she was thinking. Eugene might not want to be found. Or maybe his tormenters had struck again and he was hurt, or worse.

* * *

Katie couldn't get away from clinic until lunchtime. She saw Emmett in the hallway on her way out the door. He'd aged in the last month or so. He was tall, but seemed hunched, and his silver hair was dull. Katie hoped Nick, Emmett's son, would come back from his "sabbatical" healthy and able to work.

"Hello, Emmett," Katie said. "Any interesting patients lately?" Emmett loved to share stories of his patients with Katie. Whether it was an interesting medical puzzle or just a quirky personality, he seemed to save the good ones to tell her.

Emmett shook his head. "Not as interesting as yours, I hear," he said. He flashed her a grin that reminded her of the old Emmett, but it was quickly gone. "I remember Eugene Lowe from when he was just a little guy. It was a real shame what happened. He's been having trouble since he came back?"

"You could say that," Katie said.

"This town has a long memory, but I also believe it has a good heart. I hope the situation will resolve itself soon."

"Me, too," said Katie. She put a hand on his arm. "How are you, really?"

"Just fine," he said. When he saw her expression, he said, "Really. It hasn't been easy these past weeks, but I'm doing all right. It's Mrs. Hawkins I worry about. She's thrown herself into a Halloween frenzy. Every day there's another zombie or tombstone on our lawn. Gives me the creeps, but it keeps her busy, I guess."

"I'll have to drive by and see the display," Katie said, smiling.

"Come during the day to save yourself the nightmares," Emmett said.

They said good-bye, and Katie let herself out the back door into the parking lot.

She drove to the police station, and this time the receptionist called Chief Carlson immediately.

John Carlson ushered her into his office and sat behind his desk.

"I think I know why you're here," he said. "I'll tell you the same thing I told Gretchen Lowe. We can't start searching for an adult just because he decided to take a trip."

"I agree," said Katie.

Carlson's eyebrows shot up. "You do?"

"Of course. He's a grown man and he didn't tell his mother where he was going. If you chased down every person who did that, you'd never do anything else."

Carlson relaxed. "Well, I'm glad we agree."

"I did come to ask if there was anything you could do to keep an eye out for him," Katie said. "Gretchen insists that he wouldn't leave without telling her."

Carlson let out a sigh and rubbed his eyes. "I can have my officers watch for him, but we're all still working on Taylor Knox. *Her* parents are frantic too, and she's been missing for days."

Katie felt a wave of guilt. Of course they were still looking for Taylor. The police didn't have unlimited resources. She should have thought it through before charging into Carlson's office.

"I'm sorry, John. Of course, you're right," Katie said. "Is there anything I can do to help?"

"Other than finding Taylor alive and well?"

"You know she was doing a project on Eugene Lowe's case for one of her classes."

Carlson lowered his eyebrows. "How do you know that?"

Katie shrugged. "I recently met her professor and he told me."

"Yes, I'm aware of that project. The Ann Arbor police are looking into it." Carlson held his hands out. "It's not really my case. We're just helping them with any information we can. And, of course, searching. But she could be anywhere. She might not even be in Michigan anymore."

"Were you involved in Eugene's case?"

"Not really—it happened in Ann Arbor and Baxter had a different chief then—but I knew Eugene. He always seemed harmless to me. Maybe a little odd, but harmless. There had been that stalking episode with Alicia Stewart, but even that wasn't proven. Alicia herself never said a word against him, and I got the impression there was more to the story. But the father pushed the restraining order through, and Eugene got labeled."

"And then when he was found with the body of a young woman, they assumed he'd escalated."

Carlson shrugged. "I'm not saying they didn't do a good job investigating; they did. They had a whole list of people who they spoke to about that night. But they all had alibis except Eugene. And none of them had been labeled a stalker."

"Do you think he did it?"

Carlson put his hands out, palms up. "I really don't know. I didn't have access to all the information, so I don't know everything about the case. And Eugene never really gave a reason for why he was there. He just said he didn't hurt the girl and left it at that. He wouldn't give any more information, and I think his silence is what convicted him."

"Will you do what you can, unofficially, to try to find him?" Katie asked. "I'm worried that something has happened to him. Someone in town is out to get him, and maybe they finally succeeded."

"Or maybe he decided to cut his losses and move on to a place where no one knows him."

"In that case, why didn't he tell his mother?"

Carlson shrugged. "Do you tell your—" He broke off. "Sorry."

After the recent murder a month earlier, Katie had told John about her own mother's suicide when her cancer pain became intolerable. It was why Katie had refused to believe her patient could have killed herself. She was ever alert to signs of distress or warning signs of suicide.

"It's okay," Katie said. "You're right, he's an adult. And an adult who has been through a lot. I just hope he contacts her soon so she'll stop worrying."

"I'll put out an unofficial alert to be on the lookout, and if nothing changes in the next day or so, we can make it more official."

"Thanks, John," Katie said.

14

Katie dumped her bag on the kitchen table when she got home. After a good rummage through the pockets, she found what she was looking for. Before she'd left her office, she had written down the contact information Taylor had given her when she first started her job shadowing over the summer. At the time, Katie had thought it was ridiculous that they needed so many forms filled out just to have someone watch her work.

She pulled out her phone and dialed in the number for Taylor's roommate, Abby.

"Hello?"

She was surprised when Abby answered. Caleb had told her that no one answered their phones anymore. Everything was text or, in an emergency, voicemail. The voice sounded congested to Katie, and she briefly wondered if it was a cold or allergies. "Hello, is this Abby?"

"Yes?"

Katie couldn't tell if she was not sure of her own name,

or if Abby was just one of those students who phrased every statement as a question.

"My name is Dr. Katie LeClair." Katie crossed her fingers and plunged on. "I was hoping to meet with you to talk about your roommate, Taylor."

"Taylor?"

"Yes, Taylor Knox. She worked with me over the summer, and I know she's been missing for a few days. I'd like to help find her."

"I already talked to the police?"

Katie had her answer to the vocal tic question.

"I'm sure you did," said Katie. "This isn't anything official. I just really liked Taylor and . . ." Katie trailed off. And what? She thought she could solve the mystery of Taylor's disappearance?

"You're the doctor she worked with this summer?" Abby asked.

"Yes. I was very impressed with her."

"Taylor is impressive," Abby said. "She's my best friend." Her voice cracked and she sniffled loudly. Maybe not a cold or allergies.

"Would you be willing to meet me somewhere? I'd just like to talk to someone who knew her," Katie said.

"Okay. I know she really liked you," Abby said. "I don't want to go anywhere because of the reporters? I almost didn't answer when you called, but I thought it could be news on Taylor."

"I understand."

"You could come here, I guess?"

"I can be there in half an hour."

"Okay," Abby said.

Thirty-five minutes later, Katie knocked on the door of Taylor's apartment on campus. The hallway held the distinct dorm odor that was like no other. Part teenager, part noodle-based cooking, part old furniture. It made her briefly nostalgic for her student days.

The door swung open to reveal a tiny dark-haired girl. Hair in a ponytail, no makeup, wearing sweat pants and a T-shirt that said OH, HOW I HATE OHIO STATE, and a loose cardigan. The girl looked about twelve years old. Her red-rimmed eyes and pink nose betrayed a recent bout of tears.

"Come in," she said.

Katie lost her nostalgic feeling upon entering the apartment. The beige industrial furniture slumped sullenly in the living room. A battered dining table crouched under the weight of textbooks, papers, old mail, and takeout bags.

"Are you Abby?" Katie asked.

The girl nodded and gestured to the living room.

"Sorry about the mess," she said. "I haven't been able to focus on anything for more than five minutes since Taylor's been gone."

"I can imagine," Katie said. "You must be so worried."

Tears appeared immediately in Abby's eyes, and Katie realized how she must be struggling to keep herself under control for this meeting.

Katie looked around the apartment, wondering how she could help.

"When was the last time you ate anything?"

Abby lifted a shoulder and looked down at her bare feet.

"Let me make you some toast and eggs. Do you have that stuff in your fridge?"

Abby nodded and slid into one of the chairs at the table. Katie cleared a spot on the kitchen counter and set to work scrambling eggs. She popped a couple of pieces of bread in the toaster, and in just a few minutes, she set a plate in front of Abby.

The girl picked at the eggs at first, but after a couple of bites, her pace picked up and she devoured the simple meal in less time than it had taken to make it. Some color had appeared in her cheeks and she seemed less forlorn.

Katie sat in a chair opposite Abby. "I'm sorry to have upset you," she said.

Abby shook her head. "Everything upsets me these days. I just keep imagining these horrible scenarios. I can't take not knowing what happened to her, you know?"

"Yes, absolutely," said Katie. "That's why I'm here. I want to do something to help find her."

Abby looked up from her plate. "You think she's still alive?"

Katie didn't want to lie, but she didn't want to upset Abby any further either.

"I don't know what to think," she said. "I know that she was a very smart young woman. I hope she's just lying low for some reason, but we have to prepare for the worst." Katie hesitated, but the doctor in her knew it was unfair to give false hope. "I think the longer we go without hearing from her, the lower her chances."

Abby nodded and wiped her nose on her sleeve. "That's what I thought. So, what did you want to ask me?"

Katie had almost lost sight of her mission while tending to Abby. "I wanted to get a sense of her mood on that last day you saw her. I heard she was working on her sociology project?" Now Katie was doing it as well, making a statement into a question.

Abby rested her elbows on the table and put her chin on her hands. "That project took over her life. She was so obsessed with it?"

"Why do you think that was the case?"

"Her dad died a couple years ago? He was a cop?" Abby sat back in her chair and pulled her sleeves up over her fingers, hunching into the cardigan. "She got the idea that the guy who went to prison was innocent, and she was going to set the record straight."

Abby smiled slightly, remembering better times.

"She's like that, you know? She's always running around trying to fight injustice and help the underdog." Abby stared past Katie. "It's one of the best things about her."

"Do you know if she had started work on the paper yet?"

"The sociology paper?" Abby shrugged. "No idea. You can look in her room if you want. The police have already been in there."

Katie hopped to her feet before Abby had time to think about whether that was appropriate or not. Abby got up more slowly and led the way down a hall toward the bedrooms. The last door on the left had a nameplate on it: TAYLOR. Abby turned the knob and pushed the door open.

Taylor's room was nothing like the outer rooms in the apartment. It was fresh and bright with light-blue walls, white furniture, and black-and-white photos on the walls. Her desk was tidy, with only a few papers stacked to the right side. Katie went to it and opened a couple of the drawers. She wasn't sure what she was looking for, but thought it would stand out in all this neatness.

"Taylor had her laptop with her when she left," Abby said. "I remember her saying she would finish her research by the end of the weekend."

Katie, who was a terrible backer-upper, wondered if Taylor had a backup computer drive. She certainly was more organized than Katie had ever been at her age. The top drawer of the desk held pens and pencils, phone chargers and gum. The next drawer was more familiar to Katie—filled with odds and ends like nail polish, lipstick, batteries, hand cream, plastic animal figures, and chocolate. The bottom drawer was larger and held files. Most were labeled by class, but there was nothing there that seemed pertinent to Taylor's project.

Katie sighed. This had been a wasted trip.

"What are you looking for?" Abby asked.

"I was hoping that Taylor would have a backup for her computer, or some notes on her project," Katie said. "But it looks like she took everything with her."

"She left all these thumb drives," Abby said. "Maybe there's something on one of them."

Katie looked at the drawer Abby had opened. "Thumb drives?" Katie asked.

Abby picked up the plastic elephant figure and pulled its head off to reveal the USB connector.

Katie suddenly felt very old. "These are all memory sticks?"

Abby nodded. "She collected them. I don't know if she used them all, but she liked the animals."

Katie took the elephant, cow, monkey, rooster, pig, and shark and put them on the desktop. She debated with herself. Should she call the police and tell them about these? What would they do with them? Instead, she decided she'd have her computer hacker brother take a look, and she could turn over anything interesting to John Carlson.

"I'd like to take these with me," Katie said. "There might be a clue as to where Taylor could be."

Abby shrugged. "I think it's all just school stuff, but take them if you want. If you think it will help find her, I don't think she would mind."

Katie took a final look around the room. She picked up the stack of papers on the desk, which appeared to be flyers for concerts and events around campus. On the last flyer, a notice about a poetry reading, was a sticky note with names on it. Eugene Lowe was one of them. Katie grabbed it and shoved it in her pocket.

Katie followed Abby back out into the living room.

"Is there anyone else you can think of who might know where she would go if she wanted to get away?"

"Is that what you think happened?" Abby asked. "I don't think Taylor would just go away without telling anyone where she went." Abby's eyes filled with tears again. "It's why I'm sure something terrible has happened. She wouldn't want us to worry. And she's very close with her mom. There's no way she would put her through this. If she was able, she'd contact us."

Katie agreed. She hoped she was wrong, but thought that Taylor had definitely disappeared against her will. It was a sad commentary on the situation that not finding a body yet was the only consolation she had.

"But, to answer your question, the only other person I can think of is Colin, her boyfriend."

"They've been together for a while, is that right?"

Abby nodded. "Two years." She stared past Katie for a minute. "There might have been something going on with them. I'd never heard them argue, but I think they were going through a rough patch. Colin said she was obsessed with this sociology project. She was meeting with Professor Hunt all the time." She lowered her voice as if there were other people around who might overhear. "He has a reputation, you know."

Katie kept her face blank. "What kind of a reputation?"

"He's dated students before," Abby said in an offhand way. "It's sort of an open secret."

Katie cleared her throat. "How many students?"

Abby shrugged. "I'm a literature major, so I've never taken a class with him, but you hear stories. I mean, there are stories in my department too."

"Do you think Taylor was involved with her professor?"

Abby chewed on her lower lip, thinking. "I'm not sure. She definitely went to his office hours a lot. But I think she would have told me. And she adores Colin. But Colin might have thought that. He can get pretty jealous sometimes."

"Do you have Colin's phone number?" Katie asked.

Abby pulled out her smartphone and scrolled with her thumb. She put it back in her pocket, and Katie heard her own phone buzz in her purse.

Katie thanked Abby, stuffed the animal thumb drives in her purse, and headed out to the parking lot.

She called Colin from her car, hoping she could arrange to meet him soon, while she was still in Ann Arbor. His phone clicked over to voicemail, and she left a quick message asking him to get back to her.

Katie pulled the sticky note out of her pocket. The names were listed with phone numbers neatly written in different colored ink, as if Taylor had filled in the list as she gathered the information.

Katie glanced down the list: Hope Frost, Brad Humphreys, Alicia Stewart, Nathan Nielsen, Danny Lloyd, Russell Hunt, and Eugene Lowe.

Katie studied the names, chewing her lip. Obviously, she knew some of them. Alicia Stewart was her patient and Eugene's high school friend. She had married Nathan Nielson. Katie didn't want to think about why Russell's name was on the list. And the other three were unfamiliar. Danny Lloyd, Russell Hunt, and Hope Frost had lines through their names. Did that mean Taylor had ruled them out as suspects for her project? Or did it just mean she had talked to them? Katie wondered if the police had this information. Probably not, since it had still been in Taylor's room.

Katie pulled out her phone and dialed Hope's number. It went immediately to voicemail. "Hi, this is Hope. Leave a message."

Katie skipped Russell's name and tried Danny Lloyd.

After the second ring, a rough voice said, "Yeah?" There were loud noises in the background and men talking.

Katie cleared her throat. "Hi, my name is Katie LeClair. I'm a friend of a girl named Taylor Knox. I think you may have met her recently."

"I already told her everything I know," he said. "I can't help you."

Katie could tell he was about to hang up.

"Wait," Katie said. "I don't know if you've heard about the missing girl, but it's Taylor. I'm just trying to find out what she was up to in the few days before she disappeared."

The background noise became faint, and Katie assumed Danny had moved into a different area.

"I was sorry to hear about that, but I saw her a week before she disappeared. I don't know anything. And I don't need any trouble."

"Can I just meet with you for a few minutes? I only want to find out what you talked about. I think she was doing some research that may have put her in danger."

"Look, I'm sorry about your friend, but I don't know anything about her or her disappearance."

Katie heard a click and the dial tone. She glared at her phone.

She closed her eyes, counted slowly to ten, and took a deep breath. She pressed redial.

It rang and rang and went to voicemail. Katie called again.

The third time she called, he answered.

"What?"

Katie knew she'd have only one more chance to convince him.

"I know someone working on the investigation into Taylor's disappearance. They may or may not know she met with you. I'd be happy to pass that information along. If you won't talk to me, you can talk to the police."

Danny sighed.

"I'm working late tonight," he said. "I can talk to you for five minutes. If I get even a whiff that you're a reporter, *I'm* calling the police."

He gave Katie the address of the garage where he worked. That explained the noises.

"I'll be there in fifteen minutes."

"Yeah, okay."

Katie headed west of the main campus. The garage where Danny worked was located off Jackson Road near the car dealerships. Katie pulled into the auto body shop ten minutes later. She parked in the gravel lot and climbed out of her car. The noise from the highway and the pneumatic drill masked her steps as she approached the open bay. A red mustang convertible was up on a lift, and someone's boots stuck out from underneath. Katie was debating whether to tap the boots to get the owner's attention when she noticed a tall blond man approaching. His hair was pulled back into a ponytail, and he wore blue coveralls with combat boots.

After lightly wiping his hand on a rag, he extended it for Katie to shake. His nails were rimmed in dark oil, but his grip was firm.

"I assume you're Katie?" he said.

"Yes, thanks for meeting with me."

He narrowed his eyes. "It's not like you gave me a choice. I sensed you wouldn't let up until I met with you. And now you have. I still don't have any information for you."

He turned and walked toward a glassed-in office area. Katie followed.

He sat behind a beat-up desk piled with manuals, files, papers, and old takeout food bags. He gestured at a chair with metal legs and a cracked vinyl seat that might have been army green at one time but was now dark gray.

Katie sat gingerly on the edge. "Can you remember the date that you met with Taylor?"

Danny glanced at a wall calendar pinned behind the desk. He pointed to the second week of October. "It was somewhere in here." He gestured at a couple of days in mid-October. "I remember because she commented on a yellow Camaro we had up on the lift, and that guy picked up his car on the seventeenth."

That was the week before she disappeared, just as he had claimed. Katie wondered if he was really as nonchalant about Taylor as he seemed.

"What did she want to talk to you about?"

Danny sighed and leaned forward to rest his elbows on the desk. "She wanted to talk about Heather Stone. Do you know anything about her?"

Katie nodded. "She was killed twelve years ago on Halloween."

Danny rubbed his eyes. "Right. Heather and I dated the spring before she died. She had already dumped me by the time she died, but the police wanted to dredge up that old relationship. They seemed to think I might have held a grudge." Danny spread his hands out. "Like a brief student romance would cause someone to kill his ex. If that were true, no one would ever survive college."

"Did you go to University of Michigan as well?"

Danny shook his head. "No, I picked up a few classes at the community college, and then I opened this place."

"How did you meet Heather, then?"

"Back in our early twenties, my friends and I would crash frat parties and other events on campus. It was a good way to meet girls." He shrugged. "Too old for that now. And honestly, Heather put me off of college girls anyway."

"How so?"

Danny looked at the ceiling. He lowered his eyes and met Katie's gaze. "She was a manipulative bitch."

Katie felt the anger behind his words and reflexively leaned back away from him. Before she could respond, Danny continued. "She liked to play guys off of each other. She'd break up with one guy and then parade the new one around. She'd always act shocked if there was trouble, but she had to know what she was doing. She'd go to a party where she knew the ex-boyfriend would be. Between alcohol and male jealousy, she managed to put herself at the center of a lot of drama."

"Did she do that to you?"

Danny snorted. "She tried. But I was a little older than her usual guy and I didn't get drawn in."

"When was the last time you saw her?"

"The night she died." Danny held his hands up. "Before you say anything, we had a brief chat and I left the party. She was trying to push my buttons and I wasn't playing. Listen, I have to get back to work. I've got an owner coming in two hours and I still have to finish the detailing."

Danny stood and gestured to the door. Katie didn't think she'd get any more out of him. She was surprised he had told her as much as he had. Which made her wonder how much of it was true.

15

Twenty minutes later, Katie parked in her driveway and was disappointed to see that Caleb's car was gone. She had hoped he would help her scroll through whatever was on the thumb drives. With a sigh, she opened her car door and pulled out her messenger bag. Lunch seemed like it had been days ago, but she was too anxious to look at Taylor's files to worry about eating just yet.

She dumped her coat in the kitchen and went straight to her room to get her laptop. She flipped it open and waited briefly for it to wake up. She grabbed the elephant first and put it into her USB port. As her computer read the thumb drive, Katie chewed on her thumbnail. A box popped up on her screen showing absolutely nothing. The thumb drive was empty. The cow and rooster were the same. Empty.

There was a momentary spike of excitement when the shark yielded a folder, but when Katie clicked on it, it was just photos. Katie scrolled quickly through them and didn't see anything of interest. Most of them were snapshots and selfies dated over a year ago.

Finally, with the monkey, she got lucky. This one seemed to be her school backup. There were multiple files labeled by class with documents that seemed to be notes from class and papers. She clicked on SOCIOLOGY.

Several files popped up, but Katie's eye was drawn immediately to the one labeled EUGENE LOWE. She clicked it open and was rewarded with more files. Taylor *was* obsessed, as her boyfriend had said. She had files with police reports, newspaper articles, notes, and a rough draft of her paper.

Katie felt a frisson of unease as she pulled her notebook out of her bag. Looking through Taylor's computer files felt more invasive than she had expected. After the strange questions Taylor had asked, Katie felt she had to see what she'd been working on before she disappeared. Katie had to swallow her squeamishness and get to work.

She clicked on the first file, labeled NOTES, and a dialogue box came up demanding a password. Katie felt her eyebrows draw together. She clicked on the rest of the files and was met with the smug password request box each time.

She shut her laptop and pushed away from the table. She'd make something to eat while she waited for Caleb to get home. He could probably break through the password protection in a couple of minutes.

A text confirmed he was out with friends and wasn't sure when he'd be home. When he still hadn't returned by midnight, Katie went to bed and fell into a fitful sleep.

* * *

Katie woke up in the dark. Something had disturbed her sleep, and before she had time to think, she heard it again.

Someone was pounding on the kitchen door. She glanced at her clock, which told her it was 2:14 AM.

Her first thought was Caleb. Had he forgotten his key? She stumbled to the door, grabbing a long cardigan on her way. She met Caleb in the hallway.

"Who the hell is that?" he said.

"How should I know?" Katie said. "I thought it was you."

The two of them went into the kitchen and flicked on the light. The pounding had begun again but stopped when the lights came on.

Caleb held up his hand to Katie and cautiously approached the door.

He peeked around the curtain.

"It's some guy," he whispered.

The pounding came again. They heard a voice on the other side of the door. "Dr. LeClair, let me in, please!"

Caleb crooked his finger in the direction of the door. "It's for you."

"Well, open the door," Katie said.

Caleb left the chain on and opened the door a crack.

"Who are you?" said the man outside.

"Who are you?" said Caleb.

"I'm a patient of Dr. LeClair's. Is she here?"

Caleb glanced back at Katie, and she nodded that he should let the person in. Caleb shut the door and took the chain off. When he reopened it, Eugene hurried through the door and slammed it shut behind him.

"Thank you," he said. He flicked the bolt. "I didn't know where else to go."

Katie stepped toward the intruding patient. "Eugene, what are you doing here?"

When Katie said his name, Caleb looked more carefully at the man in front of him.

"I'm so sorry to barge in like this," Eugene said.

"Where have you been?" Katie asked. "Your mother is worried."

Katie felt like she was reprimanding a teenager.

Eugene leaned against the door and closed his eyes. "I had some things to do and I didn't want anyone following me." He held up his hands. "I know that sounds paranoid, but I feel like they're tracking my every move."

Caleb stood between Katie and Eugene. His arms were crossed, and he blocked Eugene from coming further into the house.

"Caleb, it's okay." Katie put her hand on his arm.

Caleb stepped back to allow Eugene into the kitchen but didn't change his threatening stance. Eugene looked at Caleb curiously and stepped past him into the room.

"Eugene, this is my brother, Caleb." The two men nodded briefly at each other.

"You'd better sit and tell us what's going on," Katie said.

They all pulled out chairs at the table and sat.

"I was headed back to my mom's house earlier this evening when I realized someone was following me."

"Did you see who it was?" Katie asked.

Eugene turned toward Katie. "No, he stayed in the shadows, but I know he was there."

"Why didn't you go to the police?" Caleb asked. "How did you know where we live?"

Eugene smirked at Caleb. "You think there's anyone in town who *doesn't* know where the new doctor lives? And I didn't go to the police because I'm not the sort of person they worry about protecting. I thought I would be okay if I just went home, but when I got to my street, I saw that there were people watching the house."

"What do you mean, they were watching the house?" Katie asked.

"There was a car just a couple houses down with a guy sitting in it. I might have walked right past him, but I smelled his cigarette. I waited, thinking he had just stopped to have a smoke, but he finished it and then just sat there. I'm sure he was watching the house."

"How can you be sure he had anything to do with you?" Caleb asked.

"I've spent a lot of time the last month or so watching for these guys. I recognized the car. It's one of the cars that drives past the house several times a night just to scare me."

Caleb glanced at Katie. She knew what he was thinking: that Eugene was paranoid and maybe a little unstable. But Katie wasn't so sure. Certainly, after everything he had been through, he was allowed to be on edge.

"Why did you come *here*?" Katie asked.

"It was the first place I could think of when I realized I couldn't go home," Eugene said. "You were nice to me and I figured they would never suspect I'd come here. I just blended back into the shadows and hid for a while. I wanted to be sure they were watching my house before I did any-thing else. I also wanted to be sure my mom was safe."

"So you hid for most of the evening and then made your way here?" Caleb asked, and didn't hide the disbelief in his voice.

Eugene wouldn't meet Caleb's eyes, but he nodded.

"What are you planning to do?" Katie asked.

"I'll go home tomorrow when the coast is clear."

Katie wasn't sure the coast would be clear in the morning either. She was also starting to wonder just what was going on with Eugene. Where did he have to go that necessitated all of this skulking around? Why couldn't he have told Gretchen? She started to revise her theory about what Taylor had discovered. He certainly wasn't acting like a person with nothing to hide. *And* it sounded like he planned on spending the night.

"Eugene, what happened to Heather Stone?" Katie asked. She figured she might as well be blunt. He was hiding out in her house, after all.

Eugene's head snapped up. "You think I killed her?"

Katie put her hands up. "I don't know anything about it. I wasn't here in Baxter—I wasn't even in Ann Arbor."

Eugene's shoulders slumped. "I have no idea."

"What do you mean?" Katie leaned forward, arms on the table.

Eugene sighed. "I followed Alicia to Ann Arbor." He shrugged and hesitated. "She was my only friend. I didn't think I'd be able to face every day at school without her there."

"Were you trying to bring her back home?"

Eugene nodded. "That was my plan. I thought if I could bring her home, her dad would forgive me and drop the restraining order and everything would go back to the way it was."

"It's not easy to get a restraining order," Katie said. "What did you do?"

Eugene rolled his eyes. "It sounds really stupid now, but we just had this game we played. It was Alicia's idea. We got talking about weird things people do. She'd read some story about friends who stole things from each other and earned points if it took the other person a long time to figure out what it was."

"If it was all just a game, why did it escalate so fast?"

"I don't know." Eugene looked at the table. "I thought it would be funny. I figured if I stole all of her underwear, she'd have to notice pretty quick. We were just kids, playing a prank. What did we know? Alicia thought it was hilarious, but when the police found all that stuff, it wasn't so funny."

Katie and Caleb exchanged a glance. Truth or lie?

"The night that Heather was killed. Did you argue with her?" Katie asked.

Eugene shook his head. "I never spoke to her. I had a fight with Alicia because she didn't want me to get in trouble for breaking the restraining order. I walked to my car and then changed my mind and walked back to the party. I saw Heather lying in the Law Quad. I thought it was Alicia." Eugene stopped and pulled the pink beads out of his pocket.

Katie and Caleb waited for him to continue.

He clicked the beads through his fingers and seemed to be trying to calm himself. After a moment, which seemed like an eternity and had Katie itching to grab the bracelet out of his hands, he continued his story.

"I ran over to her—she was dressed the same as Alicia. She had the same blonde hair, but I was so glad it wasn't Alicia that I didn't even think. I just stood there and then some security guard came along, and before I knew it, I was in jail."

Eugene looked up and met Katie's eyes. "It's the truth."

"But why didn't you ever tell anyone?" Caleb asked.

"I did," Eugene said. "No one believed me. Not even my own lawyer."

"That's probably enough for tonight," Katie said, then stood.

"We can give you a blanket and a couch if you want to stay here," she said, and then handed her phone to Eugene. "Call your mother. She's worried sick."

Eugene took the phone, dialed, and held the phone to his ear.

Caleb shot her an "Are you crazy?" look, but Katie ignored him.

After a brief conversation, which left Eugene blushing furiously, he handed Katie her phone back, thanked her for her offer of a couch, and followed her into the living room.

Katie pulled a blanket out of the linen closet and handed it to Eugene. Caleb hovered in the hallway.

As Katie turned to go back to her room, Caleb stepped toward her and whispered, "Lock your door."

She started to protest and then just nodded. Caleb waited while she went into her room.

She leaned against the door and took a deep breath. Did she believe Eugene? She honestly wasn't sure. Part of being a doctor meant being a good judge of people. Katie felt like she had a pretty good BS meter, but everyone got fooled once in a while. Considering the story she'd heard from Danny, maybe Heather had pushed Eugene in some way that had made him lash out. Katie only had his word for it that they'd never spoken. As Alicia's friend, would Heather have known what to say to get a reaction out of him? Had she been the kind of person who liked to mess with people just for the fun of it?

Unfortunately, only Heather could answer those questions and she had been gone for years. And Katie was convinced that Taylor had asked her cryptic question about whether to let someone get away with a crime because of her research into Eugene's case. But even that left Katie with more questions. She had said that someone had gotten away with a crime. Could Eugene have had an accomplice? Or was he innocent? And even if he *was* innocent in Heather's death, and even though he had been just a teen, the story of stealing the underwear creeped her out.

As she debated with herself, she remembered his changing story about his injuries. First he had tripped; then he'd run into a door. Either he'd fallen off a ladder or had been attacked by anonymous miscreants. Maybe he wasn't the innocent victim he claimed to be. He had lied to her before, so how could she be sure he was telling the truth now?

She was angry with herself for being so suspicious, but she'd never sleep now with her room unlocked.

She pushed away from the door, turned the lock, and then, in a moment of paranoia, pulled a chair over and shoved the back of it under the doorknob.

16

The next day was Saturday. Which would have been great except that Katie was scheduled for morning clinic. At least it would all be quick visits. Saturdays were urgent appointments only. Which could be dead boring or run-ragged busy.

After Eugene left for home, Katie had called John Carlson to tell him that Eugene was safe. Caleb had taken all of the animal thumb drives and promised to let her know as soon as he figured out how to get into the password-protected files. She was hoping to hear from him soon.

Fortunately, clinic ended up moving more smoothly than she'd expected and Angie didn't have to sigh heavily even once. She finished up her charting and was ready to leave the office by one o'clock.

Katie knew Caleb was working on his app and the thumb drives at home. She called him from the office and told him her plan.

"Okay, I'll see you there," he said, and disconnected.

Caleb was up for anything if food was used as a bribe.

She'd offered him lunch in exchange for helping her to research Eugene's case.

Just as she stepped into the parking lot, her phone buzzed. She pulled it out of her pocket and looked at the display. COLIN. Taylor's boyfriend. Finally.

"Hello?"

"Dr. LeClair? This is Colin Masters. You left a message on my phone."

Kate unlocked her car and slid behind the wheel, clutching the phone between her ear and shoulder.

"Colin, hi. Thanks for calling me back. I'm so sorry about Taylor. I'm sure this must be a very tough time for you."

"How do you know Taylor?" His voice was clipped, almost aggressive. "Are you her doctor?"

"No, she worked with me this past summer." Katie kept her voice calm and steady.

Colin exhaled and softened his voice. "I would have called sooner if I'd made the connection. She really likes you. You haven't heard from her, have you?"

Katie closed her eyes at the hopeful tone and hesitated. "No, I haven't. I'm sorry."

"Every time my phone vibrates, I think it will be Taylor." Colin stopped and released a long sigh. He cleared his throat and continued. "Telling me she's on her way back home."

"I'm sure it must be very hard for you. Just waiting."

"Plus, everywhere I go, there's either a cop or a journalist ready to pounce. They say I'm not a suspect, but it doesn't feel that way. And they say they aren't even sure she's in danger, but it doesn't feel that way either."

"Colin, did Taylor tell you anything about a project she

was working on for school? She was looking into an old criminal case?"

"She never stopped talking about it. She was obsessed. And that smarmy professor just encouraged it. In fact, we had a big fight about it a week or so ago. I told her to give it a rest."

Smarmy professor? That was two students who thought Russell Hunt was not as great as Gabrielle believed.

"Smarmy professor?"

"Professor Hunt." Colin's voice was hard. "Everyone knows he has a thing for undergrads. I *tried* to tell Taylor, but she just laughed and said she didn't care about him, only the project she was working on. She said she was sure there was something wrong with the case."

"Do you know if she had drawn any conclusions?" Katie mentally crossed her fingers, hoping Colin knew whom Taylor suspected.

"No. She wouldn't say. I know she thought the guy who went to prison was innocent, but she got sort of secretive about it after our fight. First she wouldn't shut up about the project, and then, nothing. It was like she wasn't even work-ing on it. And, to be honest, I was just as glad not to have to hear every detail. His voice became quiet. But now I wish I'd asked questions and really listened. She may have just stopped telling me about it to keep the peace. If something happened to her because of her project . . ."

Katie took a breath, debating whether to tell Colin about seeing Taylor. Instead, she switched tactics. "Were you guys getting along okay?"

There was a long moment of silence. "You're just like the cops. Always blame the boyfriend."

"No, that's not—"

Colin interrupted. "I love Taylor and would never hurt her. All I want is to get her back safely. Listen, I gotta go."

"Wait—"

But Katie was talking to dead air.

Ten minutes later, Katie grabbed a spot in the Purple Parrot and watched for Caleb. He rounded the corner just as her tea was delivered to the table.

The Purple Parrot was one of Katie's favorite places in Baxter. Run by a mother-daughter team, they made the best coffee in town and also knew how to serve pots of tea. Couches and comfy chairs huddled around coffee tables in several groupings. Books and knickknacks filled the shelves on the back wall, making the whole space feel like a cozy library. Purple and yellow dominated the color scheme, which would not have been Katie's first choice, but it gave the comfy space a bright, happy vibe. There were five or six small tables near the counter. The menu was heavy on comfort food: potpies, stews, and soups with a few salads thrown in for the virtuous.

"Hey, Katie," Caleb said. "I'm *really* hungry. I might have to have one of everything."

Katie smiled and sipped her tea. "Go for it."

"What are you having? The usual?" Caleb asked.

"I like what I like," she said. She shrugged and pointed to the potpie on the menu.

"Yeah, the chicken potpies are really good here. If I get something else and you have the potpie, I'll be jealous. But if I get something else and it's better than the potpie, then you'll be jealous and I will win the best menu choice game." Caleb pumped a fist in the air.

Katie shook her head and smirked at him.

"I didn't know that was a thing," Katie said.

"Of course it's a thing. And you win most of the time. I don't know how you do it." Caleb hunched over the menu as if studying it for ancient secrets, or coding errors.

"Just get the potpie, Caleb."

"Yeah, okay," Caleb said. "Then we'll both win." He flipped the menu shut.

Bella Peterson, the daughter of the team, arrived at that moment to take their order. She was in her midtwenties, blonde, with blue eyes and a sweet smile. She flashed one at Caleb and he grinned.

After she left, he leaned back in his chair. "I haven't had any luck yet with those thumb drives. I'll have to work on it some more this afternoon. So, what's this research project you've lured me into?"

Katie told him her theory that because Taylor had been investigating Eugene's case, maybe there was a connection. She had hoped there would be a clue in the files, but she said they could do some of their own research into the case. She thought she should learn more about what had occurred all those years ago.

"I always feel a little lost when something like this happens. Everyone in town already knows the story, and I'm just trying to figure things out. I don't have any context." Katie stirred her tea. "But Eugene's mother insists that not only was he being targeted but that he was innocent."

"Well, what mother is going to say her son was guilty?"

Caleb smiled at Bella Peterson when she brought the potpies to the table. Katie narrowed her eyes. There was an awful lot of smiling going on with these two. Bella was exactly the kind of girl Caleb liked. She wondered why he hadn't mentioned Bella before. Katie liked Bella. Maybe she and Matt could double date. It would probably go better than the double date with Gabrielle that she had ruined by interrogating Russell.

Katie reined in her thoughts. She didn't even think the two were dating, but something was up. Bella wandered off and Katie had Caleb's attention again.

"You're right, of course," Katie said. She cut into the top of the pie to let it cool. The delicious aroma of chicken, vegetables, and butter wafted up in a cloud of steam. "But the way Matt described it, Eugene was just there. No one saw him push her, or talk to her, or even had any way of showing that they knew each other."

"Okay, so where do we start?"

"I think we should visit the *Baxter Gazette* office. They must have covered the case, and maybe Linda will have something about the local perspective as well."

Caleb looked at her in a deadpan way. "I assume you've already tried the Internet? Source of all knowledge?"

Katie smiled. "Yes, but the *Gazette* archives don't go back that far. I think they've only been online for the past couple of years."

"M-kay," Caleb said, and focused on his lunch.

* * *

Linda Carlson was petite, with sleek gray hair cut in a bob. She smiled broadly when Katie stepped through the door to the *Baxter Gazette* offices.

"Katie, how nice to see you." Linda came forward and took Katie's hand in both of her own. Linda, John's wife, also believed that Katie had saved their beloved Bubba, and she was treated like royalty every time Linda saw her.

"Linda, you remember my brother, Caleb."

"Of course!" Linda turned to Caleb as if he was the most exciting person she had ever met. "It's a pleasure to see you again."

"Likewise, Mrs. Carlson."

"Linda, please, you'll make me feel old." She flapped her hand at him.

"Linda," Katie said, "we were wondering if we could look at your archives?"

"Of course. Is there something in particular you're looking for? Last time you came here, you wanted news from forty years ago." Linda laughed. "How far back are we going today?"

"Just ten or fifteen years," said Katie. "I'm interested in Eugene Lowe and any information about his arrest and trial."

Linda's smile fled from her face. "Ah, Eugene. That was a sad story."

"Do you remember it?"

"Of course. It was all anyone could talk about that whole winter. He was arrested on Halloween, and the trial was in the spring, I think. I, for one, was shocked. He'd always been a quiet, gentle kid, and I couldn't believe that he would hurt anyone."

"So, did other people in town agree with you?"

Linda shook her head. "I wouldn't say that. The town was pretty much divided on the subject. Eugene had had that unfortunate incident with the Stewarts. Alicia Stewart's father had nothing good to say about Eugene, and some people sided with him. Eugene was different and not everyone appreciated that."

"Do you think there are any stories in the *Gazette*?"

"Unfortunately, I'm quite sure there aren't," said Linda. She ran her hand through her hair and it fell right back into place. "My father was still in charge of the paper back then, and he felt that tempers were running high enough. He didn't want the paper to wade into the mess."

"Really? He just censored the whole thing out?" Caleb asked.

"Well, not censored, exactly, but remember, it all happened in Ann Arbor, and their newspaper had tons of coverage. My dad just felt like he didn't want to add fuel to the flame of either side of the argument, and it wasn't like there was *no* coverage." Linda shook her head. "I think that was when he really decided to retire. He just didn't have the heart for it anymore. He turned everything over to me the next year."

"I'm sorry to hear that," Katie said. She rapidly rethought her plan and was already mentally checking her schedule for a free couple of hours to go to Ann Arbor during the week. "I was hoping to get some background on the case. Eugene is my patient, and I hoped to fill in some of the gaps."

"Oh, I didn't say there was *no* information. Just not from the *Baxter Gazette*." Linda waved them over to a filing cabinet behind her desk. "I was fascinated with the story, so I have files on all the news reports. There are even a couple of articles I wrote hoping my dad would change his mind." She rummaged in the cabinet. "I think I had a transcript of the trial in here somewhere . . ."

Katie and Caleb exchanged a glance. Katie's look was thrilled, while Caleb's was incredulous that people still used filing cabinets.

Linda pulled out a thick file folder and brought it to the desk.

"You're welcome to look through this and see if it helps." Linda tapped a finger to her lips. "I wondered at the time whether that was the full story. This all happened right around the time of the recession, when newspapers started closing around the country. It was shortly after this that the Ann Arbor newspaper went to digital only. I know they were working with a skeleton staff."

"But you still publish a hard copy newspaper?" Caleb couldn't hide the shock in his voice.

"It's a labor of love," Linda said. "I write all the stories, businesses in town still buy ads so I can pay for the printing, and I only publish once a week. But even that will likely stop eventually."

"Too much work for one person?" Katie asked.

"Not that so much as my main paper subscribers are dying off. I publish to the website as well, and I do midweek updates. Most of the younger readers just read it online."

"It does cut down on the tree killing," Caleb said.

"You're right, of course. But there is something very satisfying and calming about reading the paper in the morning with a cup of coffee. Scrolling on the screen is just not the same."

Katie elbowed Caleb in the side to keep him from pursuing one of his favorite topics.

"You were saying you wondered about the coverage?" Katie said.

"It's just that . . . well, you'll see. There wasn't a lot of new information after the initial story. It's the kind of thing that would have warranted follow-ups and human-interest stories. They just sort of let it drop and I always wondered why."

"Do you mind if we sit over here and take some notes?"

"Be my guest," Linda smiled. "Let me know if you need anything."

Katie and Caleb sat next to each other and opened the file.

The yellowing and brittle newspaper articles had been cut from their original pages and were labeled at the top with dates in fading pencil.

Katie scanned the articles and carefully turned the fragile pages. She felt like maybe she should be wearing white gloves and working in an environmentally controlled room. The headlines ranged from subdued to sensational. *Coed Dies in Law Quad. Law Quad Killer Arrested!* And the usual editorial pieces: *Alcohol and Undergrads* and *Rape on Today's Campuses.* Even though Katie was pretty sure Heather had not been raped.

Linda's article was very well-written and had more information than any of the others. She described the Halloween party Heather had attended just before she was killed at a University-sponsored event. She hinted at the need for further inquiry into the amount of alcohol that had been smuggled in (something the other stories had failed to mention). She also had written a haunting description of Eugene sitting alone in his jail cell. Katie felt certain that if Linda's article had been published, Eugene would have had more people on his side in Baxter.

By the time they had finished skimming through the articles (which, as Linda had suggested, repeated the same information), Katie felt no closer to understanding what had happened. Mrs. Peabody and Miss Simms had provided a better synopsis.

The court transcript was dense, and Katie decided to

ask Linda for a copy. She could go over it later when she had more time.

She noticed Linda had a summary of the postmortem report but not the report itself. Cause of death was head trauma, but Katie would have loved to see the whole report.

She sighed as she flipped the last article over and closed the file.

Caleb had been assigned as note-taker, but all he had done was take pictures with his phone of anything Katie had indicated would be helpful. They both leaned back and stretched.

Linda glanced up from her computer screen. "All finished?"

Katie nodded. "Thank you for letting us look at the file."

"It didn't help much?"

Caleb shook his head. "I don't think there was much more in the paper than we had already heard."

Katie was irritated with herself. She felt so helpless in the search for Taylor, and now she had wasted more time and gotten no further information. She had hoped to discover whether there were any other suspects in the case. She had Taylor's list of names but wasn't even sure what it meant. Was it just people who knew Heather, or something more? Whom might Taylor have suspected? She had the court transcript, but that wouldn't help Taylor. Plus, she was so focused on Eugene's case that maybe she was missing something in Taylor's own life. Colin was certainly defensive, but did that make him dangerous? Katie needed to rethink her plan.

17

John Carlson sat at his dining room table warily awaiting his dinner. He had been busy all day. He'd gotten his hands on some of the interview transcripts and read them over and over again, looking for any clue about Taylor. A false-alarm sighting had had the entire Baxter police force out in the woods for most of the afternoon until they finally located a blonde woman who had been walking her dog. The witness had failed to mention the dog or the fact that the woman was in her forties.

Carlson sighed. The whole community was on alert, but that just meant that they would get lots of sightings of blonde women going about their business. He didn't want to admit it, even to himself, but Katie's mention of Taylor researching Eugene's case had set off alarm bells in the back of his head. He'd requested Eugene Lowe's file from Ann Arbor and hoped it wouldn't take more than a day to receive it.

He'd also sent a junior officer into the archives to find

anything they had on Alicia Stewart's restraining order against Eugene. But as of this evening, he had only a fake sighting and a bunch of tired and frustrated officers to show for his time. He remembered the search for Alicia all those years ago. They had hoped to find her alive and had no idea that they would find her due to another girl's death.

He heard Linda clinking silverware and sat up expectantly.

"Katie LeClair came to see me today," Linda said as she came into the room from the kitchen. She set a kale salad down in front of him.

He picked through the leaves, looking for fried chicken pieces or maybe some steak. No luck. He hoped this health kick of Linda's would wear off quickly. He'd noticed that Bubba still got chicken with *his* dinner.

Carlson nodded and said, "She said she wanted to visit Bubba."

Linda fixed him with a pitying stare.

"John." She waited until he looked up from his hunt for meat and looked at her. "She came to the *Gazette* office. She wanted to see what we had on the Eugene Lowe case."

Carlson put his fork down. He couldn't eat kale *and* focus on Linda's concerns. Well, he couldn't eat kale and do anything else. Kale took his full concentration and all of his maturity to choke down.

"She's taken him on as a patient," Carlson said. He didn't add that he was worried she had taken him on as a project as well. He adored Katie. He'd always hoped for a daughter, and when he first met Katie the night she had saved Bubba's life, he'd felt like they had a connection that he couldn't explain. Of course, he'd never tell anyone about that moment of connection he'd sensed. He'd especially never tell Linda, as their lack of children was still a painful topic between them even after all these years. "You know how she is when she senses a mystery. It will blow over soon. I'm going to find out who's been harassing Eugene, and then it will all calm down."

Linda dove into her salad as if it was the best thing since chocolate-chip cookies. She finished chewing and took a sip of water. No more wine or beer with dinner either.

"I'm sure you're right. But what if there *is* something not quite right about that old case?"

Carlson had been wondering the same thing. He took a big bite of kale to drown out his own concerns.

18

Katie spooned chili into two bowls and brought them to the table. She and Caleb had four or five meals that they rotated throughout the week. Katie always had some chili in the freezer for nights when neither of them wanted to cook or no one had been to the store. Those evenings had become more frequent this fall as Caleb worked on his app and Katie worked longer hours at the office covering for Nick's absence. They had Matt scheduled a couple of days a week to help with the overflow, but she and Emmett had both been working harder than ever just to stay afloat.

Caleb smiled as she set his bowl in front of him. He dove in and didn't seem to take a breath until it was halfway gone. Katie picked at hers and then set her spoon down.

She didn't like the direction her mind was wandering. What if Eugene was innocent, as his mother claimed, and there had been a murderer living in Baxter all these years?

But the death had occurred in Ann Arbor, she reminded herself, so there was no reason to assume the murderer would be in Baxter. So, who was harassing Eugene? Was it just people with long memories and not enough to do?

She got up from the table and rummaged through her bag. She found her notebook and a pen and brought it to the table.

Caleb looked up at her and noticed the notebook. He put his spoon down.

"Things are getting serious," Caleb said. "Do we have enough information to warrant that?"

"It helps me think," she said, and flipped to a blank page.

"Know what helps me think?" he asked. "Cookies. Do we have any?" He got up and went into the kitchen. Katie heard him rummaging in the pantry.

"Check on top of the fridge," she said.

"Why would they be there?"

"Because you never look there."

"Is this your secret stash?" He came back into the dining room with a package of Scottish shortbread. Katie's favorite, Caleb's port in a storm.

He ripped open the package and handed her a cookie. She nibbled at it while she drafted the outlines of a medical note.

Katie knew it was habit and conditioning, but she found the structure of a patient note to be helpful in thinking of solutions to a problem. Doctors were like medical detectives, and they had developed a shorthand way of communicating their thoughts through the standard patient note. There was a place for all the pertinent information, and Katie found that the structure of the notes often helped her to see patterns in her patients' illnesses. She had used this technique in a recent murder investigation, and true to her habit, she found herself sketching out a note in regard to Taylor's case. Fortunately, she remembered some of the details about Taylor's life from the time they had worked together.

CC (Chief Complaint): Taylor Knox missing.

HPI (History of Present Illness): In this case, why is she gone and was there foul play? She was recently working on Eugene's old case. Are they connected?

Social History: Did not know Eugene? Lived with friends on campus. Has a steady boyfriend for past two years.

Family History: Mother lives in Ann Arbor. Father ex-police, died recently (a year ago? two?). One sister.

Review of Suspicions: Did Taylor's recent investigation into Heather Stone's death put her in danger? Or was there some other threat in her life that had nothing to do with her project?

Differential Diagnosis (List of Suspects):

Eugene

Colin (boyfriend—jealous?)

Russell Hunt (was he having an affair with Taylor?)

Any suspects from Eugene's case?

Assessment: Need more information!

Plan:
1) Talk to Russell again and ask if he has any of Taylor's research on the project
2) Try to find old autopsy report on Heather Knox
3) Talk to Alicia about Eugene?

Katie put down her pen and pushed the notebook toward Caleb.

"Not much to go on, is there?" he said.

Katie shook her head. "I don't know what I can do to help. Taylor's missing. Eugene is being harassed or followed. I don't even know if the two cases are related. But I can't just sit around waiting to hear if Taylor's been found. She was a great person and wanted to devote her life to helping others."

"What are you going to do? I mean, I like a good mystery as much as the next person, but how are you going to find her if the police can't? And even if Eugene's case is involved, how are you going to investigate a ten-year-old murder?"

"I don't know," Katie said. "I guess I'll start with Alicia and see what she can tell me. At least I know her and she'll be likely to talk to me."

"I'm still working on those thumb drives, but I got sidetracked when the beta testers came back with problems in the game. Want to test out my app in the meantime?"

Katie laughed. "Maybe when I get back."

"Where are you going?"

"I have to go to the office and get Alicia's phone number."

Caleb put his head in his hands. "It's like you're from

the twentieth century or something. I'll get her number for you on this newfangled computin' device."

He tapped a couple of keys and turned the screen to face her.

Katie made a face and punched the number into her cell phone. She knew she was a Luddite, but living with someone who breathed new technology made her feel like she was Miss Simms's age. She closed her notebook and held it protectively on her lap. Caleb had been trying to convert her to some sort of computer journaling program for as long as she could remember, but she'd never give up her notebooks and her favorite pen.

The phone rang on the other end, and Katie was preparing to leave a message when it was answered by a male voice. She'd never met Alicia's husband. She asked for Alicia and heard a muffled conversation before Alicia came on the line.

"Alicia, it's Katie LeClair."

"Dr. LeClair?"

It was probably a good thing Katie had dialed in haste. If she'd thought it through, she would have realized how odd it was to call up a patient and begin questioning them.

"I know this sounds a little strange, but would you be available tomorrow sometime to have a quick coffee with me?"

"I think so. What's this about? It's not about Olivia, is it?"

Katie should have led with "Your kid is fine." "No, it has nothing to do with Olivia. I just wanted to pick your brain a little bit."

"Okay," Alicia said. Katie could hear the wariness in her voice. "I don't have to go to work until noon. I could meet you somewhere in town. I'd have to bring the baby."

"That's perfect," Katie said. "How about nine thirty at the Purple Parrot?"

"Okay, I'll see you then."

Katie clicked the phone off and smiled at Caleb. "She'll meet me tomorrow."

"Yes, I heard," Caleb said. "How are you going to spin this?"

"Spin?"

"You can't just sit down with someone and begin quizzing them about their past. I know that's what you do at work, but how are you going to get her to tell you anything about Eugene?"

"I guess I'll have to wing it."

19

Katie blew into the Purple Parrot on a gust of wind and had to fight to pull the door shut behind her. It had been a mild October so far, but the wind warned of the winter to come.

She ordered a pot of tea from Sheila Kazinksy (one of her patients—Katie was still not used to seeing them in the wild) and found a table by the window with two comfy armchairs upholstered in deep purple and canary yellow. She was glad to see that there were only a few customers in the room during this lull between the breakfast and lunch rushes. She didn't want any eavesdroppers, even though she knew that by meeting in public, everyone would know she had been talking to Alicia.

Alicia arrived just as Sheila set Katie's tea on the side table. The baby's cheeks were red from the wind, but she was laughing and gurgling. Alicia spotted Katie and came to the cozy corner. She asked Sheila for a hot chocolate and began stripping the coat and hat off the baby.

Olivia regarded Katie with a mixture of recognition and vague wariness, as if she couldn't quite remember how she knew this new person. Katie smiled and waved and Olivia grinned back, reassured.

"Thank you for meeting me," Katie said. "I didn't know it would be quite so blustery."

"We try to go out every day whatever the weather, so Olivia is used to it."

Sheila returned to the table with a hot chocolate and a small cookie. "Can Olivia have this?"

Olivia reached for the plate as Alicia nodded. "She'd be very upset if I said no!"

Sheila grinned. "Oh, I know. Who wouldn't be? Nobody turns down a free cookie."

Katie watched the easy rapport between the two women and realized they were of a similar age. She wondered if they had been in school together.

"How long have you two known each other?" Katie asked.

They exchanged a glance. "Since Alicia talked me into making mud pies in my best dress when we were about three."

They laughed.

"She's been getting me in trouble ever since," said Sheila. She turned to Olivia and said, "You keep an eye on your mama."

Alicia shook her head. "I'm not that bad."

"No, not anymore," said Sheila. "Domestic bliss has put a damper on your rebellious streak."

"That and sleep deprivation," Alicia said ruefully.

"Is she still not sleeping through the night?" Katie asked. It had been a major part of their well-child visit a few weeks before.

"It's getting better, actually." Alicia said. "I think she sleeps through about four times a week. Of course, that means she wakes up at five, but I'll take whatever I can get."

Sheila waved and went back to the counter to cash out her customers.

"I'm glad she's settling down for you," Katie said.

"So, what can I do for you?" Alicia sipped her hot chocolate and set it down out of reach of Olivia's inquisitive hands. She broke off a piece of the cookie and handed it to the baby.

Katie took a deep breath. It was always better to get right to the point.

"You've probably heard about the missing U of M student, Taylor Knox," Katie said. When Alicia nodded, Katie continued. "She worked with me over the summer, and I've been trying to figure out what could have happened."

"I met her a couple of weeks ago," Alicia said.

"You did?"

"She said she was doing a project for school and wanted to talk to me about Eugene Lowe and . . . all of the stuff that happened."

"That's kind of why I want to talk to you," Katie said. Something stopped her from telling Alicia that she thought Taylor might have found out something about that old case that put her in danger. "I've been trying to talk to people who had contact with her just before she disappeared. I knew she was looking into Eugene's case."

"I don't see how her research could have anything to do with her disappearance. The case is old and Eugene is out of prison now. What could she possibly have discovered that would be dangerous?"

"I don't know. That's why I'm trying to piece things together."

"Dr. LeClair, I understand you liked this girl, but how are you going to find her if the police can't?"

Katie shrugged. "You're probably right, but I can't just wait around for something to happen. I feel like retracing her steps might lead to something."

"She came to talk to me, and I did my best to tell her what I remembered. The truth is, I've tried to block most of it out. Eugene and I were good friends, and I was devastated when he went to prison. I couldn't believe that he could ever hurt anyone, but I guess you just don't always know people—even the ones you are close to."

"You think he was guilty?" Katie leaned forward. She hadn't expected this. Everyone she had talked to so far had had doubts.

Alicia shrugged. "Like I said, I tried not to think about it. The whole thing spiraled out of control. My father refused to let us see each other, Eugene was so unhappy, and I just had to get away. I've always wondered if things would have turned out differently if I had just stayed in Baxter that fall."

Olivia started to fuss when she dropped a piece of cookie. Alicia gave her a new one and the baby settled.

"Why would that have made a difference?"

"I think he followed me," she said.

"Was he stalking you?"

Alicia laughed. "God, no. We were friends. I was probably his only friend early in high school." Her face softened. "He was a really sweet guy. We both loved alternative music and walking in the woods. We just clicked." Alicia stared over Katie's shoulder, lost in memory. She met Katie's eyes. "And then everything went wrong."

Katie waited, hoping there would be more.

Alicia sipped at her cocoa and made a face. "Still hot." She looked around the restaurant and finally at Katie. "My father didn't approve of our friendship." She held her hand up when Katie started to speak. "I really don't know why, and then there was the whole misunderstanding about Eugene breaking into our house."

"What actually happened?"

Alicia hesitated, and then Katie thought she saw her come to a decision.

Alicia said, "I had to get away from my dad. His accusations and criticism of Eugene were too much for me. I went to Ann Arbor and crashed with my friend, Heather Stone. She was a couple years older and had an apartment on campus. I know it was cowardly and I shouldn't have done it."

Katie had meant "what actually happened that led to Eugene having a restraining order against him," but it was interesting that Alicia chose to skip over that part of the story.

Alicia tried her hot chocolate again, and this time she gulped it down while Olivia tried to pull the mug away.

"Eugene must have followed me. That's the only reason I can think of for him being in Ann Arbor." She shrugged. "He didn't even know Heather."

"Did you tell Taylor all of this?"

"Most of it. She wanted to talk to Nathan too. He was there that night. At the party. In fact, that was when we first started seeing each other."

"Do you know if she ever got a chance to talk to him?"

"I think she met him at his office sometime last week." Alicia deliberately checked her watch. "I'd have to ask. We don't talk about any of that if we can avoid it."

Olivia's cookie was gone and she started fussing. Alicia bounced her knee to try to soothe the baby. Alicia's phone rang. She rummaged in her large bag, taking out baby wipes, lip gloss, plastic keys, a small stuffed cat (immediately grabbed by Olivia), and finally her phone, which had stopped ringing. Alicia checked the call log.

"That was work. I'd better call them back." She clutched the phone and handed Olivia the last piece of cookie.

"Sure, go ahead," Katie said.

"Will you watch Olivia for a minute?" She stood and plopped the baby in Katie's lap.

Katie nodded, but as she watched Olivia's face crumple when her mom stepped away from the table, she had a sinking feeling that she would get no more out of Alicia at this meeting.

20

Katie left the Purple Parrot feeling out of sorts. It wasn't like she'd expected a full rundown of Alicia's past with Eugene, except that that was *exactly* what she'd been hoping for. As a doctor, it was easy to get information. People wanted to share every detail of their illness and sometimes every detail of their lives with their doctors. But in conducting her own investigation of Taylor's movements and Eugene's past with nothing to recommend her other than her dubious charm, Katie was at a loss on how to proceed.

She checked her phone and saw she had missed a call from Matt. She hoped he wasn't bailing on her for the afternoon. Debra had corralled them both into working on the Halloween festival committee. She had initially appealed to their vanity by saying how much it would mean to the committee to have such respected doctors helping out. When that didn't work, she'd enlisted Emmett, who had suggested it would be a way to get some good PR after the events of

September, when she had worked to prove her patient's suicide was actually murder and uncovered old secrets in the process. At the same time she had uncovered some problems within her own practice. Katie had finally given in to Emmett's request about the Halloween festival and dragged Matt along with her.

She listened to the voicemail and smiled when she heard he wanted to have lunch to "fortify themselves" before the meeting. She glanced at the time and sent a quick text saying she would meet him at noon at Pete's Sandwich Shop.

She had a couple of hours before she had to meet Matt.

She felt strongly that Taylor's disappearance was directly related to Eugene's old case. The timing of Eugene's release from prison, Taylor's disappearance, and the threats against Eugene seemed connected. Katie had noted Eugene's address when he came to see her at the clinic. She wanted a sense of the neighborhood to understand better what might be going on.

As if of its own volition, her Subaru steered its way toward Eugene's house. She knew this was unusual, but Gretchen had come to see her at work. Would she mind Katie dropping by to question her about her son?

Katie parked and locked her car. She stood across the street from the Lowe house. It looked like it had seen better days. The lawn was patchy and some of the bushes were prematurely brown. It was a small two-story, painted gray, but peeling near the roofline. Katie saw that the garage door had been recently painted, but it was streaky, as if someone had just slapped the paint on the door.

She climbed the wooden steps to the porch and rang the

bell. She heard footsteps from inside and adjusted her expression to one of friendly curiosity.

"Oh, Dr. LeClair," Gretchen said. "I didn't expect you." Gretchen peeked out the door and glanced up and down the street. "Come in, please."

"Thank you." Katie said.

The entryway was dark, and Katie realized that all the curtains on the front of the house were drawn closed. Gretchen gestured for Katie to follow her toward the back of the house to the kitchen.

"Have a seat," Gretchen said, and gestured to the small table. "Can I get you some coffee?"

Katie didn't want any more coffee, but she agreed. After Gretchen had finished bustling about getting the mugs, cream, and sugar, she sat and poured coffee for them both from a carafe.

Katie took a sip and was surprised at how good it was.

Gretchen sipped her coffee and looked expectantly at Katie.

"Is your son here?"

"No, he went out somewhere in his truck." Gretchen flapped her hand. "He loves that old thing. Honestly, I don't know where he goes. I worry he's going to end up breaking down along the highway somewhere. Or maybe rusty pieces will start falling off of it."

"I wanted to follow up on our conversation from the other day at the clinic."

"Okay." Gretchen looked pleased at Katie's interest.

"Can you tell me any more about what happened all those years ago? Did Eugene ever talk to you about what happened?"

"He did," Gretchen said. "He told me and everyone who would listen. He said he stumbled upon that girl's body on his way back to a party. He'd gotten it in his head that he would bring Alicia home and be the hero. He thought he could win over Franklin Stewart that way." Gretchen shook her head. "He was a tyrant. I know it's not right to say it, but I was relieved when he passed away. The whole neighborhood seemed to lighten when he died. Of course, that was before Gene came home and these recent troubles started."

"Why did Franklin Stewart dislike Eugene so much?"

"Who knows?" Gretchen said and looked out the window. "Eugene was an unusual child, and not everyone understood him. Franklin thought his daughter was perfect and every other kid was beneath her. It only got worse when she got to high school. He kept such a tight rein on that girl, I wasn't surprised when she ran away. I don't know how she even breathed in that house."

"That must have been very difficult for her," Katie said. She thought of her own teenage years and how she would have rebelled at the first sign anyone was trying to tell her what to do. She had not been above doing the opposite of what was expected just to prove she could.

Gretchen's face softened. "I think it was. But she was always so kind to Gene. They were really good friends. Of course, he wanted it to be more. What teenage boy wouldn't, with such a pretty girl? But as far as I know, nothing of that sort ever happened."

"Do you have any idea if there were other suspects in the case of Heather Stone's death?"

Gretchen pursed her lips and slowly shook her head.

"I really don't know. Being found outside like that on a college campus, I would think just about anyone could have killed her. My Gene was just in the wrong place at the wrong time."

A few minutes later, Katie thanked Gretchen for the coffee and said good-bye to her on the porch. As she walked to her car, she felt a prickle on the back of her neck. She turned to see who might be watching her but didn't see anyone. The feeling gave her a chill, and she quickly unlocked her car, climbed in, and started the engine.

She felt better when she turned off of Gretchen's street and headed for home. She reflected that a mother's view of her children could never be completely relied upon. There were so many layers of memory, one on top of the other. From that delightful toddler to the inquisitive child to the moody teen. They were all there at once, clouding her view. Katie wondered how much Gretchen's memories were obscuring the man her son had become.

She parked in her driveway and noticed that Caleb's car was missing. Her shoulders slumped. She'd been hoping to talk to him and see if he had any more bright ideas on how to proceed. She pushed open the back door and set her bag on the kitchen table. The room was spotless. This made Katie worry. Either he was bringing someone back with him or he had done something Katie would not be happy about. Not that he didn't clean up after himself, but he pretty much thought the job was done if he put his dishes in the dishwasher. The idea of wiping down the counters and rinsing the sink was a foreign concept. Or so Katie had thought. Apparently, he knew all about these details and chose to use them only on occasion.

She sat at the table and pulled her notebook out of her bag. She put a checkmark by *Talk to Alicia*, but didn't feel that she was any further along. She needed more, but where could she get it? John Carlson? He might not know much more than anyone else in town, since the investigation had happened in Ann Arbor. She moved back to the first to-do, *Talk to Russell again*. That wouldn't be easy without telling Gabrielle. She hadn't wanted Katie to ask him about the case when they went out; she certainly wouldn't be thrilled with Katie doing a follow-up visit. Especially if she knew the reason was that Russell had a reputation for dating students. And the fact that Katie just didn't trust him. Between his smug demeanor and the things she had heard from Taylor's friends, she hoped this was one of Gabrielle's shorter relationships.

Katie went into her room and opened her laptop. She felt like a stalker herself, tracking down personal information on the Internet.

She searched for Eugene Lowe and got a few hits about Heather Stone's death, but none of it had any more information than she already knew. It was as if there were one or two original articles and the rest just rehashed the same thing. Several articles focused on Heather's potential and the loss of a young, beautiful woman. When she searched for Heather Stone, the same articles popped up as well as the tribute page that had been set up by Heather's sorority.

She heard the kitchen door slam and knew Caleb was home. She got up to go into the dining room and involve him in her research when she heard a female voice. She listened from the hallway and thought she recognized it.

Hmm.

"This is so cool, Caleb," the woman said. "I can't believe you designed your own game."

"I'm just hoping it works when I release it."

Katie tiptoed back into her room and pulled the door shut quietly. She'd have to do this on her own for now. She opened her computer again and started clicking on links to read the stories of Eugene's arrest and trial.

What she thought was a few minutes later, Katie glanced at her watch and snapped the computer shut. She'd lost track of time, as one did when following the breadcrumbs of the Internet.

She ran out of her room and startled Caleb and Bella Peterson.

"Can't talk now; I'm late," Katie said as she rushed through the room. "Nice to see you, Bella."

She grabbed her keys and bag and dashed to her car.

21

The wind had not died down as the day progressed, and Katie found herself wrestling open the door to Pete's Sandwich Shop just as she had at the Purple Parrot. Once inside, she shook her hair out of her eyes and surveyed the room. She spotted Matt at the back in a corner booth. He was focused on his phone, and she took a moment to admire the view. It was no wonder half the medical residents had had a crush on him when he was the senior resident. His dark hair had fallen over his forehead, and she knew he'd brush it back impatiently when he looked up. As if he sensed her watching, he did look up and met her eyes with his own intense brown-eyed gaze. He raised his hand and smiled while Katie wended her way through the tables.

He stood and kissed her on the cheek. Katie felt her face get warm and glanced around the restaurant. She was still getting used to being in a relationship *and* living in a small town where everyone knew your business. Matt grinned at her. "Already checked that the coast was clear."

She was sure her face was even redder when she turned away to take off her coat and toss her bag onto the seat of the booth. Guessing she looked windblown and embarrassed, she decided it didn't matter and leaned toward Matt for a proper kiss. People seemed to find out everything anyway; might as well give them something to talk about. They slid into the booth and grinned at each other.

Pete arrived, belly first, with an order pad in his hand. His smooth head gleamed in the overhead light. "What'll ya have?" Katie was always amused at Pete's aloof manner. No matter how long any customer had been coming to his place, he acted like he'd never seen them before. He was all business, no chitchat.

They ordered and Pete wandered off without another word.

"What are we in for today?" Matt asked.

"I'm not sure, actually." Katie thought of how keen Emmett had been to have her work on the committee. "I'm a little worried that Emmett has tricked us into one of the more difficult community outreach jobs. He's been on every committee Baxter has ever created, and he didn't say it was fun, just that it would be good for the practice."

"I don't know. He really seems to like you," Matt said. He reached across the table and covered her hands with his own. "Maybe he's giving you an easy job in the hopes you'll want to do more."

"Either way, it's a trick," said Katie. "But I *would* like to get to know some of the other people in town. And I love Halloween."

Katie felt warm and safe sitting with Matt in their back

138

corner booth. The bell on the door rang occasionally as more diners blew in from outside. Each time, a cold blast of air ripped through the restaurant and ruffled the napkins on the counter.

"Any more news on Taylor?" Matt asked after another gust receded.

Katie shook her head. "No more than I told you yesterday."

"Where could she have gone? And why?"

Katie shook her head. "I wish I knew."

"Hey, I remembered why Russell looked familiar to me," Matt said. "He was a grad student when I was an undergrad. There were rumors he was dating Heather, and he was at the party that night."

"Are you sure?"

"I never forget a face," Matt said.

"He dated Heather?" Katie asked. "I wonder why he didn't mention it?"

"Maybe he didn't want to talk about it in front of Gabrielle?"

"It was years ago. Gabrielle wouldn't care."

"Still, it would have put a damper on things."

"I've heard some rumors about Russell from students," Katie said.

"That he's a womanizer and not above dating students?"

Katie's eyebrows ticked upward. "Yes, something like that. What have you heard?"

Matt shook his head. "Nothing lately, but once I remembered who he was, I remembered the rumors." He held up his hands. "I never heard anything dodgy about him, just that he sometimes dated his students. At that time, he was a teaching assistant, and it's not like it's unheard of for TAs to date students, but he did have a bit of a reputation for it."

"I should tell Gabrielle," Katie said as she looked down at the table.

Matt squeezed her hand until she looked up again. "People change. I'm not sure you want to wade into her relationship."

"But she's my friend," Katie said. "I'd want to know."

Matt sat back and crossed his arms. "What good will it do to tell her? Either she'll confront him and he'll deny it and then you'll look like the bad guy, or she'll confront him and they'll break up. Or she'll keep quiet and watch his every move. Any of those reactions will ruin their relationship."

"But—"

"She's your friend and you know her best, but telling her about a rumor from ten years ago, or even a rumor from now, will only cause trouble."

Katie also sat back and stared at the ceiling for a moment. Matt was right. She would only cause trouble, and she didn't actually know Russell had done anything wrong. There was just something about him that rubbed her the wrong way. He was too sure of himself, and she didn't like how quickly Gabrielle had fallen for him. Katie just felt it was going to end badly.

"You're right," she said. "I'll stay out of it. *Unless* I hear something real."

Pete rang the bell on the counter to signal that their order was ready, and Matt hopped up to grab the tray.

Katie enjoyed a moment watching Matt joke with Pete.

He had a brilliant smile. Matt had the exceptional gift of knowing exactly what kind of person to be for each interaction. Just by this chameleon trick, he could establish rapport with anyone, from a tattooed motorcycle dude to a four-year-old glitter-loving ballerina. After earning a rare smile from Pete, he returned to the table with their lunch.

Matt's Reuben dripped with cheese and the rye was grilled perfectly. Katie looked at her own roast beef and cheddar and wondered if she had lost Caleb's best-ordering contest. She took a bite and was no longer concerned. They shared a basket of Pete's house-made potato chips. It really didn't matter which sandwich was chosen if the chips were involved.

The sandwiches took their attention for the next few minutes, and except for the crunching of chips, a comfortable silence fell over the table. Matt took a swig of soda and sat back in his chair.

Katie set her sandwich down and leaned toward Matt. "Do you know anyone who works in the morgue at the university?"

Matt laughed. "You do have a way with mealtime conversation."

"I'm hoping to get Heather Knox's autopsy information. I've seen the short version that it was head trauma, but I'd like to see the complete report."

"Yeah, I know a guy," Matt said. Matt always knew a guy.

"I know I can request a copy, but I figure it will take weeks to get it," Katie said. "Do you think your friend could get it soon?"

"He's not exactly a friend, but I'll reach out to him after the meeting."

Katie thanked him and went back to her sandwich.

"I hope we won't have to get too crafty at this meeting," Matt said. "I'm not that good with construction paper."

"I think you're safe," Katie said. "Emmett made it sound like it was just a planning meeting. How much planning does a Halloween celebration need?"

* * *

Half an hour later, they entered the main doors of Baxter High School. The smell of linoleum, lockers, and food cooked in industrial pots hit her with a wave of nostalgia. Not all of it pleasant. Every high school she had been in had that ambience of trapped adolescent energy embedded in its walls. Katie had attended several high schools as she and Caleb were shuttled from one family member to another. She shivered a bit and felt grateful she had made it through those years.

Matt grinned. "This brings back memories," he said.

"You didn't go to school here, did you?"

He shook his head. "In Ann Arbor, but it still feels the same."

Katie thought fleetingly that Matt might have been one of those people who actually *liked* high school. She wondered if that pointed to a bone-deep difference in their approaches to life. He took her hand then, and she felt briefly what it might have been like if she had spent more than a year at any given high school. She imagined having Matt as a boyfriend in high school. Nope. She couldn't see it. She had been too angry about her past and too driven about her future to fit with someone as easygoing as Matt. This was their time.

They had been told to meet the rest of the committee in

the school gym. That should have been Katie's first clue that the meeting was going to be more than she had bargained for. They wandered the empty halls, their footsteps echoing off the metal walls of lockers and shiny linoleum floors.

They followed the signs to the gym and pushed open the heavy double doors. Katie gasped. Matt chuckled.

"I don't think anyone has seen us," he whispered. He tugged on her hand. "We still have time to make our escape."

"There you are!" a familiar voice said. Matt dropped her hand as if it were hot. Debra Gallagher trotted over to them and ushered them further into the room.

The gym was filled with people. Tables had been set up in opposite corners with signs saying FOOD, DECORATIONS, ENTERTAINMENT, and PARADE. People milled around the tables in what appeared to be organized chaos. Katie wondered who would actually *attend* the event if the whole town was involved in working on it.

A siren sounded and echoed throughout the room. Everyone fell silent and looked for the source of the noise. A thin, elderly woman with bright-pink lipstick and a helmet of dark-gray hair smiled benignly and held up her bullhorn.

"Now that I have your attention," she shouted into the horn, which squeaked and reverberated. She glared at the device and held it away from her mouth. "I need all team leaders to meet with me on the bleachers in five minutes," she said.

"Who is that?" Matt asked.

"I think her name is Delores Munch," Katie said.

Debra nodded. "She's head dictator of the Halloween festival every year. People draw straws to see who has to lead each team because she gets very bossy as Halloween approaches."

"I don't know which team we're on," Katie said.

"You can join our group," Debra said. "We need all the help we can get."

Debra dragged Katie and Matt toward the table labeled PARADE.

"I thought this was going to be like a trunk-or-treat thing," Katie said. Katie had seen flyers when she was in medical school about trunk-or-treat events. It was a Halloween party where the kids could walk around a parking lot and collect candy at each car. It didn't sound nearly as fun as going door to door, but maybe it made the parents feel better.

Debra laughed as if Katie had made a very clever joke. "No. This is serious stuff. As long as Delores is in charge, it's a full-on takeover of the town."

"How long has she been doing this?"

Debra shrugged. "As long as I can remember. It's great when you're a kid and all you have to do is show up for the fun."

Debra glanced at the crowd milling around the parade table.

"Here, come check in with our team leader." Debra pulled Katie off to the side.

Team leader? Debra made it sound like a military exercise. Between Munch and her bullhorn and the general high level of energy in the room, Katie was quite sure she had been tricked into way more than she had planned on.

Debra approached a woman with light-blonde hair

pulled into an elegant updo. Katie's stomach sank. Cecily Hawkins. Nick's wife. Katie still didn't know exactly what had gone wrong between them, but Cecily seemed to barely tolerate Katie's existence. Katie wasn't sure if Cecily blamed her for Nick's need to take time off from work (as if it were Katie's fault that Nick had a drug problem) or if she suspected that Katie had learned Cecily's deep dark secret while investigating a sudden death in September (she had, but she wasn't going to admit it). Perfect Cecily claimed to come from a wealthy family on the East Coast, but she had, in fact, put herself through school by working as a stripper. Katie was pretty sure Nick didn't know, and Katie wasn't going to tell him.

Cecily turned, saw Katie, and her smile faltered before she turned it up to its highest wattage.

"New recruits, Mrs. Hawkins," said Debra. For someone so in tune with the events in Baxter, Debra seemed oblivious to the tension between the two women.

"Katie, how nice to see you," Cecily said. "And Matt, I hope everything is going well at the clinic?"

Katie and Matt nodded warily.

"I have just the job for you two," she said. She held a clipboard up and made a mark on the paper. "Katie, you will be on our lead float for the parade. You can be the pumpkin. It's a big hit every year."

Before Katie could respond, Cecily continued.

"Matt, you can be our pirate leader. Nick used to take on that role, but he won't be here this year, as you know." She gave them an icy smile.

Matt brightened up at the idea of playing a pirate and

cast a commiserating glance at Katie and her pumpkin assignment.

"You'll be in charge of the pirate crew," Cecily continued.

"Crew?" Matt asked.

"Yes, the first- through third-grade students act as our pirates. You'll just have to shepherd them through the parade and keep track of them all. I think we have forty-five kids signed up this year."

"Forty-five?" Matt said. His voice rose into the terrified octave range. "Does the pirate leader get an assistant?"

Cecily laughed and patted his arm. "Of course. Two experienced teachers." She waved her arm in the direction of the bleachers. The only two sitting there were Mrs. Peabody and Miss Simms.

Katie cast her own sympathetic glance at Matt, who was looking decidedly less thrilled with his assignment.

"You can both go report to our costume director and then help the float design team with whatever they're up to." Cecily waved her hand in dismissal and turned away. She strode toward Delores Munch, and the two women began comparing clipboards.

"Wow, you get to be the pumpkin," said Debra. "I always wanted to do that. Until I realized that I'm claustrophobic. And I have to pee every couple of hours . . ."

Katie and Matt straggled in the direction Cecily had pointed and asked other parade team members about the costume director.

"I think he's out in the hallway," a teenager said, and pointed to a door.

They pushed open the door, but no one was there.

Katie looked up and down the hallway. They heard voices and followed them around the corner to an open doorway.

Two men stood by a pickup truck in the lot. Their tense faces made Katie think they were arguing, but she couldn't hear what they said.

A tall man with short blond hair and the thick build of a weightlifter turned toward them as they came down the hallway. Katie thought he looked vaguely familiar but couldn't place him.

"Can I help you?" he said.

"We're looking for the costume director," Matt said.

"You've found him," he said. He put his hand out. "Nathan Nielsen, nice to meet you. Although costume director is a lofty title for what I do."

They shook hands and introduced themselves. Nathan nodded at the other man and introduced him as Mike. Mike said hello and then strode across the parking lot and got into a minivan.

"Dr. LeClair. My wife, Alicia, speaks very highly of you," Nathan said. "She brings our daughter to you for her checkups."

They chatted for a moment about babies and sleep deprivation. Then Nathan got down to business. He also had a clipboard. He consulted it when they identified their assignments.

"The pumpkin costume is here." He pointed to a large green tarp covering an unwieldy shape. "I have a rented storage place and I keep it there during the year. I was just unloading it to store it in the drama department at the end of the hall," he said. "If you don't mind helping, we can wrestle it inside together. The toughest part about being the pumpkin is that you can't sit down, so you'll have to be careful when the float is in motion. We've had more than one pumpkin fall over while riding the float, and then we have to stop the parade to get the pumpkin standing again. You can't do anything from inside the costume."

Katie sighed.

Nathan and Matt pulled the tarp to the edge of the truck bed and gently set it on the ground. The pumpkin was awkward but not heavy, and the two men carried it down the hall while Katie held the door open and then ran ahead to open the drama room door.

They set the tarp-covered costume on the ground.

"The pirate costume is right here." Nathan pulled a hanger off the clothing rack that leaned against the wall. Black pants, a brown vest and long coat, and a white puffy shirt hung above dark-gray, tall, cuffed boots. With an earring and the tricornered hat Katie saw sitting on top of the rack, Matt would make a very convincing pirate. "You can embellish it if you want. Sometimes Nick wore a fake beard and braids like Captain Jack Sparrow. But don't make it too scary. The little kids will be hopped up on sugar as it is, and you don't want to give them even more reason to act crazy."

With a flourish, Nathan pulled the tarp off the pumpkin. Katie had imagined a light wire ball with orange fabric over it. She'd figured her head would stick out the top and she'd have to wear a green hat and makeup.

The reality was worse. The costume was quite large, with green gloves hanging off the sides. There was a two-foot hole in the bottom and no hole at the top.

"Where does my head come out?" Katie asked.

"It doesn't," Nathan said. "When you're inside, you can put your hands in the gloves—most people have a wingspan long enough to reach." He broke off his explanation. "You don't have short arms, do you?"

Katie shook her head. "I don't think so."

"Good. It helps you keep your balance if you can get your hands into the gloves. Just gives another level of control."

Katie nodded without understanding a thing he said.

"Anyway, there's a strip of fabric that is thinner than the rest, and you can see out through that when you're inside."

"That's good," Katie said.

"You can't walk very easily because there isn't much space to take a full step. Fortunately, all you need to do is stay standing."

Nathan had a walkie-talkie strapped to his belt, and it crackled to life.

"Team leaders, please come to the gymnasium."

Katie recognized Munch's voice, and her sympathy quickly switched from herself to Nathan.

"I'd better go," Nathan said nervously. "I can help you try it on at the next meeting." He headed back down the hall and broke into a slow jog as he approached the door to the gym.

Katie and Matt followed him to see what other unwelcome surprises awaited them among the float-building crew.

22

Across town in the police department, Carlson smiled politely and offered Gretchen Lowe more coffee. This would be her third cup, and short of pushing her out the door, he was unsure of how to get her to leave his office. They had been in school together, and when she had shown up at his house, Linda had sent her up to the station where Carlson was trying to take advantage of a quiet office to finish paperwork.

"It's very kind of you, John," she said. "But I think I've had enough."

Carlson felt his shoulders relax. Perhaps she was getting tired of quizzing him on every aspect of his protection plan for Eugene. The trouble was, Eugene was an adult who was perfectly within his rights to leave town for the day without telling his mother where he was going. But since he had returned, Gretchen was on a mission to protect him from the "town bullies." She seemed to think Eugene hadn't aged a day in his decade in prison. She talked about him as if he had just graduated from high school. Although, as Gretchen had informed him, Eugene had never graduated. He'd been arrested, tried as an adult because he was already eighteen, and sent to prison during his senior year of high school. The GED earned in prison and the remote coursework he had done toward his bachelor's degree "wasn't the same" as watching him walk across the stage at Baxter High School.

Carlson stood and held out his hand. "Thank you for stopping by, Gretchen. I'll do my best to find out who is bothering Eugene."

She took his hand and shook it. Standing slowly and gathering her purse and jacket, she looked old. The years of her son's imprisonment had not left her unscathed. Carlson walked her to the front door and held it open for her. She smiled weakly at him and headed up the street face-first into the wind.

Carlson walked back to his office, wondering what else could be done. Despite his assurances to Gretchen Lowe, he was worried about Eugene. Someone or several someones in town didn't want him there. Carlson wished he had more manpower to protect Eugene, although the man himself had refused any help. He didn't want a bunch of "cops following him around." Carlson couldn't blame him. It seemed all Eugene had wanted was to slip back into his old life unnoticed and unmolested.

He sat at his desk and pulled Eugene's file out of the stack. Who in town had been harassing him? And had Eugene known more than he said?

The file from the old investigation of Eugene had been

unearthed from the basement archives. Carlson flipped it
open again and found the spot where he had left off. He had
moved past the complaints lodged by Alicia's father, Franklin Stewart. He flipped to a page that listed everyone who
had been interviewed after Heather Knox's death. He hadn't
noticed the first time through that Heather's two roommates had eventually married each other. Hope and Brad.
He flipped to their interviews.

They both said they'd left the party early and went
home. Brad said he'd had a lot to drink and gone straight to
bed. Hope claimed the same. But Hope also said she'd seen
Heather have a fight with an ex-boyfriend, and other witnesses put that fight at about eleven thirty. Was one of them
lying, or were they just drunk kids who didn't pay attention
to the time?

23

Monday morning clinics were always hectic. Everyone who had gotten sick over the weekend, or who had put off coming in the week before, was suddenly at emergency status. Katie put her head down and focused on working her way through the list. She did not think about Taylor or her disappearance. Or about Eugene and his injuries. She avoided thoughts about being a pumpkin in the Halloween parade. And she denied the feeling that her adopted town of Baxter harbored violence and intrigue just under the surface.

At lunchtime, Katie escaped to her office and shut the door. She wanted a few minutes to decompress after the morning of listening and advising, cajoling and threatening. Her office phone buzzed. She ignored it.

A few minutes later, she heard Debra's voice in the hall. "Have you seen Dr. LeClair?"

A rapid *tap-tap-tap* sounded at the door. Katie sighed. "Come in, Debra."

"Hi, Dr. LeClair," Debra came into the small office

looking just as frazzled as Katie felt. Her hair stuck up more than usual, and her mascara had settled into dark rings under her eyes. "I tried to call you on your phone, but I must have missed you."

A pang of guilt hit Katie as she realized her momentary rebellion had forced Debra to wander the building looking for her.

"Sorry, Debra," Katie said. "What do you need?"

Debra clasped her hands at her waist and seemed to steel herself. "I'm really sorry; I didn't know what to do."

Katie's pulse bumped up a few beats. What could have Debra so flustered?

"What is it?"

Debra wrung her hands a bit more and took a deep breath. "Delores Munch is here to see you."

Katie frowned. "I thought she was Emmett's patient."

Debra nodded. "She is. She's not here as a patient. She says she has important information for you and she has to see you right away. I told her you had a full clinic. She's been waiting out there for half an hour."

"Okay. Put her in the conference room and I'll be right there."

"Thanks, Dr. LeClair. I don't like to get on her bad side so close to the Halloween festival. She can make your life miserable if she wants."

Katie wondered if one of the tortures was being forced to wear the pumpkin suit.

"She doesn't have her bullhorn, does she?"

Debra laughed. "I don't think so, but her purse *is* big enough to hide it."

Katie took a bite of a protein bar and a swig of cold

coffee and walked down the hallway to the conference room. The thought occurred to her that the conference room had seen a lot of traffic lately.

She straightened her shoulders, took a deep breath, and pushed open the door. "Hello, Mrs. Munch. How can I help you?"

Delores Munch sat up taller in her chair and brushed imaginary lint from her skirt. "It's how I can help *you*, not the other way around."

"Oh?" Katie sat across the table from Mrs. Munch and assumed a polite smile.

"I heard you've been asking around about Eugene Lowe."

Katie closed her eyes and nodded. She still wasn't used to everyone knowing every move she made.

"Well, you won't get any help from that Alicia Nielsen, née Stewart." Delores punctuated this with a sharp nod.

Katie tamped down the irritation that when people knew exactly what she was up to, they had no trouble commenting on it. She clenched her jaw and tried to keep her voice even. "Why not? I thought they were friends."

"Maybe a lifetime ago, but now she's married to Nathan Nielsen. He's not the kind of man to let his wife get involved with your kind of malarkey."

Katie bristled at this but kept her face neutral. She had years of experience with hiding her reactions. "What kind of malarkey is that?"

"You must be trying to prove he was innocent all those years ago." Mrs. Munch leaned forward. "You should leave the past in the past. I would have thought you learned that lesson last time."

This was really going too far, but Katie sensed

Mrs. Munch had something more to say, so she tolerated the rebuke. But she couldn't resist a little pushback.

"Actually, I was trying to protect my patient from further harm. I'm not trying to prove anything." And she wasn't, yet. But what if Eugene was innocent? That would mean someone else had gotten away with killing Heather. It might have been an accident, but still. The other person had been walking around free, living his life, while Eugene was only now able to start putting his life back together. And maybe Taylor had discovered who that person was.

"Humph," said Munch.

"Is there something you want to tell me?" Katie didn't want to encourage Delores, but she also knew she wouldn't leave until she had delivered her message.

"Don't trust Alicia. Even if Nathan hasn't warned her off, she isn't reliable or trustworthy."

Katie raised her eyebrows and pushed away from the table. "Okay, thank you for the warning. I'll keep it in mind."

Delores scowled at her. "You don't fool me. You're just agreeing to get rid of me." Here she pulled out a long bony finger to waggle at Katie. "You'll be sorry."

For a moment, Katie felt like Dorothy confronting the Wicked Witch. But Delores was right; she *was* just trying to get rid of her.

Delores stopped scowling and bent to her bag. "Here, I brought you these. You look like you could use them." She pushed a bag of cookies into Katie's hands. She could just make out the shapes of pumpkins among the blobs.

Katie forced a smile and thanked Delores for her cookie rejects.

24

Eugene had a plan at last. The fact that it involved Alicia and that she had no idea about this plan did not dampen his enthusiasm. He knew the cabin in the woods would be deserted. The people that owned it were away and not returning anytime soon. It would be the perfect place to hide.

He parked his truck behind the house, creaked open the door, and climbed out. The woods were silent, as if waiting to see what this new intruder would do. After a few minutes, he heard the birds begin their noises again and the small creatures rustle in the leaves. The sun dappled the yard and flickered with the breeze. Eugene felt himself relax.

His only concern was where to put the truck. If he was going to hide, he couldn't have his truck sitting in the yard, or anywhere near the place. He was pleased to see his memory had been correct: there was an old outbuilding at the back of the property, more shed than garage, but he thought the truck would fit. He strode to the back of the yard and pulled on the double doors.

His breath caught in his throat as the door swung wide. There was already something there. A tarp covered it, but it was a small car. Eugene stepped forward and tugged. He felt that he knew what he would see before the fabric fell away, but it was still a shock. The little blue Fiat, with its round headlights and curved grille, that had been featured on all the missing posters seemed to smile at him from the gloom.

He remembered the girl who drove it. She had been so lovely.

He had stood at the window, pink beads in his hand.

Watching her as she approached the house, he'd felt as though she looked familiar. He'd realized with a start that this girl looked like Alicia from ten years ago. It was like watching Alicia walk up his front steps the way she had done so many times before. If he had known the girl looked like this, he wouldn't have avoided her calls. He'd thought she was just another reporter, or a curious true crime junkie.

As she got closer, he'd noticed she also resembled another girl from long ago. He'd shaken his head. He didn't think about that. Ever.

The doorbell had rung and the cat had run up the stairs—a white streak, like a ghost. Before he could answer the door, his mother had been there. She was always there. He knew she was keeping watch over him, but he'd been too tired to care. How could he tell her it reminded him of prison? Always being watched. But how could he also tell her it was almost comforting, after so many years, to *know* he was being watched? Keeping him safe from himself.

He'd stepped toward the door as the girl entered and put out his hand to shake.

She'd clasped his hand in a firm grip. This girl had not been weak or frightened of him. He fought the prickle of tears at the back of his eyes and in his throat at the thought that a girl like that could shake his hand without fear. It was the same way he'd felt with Dr. LeClair. Accepted as a regular person, not a monster.

He had smiled and slipped the beads into his pocket.

But this car, grinning at him in the shadows of a falling-down shed on a deserted property, told a different kind of story. Someone else had been here. And whoever it was must know what had happened to Taylor Knox.

25

After Delores left, Katie stacked her charts with a promise to herself that she wouldn't let them pile up all week. She texted Matt that she would meet him in thirty minutes, grabbed her bag, and went to the parking lot. It was a cool, crisp October day, and Katie was glad to be out of the office for the afternoon. The path through the woods that led to the hospital was covered in orange, red, and yellow leaves. Katie wished she could take a long walk along the pathways. But she had somewhere else to be. Matt had arranged a meeting with his "guy" who worked in the pathology department. Katie thought it was strange that Linda had only the summary page of Heather's autopsy. Was that just an oversight? Was that all she had been able to obtain? Maybe it was routine practice for a court case, but Katie had been trained to examine the whole pathology report, not just the conclusions. Was there something there that would shed light on Eugene's case? She hoped to find some answers in Heather's full autopsy report.

If that led nowhere, she still wanted to talk to Russell again and might even try to track down Colin. They hadn't ended their last conversation on a good note, and she hoped to figure out why he was so defensive.

She climbed into her car and turned it in the direction of I-94. There were a couple of small towns between Baxter and Ann Arbor, but all she could see from the highway was trees.

She turned left at the exit to head into Ann Arbor and the medical campus. There was a more direct route, but Katie liked to drive along Main Street and then through campus. The medical center was located at the center of Ann Arbor but north of the main campus. This was her favorite time of year in Ann Arbor. The campus had come alive with all the student activity, the leaves were changing colors, and it was still warm enough to be outside. She didn't much like football (a secret she kept from almost everyone), but she did like football weather.

She skirted the edges of campus to avoid the traffic that was always slow due to the pedestrians who obeyed no traffic laws. She wound her way around the familiar streets and snagged a parking spot that would likely earn her a ticket. Every parking space in Ann Arbor seemed regulated in some way, either requiring a permit or having a time limit.

She met Matt in the newly redesigned lobby. The glass front and soaring ceiling gave the space a bright, light feeling. A woman sitting at a large central information center prepared to dispense directions. Matt nodded at her but didn't stop. Katie followed him into a back stairway that had been missed during the renovation, and they ended up in a small white hallway. They checked the directional arrows on the wall and wended their way to the office of Matt's guy, who was a lab assistant in the pathology department.

Charlie McQueen was well over six feet tall, with broad shoulders and muscled arms that would have been at home on the football field. He was bald and wore a little cap over his long hipster beard. The beard sock would have looked ridiculous on anyone else, but Charlie carried it off. He greeted Matt warmly with a couple of pats on the shoulder that almost knocked him off balance. Katie stuck her hand out, hoping to get away with a handshake and avoid anything more violent.

"Hey, guys," Charlie said. "I don't get a lot of visitors here at work." He had an infectious, warm smile, and Katie liked him immediately.

Introductions and small talk ensued. It turned out that Charlie had indeed spent some time playing football in college. He and Matt discussed some old acquaintances while Katie smiled and hoped they would get to the point.

"I mentioned on the phone that I had a favor to ask," Matt said.

"Yup, I've got it right here." Charlie pulled a file out of a teetering stack. "I had to call in some favors with the ladies in the records room. They don't want to give out the impression that records requests actually only take a few minutes to fulfill. The long wait discourages most people from even asking." He winked and bestowed another smile along with the file.

"Thank you, Charlie," Katie said. "I really appreciate it."

"Sure, no problem. Hope it helps." Charlie's smile faded.

"I remember that case. I had just started here. It was such a tragedy."

"Do you remember anything about the autopsy?" Katie asked.

Charlie tugged on his beard and shook his head. "It was so long ago. I just remember she had hit her head on a brick or some sort of building material."

"We'd better let you get back to work," Matt said. "Thanks again."

"The records ladies did say something interesting," Charlie said as they turned to go. "They said this was the second request for that report in the last couple of weeks. But whoever requested it hadn't picked it up yet."

Katie glanced at Matt and knew he was thinking the same thing: Taylor.

* * *

They had one other stop to make in Ann Arbor. This one was tricky. Matt had tracked down Russell Hunt's office hours, and they planned to visit him to ask a few questions. Katie knew that once Gabrielle got wind of it, there would be some apologies to be made. She had always hated that saying about asking permission and begging forgiveness, but in this case, she would just prepare to grovel.

They decided to take Katie's car back onto the main campus, since she wanted to rescue it from her illegal parking spot. They saw the parking enforcement officer working his way down the line of cars toward Katie's Subaru. With the reflexes born in the parking jungle of Ann Arbor, they both broke into a run and jumped in the car. Katie sometimes felt she could have purchased a whole new car with the amount she'd spent paying parking fines as a resident. Another nice thing about Baxter—parking was free everywhere.

She drove to the main campus and found a spot at an actual meter. They rummaged in pockets and wallets for change and slid the coins into the slot. The sun was lower in the sky and bathed the campus in the golden light of fall. Students lounged on the Diag, reading, eating, feeding squirrels. Katie remembered those days through a soft lens of nostalgia. She chose not to remember the late nights, final exam stress, and slogging across campus in snow and slush.

They made their way to the literature, science, and arts building, where Russell's office was located. They climbed the steps to his floor, got turned around twice looking for his office number, and finally found his office with the door closed and a sign saying PLEASE WAIT. IF THE DOOR IS CLOSED, SOMEONE GOT HERE FIRST.

They sat next to each other on plastic chairs in the hallway. Fortunately, no one else was waiting, but Katie checked her watch and noticed there were only fifteen minutes left in his office hours schedule. She hoped he didn't have an afternoon lecture.

"Feels like waiting for the principal," Matt said.

"You never had to wait for the principal, did you?"

"Oh, I haven't always been the upstanding citizen you now know. I was a rebel."

"A rebel?" Katie laughed. "What did you do?"

"I do like a well-planned prank . . ."

"You're kidding," Katie said. "I saw you as a diligent student who got straight As and dated the cheer captain."

Matt swiveled in his chair and looked at her in shock. "It's like you don't know me at all," he joked. "I did get good grades, but alas, no cheerleader for me. I always thought they were overrated. All that bubbly excitement, and perfect hair. Who wants that?"

"Most high school boys," Katie said.

"Not if they're rebels." Matt sat back and folded his arms.

Katie was about to pursue this interesting line of information when the door to Russell's office swung open and a pretty young woman with too much makeup, skinny jeans, and high heels came into the hall.

"That was sooo helpful, Professor Hunt," she said. "See you in class." She tottered down the hall and turned the corner.

"Who's next?" Russell said as he peeked his head out of his office. He saw Katie and Matt, and looked up and down the hall as if for an explanation. "Oh, it's you. Are you here to see me?"

Katie and Matt stood. Matt nodded and said, "If you have a couple of minutes, we'd like to talk to you about Taylor."

Russell narrowed his eyes and gestured that they should come inside. He shut the door and walked around to sit behind his desk. Matt gestured for Katie to take the student chair, and he leaned against the wall. Russell's office was like many others, with bookshelves on one wall, diplomas framed and hung behind the desk, and a couple of potted plants that were actually healthy. What he didn't have was piles of paper everywhere. Katie wondered what he did with all the papers and handouts he must collect.

"What can I do for you two?" he asked. "I don't know anything about why Taylor is missing."

"I know this is unusual, Russell," Katie began. "I've been looking into some things, and I'm worried that maybe Taylor's project put her in danger. If she had been interviewing people from Heather's past, maybe she found out something that she shouldn't have."

"What could she have found out?" he said. "The case was closed years ago. The responsible party went to prison, and now he's out."

"It's just that he always maintained his innocence."

Russell snorted. "They all do, don't they?"

"How well did you know Heather?" Katie asked.

Russell looked down at his desk. "I didn't know her, not really."

"I remembered why you looked so familiar the other night," Matt said. "You were dating her just before she died."

Russell looked up quickly, a flash of anger in his eyes that was quickly extinguished. Katie saw him relax his shoulders and take a deep breath.

"Yes, we had been dating, but it wasn't serious," he said. "In fact, I was sure she was seeing other people. I had started seeing someone else as well. Look, I don't see how this is any of your business. The police investigated at the time."

"You didn't mind Taylor looking into the case?" Matt asked.

"Are you accusing me of something?" Russell sat very still, but Katie could sense the tension under the surface. She wondered if they had gone too far. They certainly weren't going to have any pleasant double dates in the future.

"No, we aren't accusing you," Katie said. "I really like Taylor, and I think she has a lot of potential. I'm just worried about her and want to do something to help find her."

Russell seemed to relax at this. "I really like her, too. She's a rare student—enthusiastic, bright, original. I'd love to help, but I don't know anything." He held his hands out, palms up. "I don't even know what she was working on exactly. She gave me a thumb drive with her outline and notes. I know it's a little intrusive, but I like to be sure the students aren't procrastinating too much, so I have a couple of checkpoints throughout the semester."

"What's on the thumb drive?" Matt asked.

Russell shrugged. "I have no idea. She turned it in before she . . . disappeared. But it's password-protected. I don't know if she forgot to take the security off or if she was being snarky, but I can't access it."

Katie and Matt exchanged a look. "Would you mind letting me take a look at it?" Katie asked. "I know someone who might be able to open it."

Caleb would be thrilled with another USB to crack.

Russell opened a desk drawer and pulled out a small plastic storage container. He dug through it and pulled out a gray metal thumb drive with TAYLOR KNOX written on a piece of masking tape stuck to the side. He handed it to Katie.

"Send me the file if you manage to open it. I'm curious now about what might be on there."

"Why didn't you give this to the police?" Katie said.

Russell shook his head. "It didn't even occur to me. I have papers she wrote earlier in the semester, and I didn't turn those in. I wasn't even thinking about it. This is likely to just be an outline and some scanned newspaper articles. I figured if something had happened to her, it had to do with her private life, not a school project."

Katie stood. "Thank you for talking to us. Sorry for the intrusion."

Russell nodded. Katie and Matt opened the door and stepped into the hall.

They headed down the hall to the stairwell, and after they had turned the corner, Matt leaned toward Katie and whispered, "He's lying."

26

She drove home in the fading golden light of a Michigan fall day. The air was crisp and the leaves bright on the trees. She knew that this time only lasted a short while, and it seemed every year she berated herself for not appreciating it enough during its brief moment.

She thought about Matt's conviction that Russell was lying. She knew Matt was a good judge of people. Anyone working in the emergency room had to develop a sixth sense about whether someone was telling the truth. So many accidents occurred in ways that patients would rather not describe. So many people drank or did drugs more than they claimed. Even in her own work in her clinic, Katie herself had developed the talent. Being lied to on a daily basis imparted the ability to detect a fabrication. And a cynicism Katie had never expected.

But Matt had said it wasn't just his innate lie detection system that had set off an alarm. He knew that Russell and Heather had been more than casual. She had told him so when she invited him to the Halloween party. The question Katie now struggled with was why. Why would Russell lie about something that happened ten years ago? She hoped whatever was on the memory sticks would help her figure that out.

Caleb's car was in the driveway, which meant he was likely home. She banged into the house through the kitchen door and dumped her tote bag and purse on the table.

"Caleb?"

"In here," he said.

He was ensconced, as usual, at the dining room table with papers and drawings spread around him. His laptop was open, and he had a large coffee cup steaming next to him. Caleb claimed he wasn't a coffee drinker, that he only drank it occasionally when he needed the caffeine boost for late-night programming sessions. Katie thought that if you drank coffee every day and late into the evening, you were a coffee drinker, but who could argue with denial?

He stretched his arms over his head and suppressed a yawn, which triggered a yawn in Katie until they both started laughing.

"You're too empathic," Caleb said.

"Goes with the job, I guess."

"I don't think so," he replied. He studied her for a moment as if considering saying more.

"Look what I have," Katie said. She pulled the memory stick out of her pocket and handed it to him.

"Ooh, what's on here?" Caleb loved breaking into password-protected devices. It was like a hobby for him. Some people liked crosswords; he liked computer hacking.

"I'm not sure, but I'd love to find out."

"It's got a password?"

Katie nodded.

"How many of these are you going to bring home?" Caleb asked. "I haven't even cracked the other ones yet. But I do need a break from worrying about this app."

Only Caleb would see hacking into a thumb drive as a break from coding an app.

Katie went to her room and changed into jeans and a sweatshirt. She wasn't planning to go back out again and always changed out of her work clothes as soon as she could after getting home. It was like taking off a costume. Gone was the efficient physician who advised people about their health all day, listened to complaints and worries, and always maintained a professional distance. She could rid herself of Dr. LeClair and become Katie again. Sometimes unsure, occasionally doubtful of her own skills, but dedicated and passionate about her career. It was exhausting sometimes to keep up the facade of objective, but warm, efficiency.

She went out to the kitchen to see what the refrigerator might offer for dinner. Finding some chicken breasts close to their expiration date and salad makings that also had seen better days, she began making a quick chicken salad with mustard sauce. "Are you here for dinner?" Katie called into the dining room.

"If you're cooking, I'm staying home for dinner."

Katie rolled her eyes. Caleb seldom thought of food until he was starving and then ran out to fast-food places. He had a couple of standby recipes he could make, and Katie tried to keep the ingredients on hand in case he was inspired. They had both been too busy to shop recently, hence the scrounged dinner.

She put in her headphones and listened to Frank Sinatra while she cooked. No one could help her forget her worries like Frank.

27

At nine o'clock that evening, Caleb triumphantly presented a folded piece of paper.

"You did it?"

"The regular one was easy to crack, and that helped me to open the animal ones. Sorry it took so long," Caleb said.

Katie couldn't wait to see what was on the memory sticks.

She found her laptop under some unfolded but clean laundry on the table in her room. The computer woke up slowly as she put the gray memory stick in the slot and waited.

Staring at the screen, she sat back and watched as one file popped up. It was a sketchy outline of her project and a couple of pages of notes. Just as Russell had said, it wasn't very helpful. Katie's shoulders slumped.

She pulled out the metal thumb drive and replaced it with the monkey. This time, file upon file scrolled in the USB window. It was as if Taylor had been running a full

private investigation. She had police reports, some interview excerpts, and notes. Lots of notes. Taylor had really
taken this project seriously. Katie wondered why she hadn't
shared all of this with her professor. It made Katie sad,
looking at all her hard work and wondering if her diligence
had put her in danger. Could she have found some missed
piece of evidence that had made one of her interview subjects nervous?

If these notes pointed to a different killer, then someone
did have a dangerous secret. And that caused a cold shiver
of dread.

She flipped open her notebook and got to work.

She clicked on the NOTES file, hoping that it would give
her a summary of what Taylor had been thinking. Instead,
it led to more questions.

Katie opened the file marked TIMELINE and saw that it
focused on the night of the party. It was a scanned copy of
notebook paper with multiple erasures and cross-outs. Taylor had written in the arrivals and departures of Heather
and her close friends. From what Katie could tell while
squinting and trying to read Taylor's handwriting, things
had gotten messy around ten o'clock. It was unclear who
had still been at the party, who had seen Heather last, and
when people had left. Katie wasn't surprised. She would not
want the job of tracking movements during a large college
party where alcohol was the main entertainment.

Katie closed out that window and scanned the list of
files. Why wasn't there one labeled SUSPECTS or MURDERER?
That would have been helpful.

Knowing that Hope Frost and Brad Humphreys were

on the sticky note she had found at Taylor's apartment, she clicked on Hope's name. There were scanned newspaper clippings of her wedding announcement and pictures that looked like they had been pulled off of social media of her graduation and her kids.

Brad Humphreys had the same type of information in his file. Katie wondered what Taylor had been thinking. Why the pictures and the announcements from their lives years after Heather's death? Did she suspect the room-mates? And if so, what was their motive?

Katie had just started writing out a list of questions when her phone rang.

She was on call and looked at the screen with trepida-tion. Ugh. The Baxter ER. That was never good news. She answered the call as she shut down her computer and flipped her notebook shut.

28

"This is police harassment."

Carlson shook his head. "I'm not harassing you. I haven't even touched you."

He stood on Nathan's small porch and glanced up and down the street in the fading light. Some teens were throwing a football in the street and a couple of younger kids sped along the sidewalk on bicycles. Carlson turned back to face Nathan's tirade.

"You show up at my house and accuse me of assault." Nathan's face had become dark with anger. "You do nothing to protect my wife when her stalker gets out of jail. Now you're telling *me* to stay away from *him*?"

This was not going the way he wanted, but Carlson had to admit it was going about the way he'd predicted. He held his hands up in a placating gesture.

"Mr. Nielsen, I merely asked you if you knew who might be vandalizing Mr. Lowe's property." Carlson had to admit that Nielsen's response was not casting him in the light of innocence.

Nathan took a deep breath and visibly tried to control his temper. Carlson could almost see him reining it in and tamping it down. The thought crossed his mind that this was a man with too much anger near the surface.

"You're right, Chief Carlson," Nathan said in a calmer tone. "I apologize."

"I know this has been a stressful time for you," Carlson said.

"I just don't want that guy anywhere near my wife. The whole trauma of Heather's death took a long time for her to get over, and now that *he's* back, the whole thing is being dredged up again. And I don't trust him. I know some people thought he was innocent, but I'm sure he did it."

Carlson cocked an eyebrow. "How can you be so sure?" Did Nathan have information he'd withheld from the police at the time? He tried to remember where Nathan had fallen in the whole affair. He'd known Heather, but how well? Carlson decided to do just a touch of research when he got back to the office.

"It's obvious," Nathan said. "He's a weirdo stalker type. He has no friends. Heather was beautiful and popular. He probably saw her when he was stalking Alicia and decided to switch targets."

This was a theory Carlson had heard before—the idea that Eugene had followed Alicia to Ann Arbor that fall and had seen a girl he liked even more. But it had never made sense to Carlson. Why would a shy kid like Eugene, who had only ever cared for Alicia—if the gossip could be believed—suddenly decide not only that he was in love with another girl but also become violent about it? He would still need to look into it. Carlson knew that when emotions got involved, things didn't always make sense to an observer.

"So, I take it you have no idea who might be harassing Eugene now?" Carlson got back to his original question.

Nathan ran a hand over his face and shook his head. He focused on a spot just over Carlson's shoulder and said, "No idea."

"Okay, well, thank you for your time." Carlson made his way down the steps and to his car parked in the street.

He unlocked his car and pulled the seat belt across his stomach. With a sigh, he stared out the windshield.

Nathan Nielsen was lying about something. He could feel it.

* * *

Instead of heading home to another healthy dinner, he swung by Pete's and picked up a grilled turkey, bacon, and cheddar sandwich and fries. He texted Linda to say he'd be home late and (somewhat gleefully) took his bag of food back to his office.

He flipped through the reports that had been left on his desk. After they had realized Taylor had been in Baxter just before she disappeared, he'd asked Linda to put a notice online asking for any information that might help the investigation. His officers had interviewed several people who'd claimed to have seen Taylor in town. Delores Munch had reported seeing her having coffee in the Purple Parrot that afternoon. She'd said she thought the girl was alone. Mike Sherman had claimed he had seen her going into Eugene's house that evening. Since Mike lived across town from

Eugene, Carlson wasn't sure what he'd been doing near Eugene's house, but because he was Nathan's best friend, Carlson was suspicious that he might be one of Eugene's harassers. He'd asked Molly Hart to follow up on that report. She had apparently found someone who could place him at the Riley's Grill bar at the same time he claimed he'd seen Taylor. So who was he protecting?

Thinking that it was often what was not said that carried the most weight with him, he pulled his bag of food over to a clear space on his desk.

He was halfway through his sandwich when something niggled at him. The kids who had lived with Alicia hadn't been interviewed until late in the day after Heather was killed. They'd had plenty of time to organize their alibis. Nathan had seemed so insistent that Eugene had killed Heather. Katie's voice nagged at him. "What if Eugene was innocent and Taylor had discovered evidence?"

Was Nathan protecting someone?

Carlson flipped through the file again. The two roommates had covered for each other, sort of. As he had noticed before, Hope had likely been at the party later than she claimed. But it didn't matter, did it? Carlson couldn't see a way that lying about their timing could have benefited either of them. So why had they done it? Had they just been drunk and confused, or had they planned it?

Alicia had also changed her mind about the timing quite a bit. At first, she'd said she'd come back to the apartment at midnight; then she'd changed her mind and said she was home by ten thirty. The officers finally got her to admit that she had been drinking and had no real idea what time it was. But she was sure she hadn't seen Brad or Hope until the next day. The only person she had seen at the apartment was Nathan. He'd walked her home and then stayed with her until she fell asleep.

Alicia had claimed that she and Nathan were "just friends" and that he was Heather's boyfriend. She had later revised that to say Heather and Nathan had recently broken up.

Carlson looked at his watch and sighed. The whole thing sounded like a teenage soap opera. He had to get some sleep. He put the file in his bottom desk drawer and locked it. He suddenly felt like maybe Katie was right and something about Eugene's case had come forward in time to threaten Taylor Knox.

29

The call from the ER had been for an elderly patient with pyelonephritis. In a young patient, a kidney infection could be treated with oral antibiotics at home. In an elderly person, it could be extremely dangerous. Katie had admitted him and started antibiotics for the infection. She probably could have left it to the nurses, but Katie wanted to be sure he was stable before leaving the hospital. By that time, it was almost two in the morning. After just a few hours of sleep, she'd doubled up on the caffeine and made it to Tuesday's clinic only fifteen minutes late. Halfway through the morning, Katie came out of an exam room to find Debra waiting for her. She was pale and her lower lip quivered.

"I just heard from Sean," Debra said. Sean was Debra's husband and an officer on the Baxter police force.

Katie's first thought, as always, went to Caleb—was he hurt?

Katie grabbed Debra's hand. "What is it?"

"Mrs. Munch found a body in the woods. She was walking that yappy cairn terrier of hers and they stumbled on a body."

"Whose body?" Katie's heart hammered in her chest.

"Sean said it was a university student." Debra's voice cracked, and she put her hand to her mouth. "They found her ID in her purse. It was Taylor Knox."

Katie felt dizzy and sat down hard in the nurse's chair at the desk. Taylor was dead?

It wasn't a complete surprise; after she'd been missing for almost a week, Katie hadn't really thought they would find her alive. But still. Katie felt like she had failed this young woman with so much promise.

Katie looked up at Debra, who was wringing her hands and looking helpless. "Could he tell how she died?"

Debra lowered her voice. "He said they think she was strangled."

"Where . . ." Katie cleared her throat. "Where did they find her?"

"She was in the woods at the far side of the hospital property. She was just covered in some leaves. It was like whoever left her there wanted her to be found. But Sean said it looked like she'd been dead for a while. The medical examiner thought it had been at least a few days."

"I need to . . ." Katie started. But what did she need to do? There was nothing she could do now.

"I'm sorry, Dr. LeClair," Debra said. She put a hand on Katie's shoulder. "I know you really liked her. We all did. She had such great . . . energy." Debra's voice cracked, and she pulled a tissue out of her pocket.

Katie looked up at Debra. "I'm sorry, too." She stood up and turned toward her office. "I have to make a couple of phone calls. Will you ask Angie to tell the patients I'll just be a few minutes?"

Debra nodded and went in search of Angie.

Katie had to call Gabrielle and let her know. She'd want to tell Russell.

After she got off the phone to Gabrielle, she pressed Caleb's number on her cell phone.

"Katie, hi."

"Caleb, listen. Taylor Knox is dead."

"Yeah, I know. I was just about to call you."

"How did you find out?"

"Eugene. He showed up here again."

Katie could hear muffled noises on the other end of the phone. Then she heard a door close.

Caleb spoke again. "He's a mess. He said he saw the police cars and his mother went to see what had happened. She came home in a panic because the girl was dead and people were already muttering that Eugene must have done it."

"And he just left his mom at the house?"

"No, she grabbed a bag and she's headed to her sister's house over in Denton. He came here because he figured no one would look for him here."

Eugene was becoming a higher-maintenance patient than she had bargained for. She couldn't hide him at her house. What if he *had* done it? Could she have been wrong about him all along? If the police were looking for him now that Taylor's body had been found, she and Caleb could be breaking the law. Harboring a fugitive? Accessory after the fact? Katie didn't know, but it was something for sure. Something that she didn't want to do. It was one thing to advocate for a patient with the police; it was another to *hide* him from the police. *If* the police were even looking for him. But, if the police weren't looking for him, the gang that had been harassing him certainly would be. He'd be safer in the jail than anywhere else.

"Katie?" Caleb said.

She should be focused on her phone call, but her mind was already spinning scenarios of doom.

"I need to call John Carlson. We can't hide Eugene there. If the police are looking for him, we'll be in trouble. If the people who have been bothering him are looking for him, we'll be in trouble."

"Okay, but you'd better tell him. He's not a big fan of mine. It's like he only trusts you."

Great. No pressure there. Katie had no idea if she was doing the right thing.

She clicked off her cell phone and buzzed the front desk. "I have an emergency at home, Debra. I'm going to ask Dr. Gregor to cover for me. Can you reschedule the afternoon patients and shuffle the rest into his schedule?"

"Sure, Dr. LeClair. Is your brother okay?"

"He's fine. I just need to get home."

Katie headed into the next hall and found Matt just stepping out of a room.

"Hey," he said. He looked up and down the empty hallway and lowered his voice. "Couldn't keep away, huh?"

Katie smiled in spite of her nerves. "I need to talk to you."

She took his hand and dragged him down the hall to his office. When they stepped inside, she closed the door.

"You don't look like you dragged me in here because you missed me."

Katie shook her head and felt the tears flood her eyes. Matt took her in his arms.

"What is it?" he asked. She heard the concern and confusion in his voice.

She swallowed to stop the tears and rubbed her cheeks with her sleeve.

"Taylor Knox was found dead not long ago."

"Oh, no. I guess it's not a shock, but at the same time, it is. What happened?" Matt asked.

"I don't know yet, but Caleb says that Eugene is hiding out at my house. I have to go over there and convince him to go to the police."

"Do you think he did it?" Matt asked. And then, without waiting for her answer, "I don't think you should be alone with him."

"No. I don't think so," Katie said. But even *she* could hear the uncertainty in her voice. But regardless of whether he was guilty or not, she didn't want him staying at her house. "I just don't think it's going to be safe for him with the vigilante gang out there. If they were after him just for moving back to town, I can't imagine what they'll do if they decide he killed Taylor."

"Okay, what can I do?"

"Will you cover my clinic for me, please? I'm canceling the afternoon, but there are a few sick visits already checked in."

"Of course. My schedule is pretty light. I'll head over there and tell Angie what we're doing."

"Thanks, Matt." She stood on her toes and kissed his cheek.

"Let me know how it goes," he said. "I'll take you out to dinner tonight, if you want."

"I'll call you later," Katie said on her way back to her office.

She grabbed her bag and headed out to the parking lot.

30

Katie unlocked her Subaru and climbed inside. She stuck the key in the ignition and hesitated before turning over the engine. Had she been wrong about Eugene? She hardly knew him, after all. Just because he was a patient didn't mean he wasn't capable of violence.

If Eugene had in fact killed Heather long ago, did that mean he had killed Taylor because she had gotten too close to the truth? But that didn't make any sense. Eugene had already served his time. Or was he some kind of lunatic who couldn't stop himself from stalking and killing young blondes? Alicia, Heather, and Taylor were all blonde, thin, and pretty. He had been caught breaking into Alicia's house. Katie only had his word for it that it had been a prank.

If Eugene *had* killed Taylor, Katie would never forgive herself. That's what it had all come down to in that initial moment of hearing about Taylor's death. It looked like the 'it's all about me' mentality that Katie despised in others was also alive and well in her own brain. She let her head fall back onto the seat and closed her eyes.

She felt her way past the selfish concerns and tried to think logically. It had been one of the first lessons of medical school. It wasn't taught in any specific class; it was entrenched in all the classes. *Nothing* was about her, the physician. It was *all* about the patient. And emotions, reactions, and self-involved thinking didn't help the patient. She was very good at compartmentalizing. Watching her mother lose her battle with cancer, watching her father struggle with alcohol, feeling like an orphan as she shuttled between family members—all of it had helped train her to be "good in a crisis."

It wasn't until residency that she had learned the other side of that lesson. Which was that, after shoving all those thoughts into the compartment that kept them separate from the job, she also needed to let them out or they would overwhelm her. It wasn't weakness; it was human. It was the only way she knew to be. So sometimes she had to take an evening and write everything down, or listen to sad music until she had cried all the pent-up tears of the week or the month or the year. And sometimes she had to sit in her parked car and enjoy the beauty of solitude.

She took a deep breath, turned over the engine, and steeled herself for what she would find at home.

* * *

Caleb met her at the back door. His look conveyed both irritation and concern.

"He's in the living room." Caleb tilted his head in that direction. "He hasn't said much."

"Thanks, Caleb." Katie squeezed his arm.

Eugene sat on the couch staring at the pink beaded

bracelet in his hands. He was clicking it like some sort of rosary.

"Eugene?" She stepped into the room and took a seat in the chair opposite. She sat for a moment, watching him. "Where did you get the beads?"

His hand stilled and then started up again. "Alicia gave them to me a long time ago."

He looked down at the beads resting in his hand. "I left them with my mother when I went to prison. I didn't want anything to happen to them. One day, after a horrible day at school, Alicia and I walked in the woods. I didn't even have to tell her what had happened; she just seemed to know." Eugene glanced up at Katie. "Have you ever had a friend like that?"

Katie nodded, thinking of Caleb.

"Well, high school was tolerable for her, but it was torture for me. As we walked along, I started to feel better just to have someone with me who understood. She stopped in a shaft of sunlight that had burst through the trees. She looked so beautiful. She took my hand and slipped the pink beads from her wrist to mine. 'Now, I'll always be with you,' she said. 'Just hold this bracelet and you'll know I'm thinking of you.'"

Katie sat, silent and surprised. She had assumed that Eugene had a one-way crush on his high school friend. But maybe Alicia had really cared for him.

"I can see why you still have them," Katie said.

Eugene blushed a blotchy red. "I've never told anyone that story."

"It'll be our secret."

"I'm sorry to keep involving you in this mess," he said.

"You don't deserve it. It's just that you were kind when no one else was. I guess what they say is true—no good deed goes unpunished."

Katie took a deep breath and decided to plunge in. Maybe she would get a real answer now that they were sharing this moment.

"Eugene, did you meet with Taylor before she disappeared?" Katie asked. "It's just that I know she'd been interviewing people involved in your case."

He looked at her then. His eyes were sad, and she saw something else there. Fear? Anger?

"I did. She was very nice," he said. "She said her father was a police officer and he'd never believed I was the one who killed Heather. She was trying to find out who did."

"She was?" It made sense now that Taylor's files were so thorough. Katie remembered that Taylor had said her father had died in the last couple of years. She must have seen this project as a way to finish her father's work. No wonder she'd been so desperate to clear Eugene. "Who did she think did it?"

Eugene shook his head. "She didn't say, and I'm not even sure she had narrowed things down. She just asked me about that night and we talked a little about prison and that was it. She left, and the next thing I heard, she was missing."

Katie thought about how to phrase the next question. Would he even tell her the truth if she came right out and asked him if he had harmed Taylor?

"You didn't see her later that night, or in the morning?"

Eugene narrowed his eyes. "I didn't kill her, Dr. LeClair. I hardly even knew her."

Well, that was easy, Katie thought as she squirmed

uncomfortably under Eugene's stare. She wasn't accustomed to accusing people. She liked the role of advocate and helper much more than opposition and confronter.

"I'm sorry, Eugene," Katie said. "I felt I had to ask. The police will ask."

He shot her a look. "I'm not talking to them."

"I think you should. You were possibly one of the last people to see her alive. It's only natural that they'll want to talk to you."

He started to speak, and she held up her hand to stop him. "I think, more than cooperating with them, you should go to them for protection. Think about these people who have been targeting you over a girl who was killed years ago in another town. How do you think they'll react to a murder in Baxter?"

Eugene's shoulders slumped. "I can go away again. I'm good at hiding."

Katie shook her head. "That will just mean that the police have to look for you, and that will pull them away from finding the real killer."

"And what if they think they've already caught the real killer?" Eugene said. "You want me to walk in there and turn myself in. And you think they'll continue to investigate? They'll just all go out for beers and toast their policing skills while I sit in prison and wait to be sent back to Jackson."

"That's not . . ."

"I can't go back there, Dr. LeClair," Eugene said so quietly Katie almost didn't hear him. "I barely survived the first time. Look at me. I'm not exactly the kind of guy who inspires fear. I had to be vigilant every hour of every day for ten years."

"Okay, let me talk to Chief Carlson. I'll try to figure out what they're thinking, and then we can reevaluate."

Katie stood up, and Eugene regarded her with such undisguised hope that she had to look away.

"You stay here with Caleb," she said. "You can trust him."

Eugene nodded, and the beads began to click.

31

John Carlson stood in the woods watching the Ann Arbor team go over the area and photograph the body of the young woman. He had sent Mrs. Munch back to her house with Molly Hart, a young female officer. He knew that Officer Hart had glared at him behind his back, but she was really good at dealing with victims and witnesses. She thought he chose her to keep her away from the action, but he chose her because she was the best officer for the job. He had a hard time navigating all the rocky waters of gender bias and usually tried to ignore it as best he could. He'd have to deal with it eventually, he knew.

Taylor Knox had been beautiful. But lying in the leaves, her face gray, eyes bloodshot, and with angry red marks on her neck, she merely looked dead. The crime scene team had already told him that she had been dead for a while. Carlson swallowed hard and turned away.

He had welcomed the job as chief of police in this small town knowing that it was unlikely he'd ever have to deal with a murder of a young woman. He'd watched Andy

Griffith reruns as a kid and imagined the job of dispensing wisdom and fishing with his son as the best one could hope for. The son had not materialized, and now neither had his fantasy of a quiet town where the worst criminal was the local drunk.

Carlson felt the anger rising up from the pit of his stomach. How had this happened? Why? What was she doing here? Did she have a connection to Baxter? He would have to begin the process of digging through Taylor's life and uncovering every person she had known. Fortunately, the AAPD had done a lot of that work when she was missing. It all felt so invasive. As if that was the true violence against the victim. He knew this was an unusual stance for a police officer. His wife, as a journalist, was comfortable invading people's privacy. He wondered sometimes if she believed anyone deserved privacy at all.

But this wasn't a missing person case anymore. This was murder. He sighed and smoothed his sparse hair over the top of his head.

If Taylor had been researching Heather Stone's murder, as Katie suggested, how would he be able to connect the dots? He'd have to look into Taylor's life *and* reopen the old case to see who could have felt threatened by a twenty-year-old sociology student.

He flipped open his notebook. His list was short for Taylor. Her roommate had said everyone liked her and she had no enemies. The boyfriend had seemed distraught, but Carlson had learned that that didn't always mean innocent. The problem was that since no one was exactly sure when she had disappeared, it was hard to check alibis.

Carlson made a note to find out where Taylor's boyfriend

and roommate were on the evening Katie had met with Taylor.

His cell phone buzzed in his pocket, and he pulled it out. The name KATIE LECLAIR popped up on the screen. Think of the devil . . .

He clicked it open. "Hey, Doc," he said. "I can't talk right now; can I call you later?"

Katie ignored him and said, "I need to talk to you. How soon can we meet?"

"I'm in the middle of a murder . . ."

"I know. That's why I'm calling. I have information."

Carlson's shoulders slumped. Of *course* she had information. She'd probably have the case wrapped up by dinnertime.

He looked at his watch.

"Meet me at my office in half an hour."

32

The cheery yellow door mocked Katie's dark mood as she pulled it open and entered the police station. The same young woman sat at the desk, but she was not chatting on the phone. She was fielding what sounded like real phone calls and not enjoying it one bit.

"No comment," she said, and pressed a button on the phone.

"I can take a message," she said to the next caller. Then, "Hold, please."

She glanced at Katie and gestured that she should go back to Carlson's office.

John Carlson had just arrived. He hung up his jacket on the hook behind his door and gestured for Katie to have a seat in the molded plastic chair in front of the desk.

"What can I do for you, Doc?" he said wearily as he eased himself into his chair. Carlson rubbed his face with both hands. His eyes were red and tired looking.

"Eugene Lowe is at my house," Katie said.

Carlson perked up at this. "What? Why?"

"He says he didn't hurt Taylor." Katie held up her hands when Carlson started to interrupt. "But he did see her just before she disappeared. He may have been the last person to see her before she went missing."

"This was for the project you told me about?"

Katie nodded.

Carlson put his head in his hands. "Why?" he said to his desk.

"Why?"

"Why was she interviewing Eugene?" Carlson put his hands down and looked at Katie.

"Apparently, her father was a police officer who had worked on the Heather Stone case. He always thought Eugene was innocent. I don't know if she took the class in order to do this project or if it was a coincidence, but she used her father's notes and researched the case on her own."

Carlson looked at the ceiling in the same way her mother used to when she and Caleb had been particularly challenging. "I don't suppose you have any of these notes?"

"I do, actually." Katie slid the thumb drive across the desk along with the password.

"Do I want to know how you got this?"

Katie shook her head. "I don't think any of it will be news to you. It mostly references interviews and reports that her father had."

"And why is he at your house and not here in the station to give a statement?"

"He's afraid," Katie said. "He's afraid he'll be accused of this new murder and afraid that whoever has been harassing him will ramp up their efforts with this new death."

"He's not wrong," said Carlson. "We need to talk to him if he saw Taylor close to the time she disappeared. And whoever is bothering him is not likely to wander off and leave him alone at this point."

"I agree," Katie said. "I told him I'd talk to you about the best next steps. I told him he could trust you."

"Katie, I can't promise anything." Carlson rested his arms on his desk and leaned forward. "I need to talk to him, and if his story is suspicious, I'll need to keep him here until we figure this thing out."

"Yes, good," Katie said.

"Good?" Carlson looked at her in surprise. "You want me to arrest him?"

"I want you to keep him here for at least a couple of days," Katie said. "It will be safer here than at his house."

"I see," Carlson said. "Do you want me to pick him up for his staycation, or will you bring him in?"

"I think you should pick him up," Katie said, ignoring the sarcasm. "And be sure to use the sirens."

"You want a big production?"

"I want everyone to know he's in police custody," Katie said. "It will be safer for him and for his mother."

* * *

True to his word, Chief Carlson arrived at Katie's house with sirens blaring. She had explained to Eugene that the safest course for now would be to cooperate with the police and to do it in a very public way. She didn't want Eugene's mother to be in danger and wanted whoever had been harassing Eugene to know he was in custody and untouchable.

Katie led the chief into her living room where Eugene sat, still running the beads through his fingers.

Carlson stood in front of Eugene. "Eugene, we need to take you down to the station to answer some questions," he said in a soft voice.

Eugene nodded and stood up. He cast a desperate look at Katie—a combination of fear, relief, and (most upsetting to Katie) trust.

She hoped her gamble would pay off. He would certainly be a suspect in Taylor's murder, and she herself wasn't sure what to think. Even knowing the beads were Alicia's gave her a shiver of apprehension.

The noise and flashing lights had drawn the neighbors out onto their porches to watch the spectacle. Katie realized too late that it wouldn't reflect well on her own reputation to have someone dragged out of her house in handcuffs.

Fortunately, no dragging was necessary and Carlson didn't use cuffs. Eugene got into the back seat and gazed gloomily out the window as the car pulled away from the curb.

Caleb slung an arm over her shoulder as they stood on the porch and watched the police cruiser disappear around the corner. "I hope you know what you're doing," he said.

"Me, too." Katie turned to walk back into the house. "Let's get to work."

33

They sat together at the dining room table, laptops open, huge mugs of steaming coffee at the ready. Katie pulled the autopsy report out of its large yellow envelope and began reading. She wondered why Linda hadn't been able to obtain the full autopsy report at the time of Eugene's trial. In reading the trial transcript, it hadn't seemed as if the full report had been submitted then either. Were the prosecutors hiding something? Something that made Eugene seem less guilty? She'd already scanned the list of conclusions but wanted to go back over the physical exam section itself.

Detailed description of the head wound was included along with photos. Something that surprised her was a note about bruising to Heather's upper arms and marks on her neck. There were no photos of the bruises, which also seemed unusual. Katie didn't read autopsy reports very often, but it seemed like bruising on the victim of a violent death would be worth a photo. She flipped to the end again—there was no mention of the bruises. She'd seen only a photocopy of the final page at the *Gazette* offices.

She'd assumed Heather had been pushed and accidentally hit her head. But bruising—described as recent—painted a picture of a different kind of assault. And why were there no defensive wounds noted? Surely she would have fought back. Eugene was a stranger to Heather. Katie found it hard to believe he could have tried to strangle her, as the bruising suggested, and then pushed her away so that she fell and hit her head on a brick without any broken fingernails or other evidence of a struggle. Unless she knew her killer and trusted him. Could she have let someone she knew get close enough to put his hands on her neck and not fight back?

Katie's initial examination of Taylor's files had focused on the police interviews with Eugene and the files on Heather's roommates. The interview with Eugene had yielded no new information, as Eugene had refused to say anything more than his initial "I found her like that." She still needed to go through the other interviews.

She pulled up the files on the computer to see if Taylor had noticed anything about the pathology report. Katie couldn't tell. Taylor had not included a mention of it in her notes and had just listed the pathologist's summary. Then she remembered that there was an unclaimed report back at the pathology department. If Taylor had ordered it but had never seen it, then there was something besides the autopsy report that had made her suspicious.

Katie explained all of this to Caleb, and he agreed it seemed strange. The two of them split the rest of the interviews and notes and began to read.

Katie's files included Heather's two roommates, Hope
Frost and Brad Humphreys. She reviewed the information.
They had both been at the party that night, but Brad had
left the party early and Hope had remembered leaving right
after she saw Heather fighting with one of her exes. She said
Danny Lloyd had grabbed Heather's wrist, but he let her go
and stormed off when some of the other guys at the party
stepped in. It became clear to Katie that the party had been
huge and that no one had been sober. What a mess it must
have been at the time. Trying to get a bunch of college kids to
put together a timetable of events seemed an impossible task.

"Caleb, have you looked at Danny Lloyd's interview yet?"

"Nope, I'm still reading the report from the campus security guy who found Eugene hovering over Heather's body."

"I'll take that one," Katie said. "You can take Brad
Humphreys."

"'Kay."

Katie opened Danny's file but was disappointed almost
immediately. He said he had stormed out of the party, but
two of his friends had followed him and all three had gone
home from there. The timing was iffy; two of them claimed
they left at ten, but Danny said it was later. Either way, he
couldn't have killed Heather if he had left the party while
she was still alive. But could he have gone back to the
party? Katie went back to Hope's interview. Hope said
Danny and Heather had been together in the spring. She'd
thrown him over for Nathan Nielsen. Hope made it clear
that she approved of the decision.

Katie scrolled down the files, looking to see if Taylor
had taken notes on her meeting with Danny. She found a

to-do list and his name was on it. *Eleven a.m., October 16, meet with Danny Lloyd.* That was the Thursday before she'd gone missing. There were no notes from that meeting, but Russell had said she'd given him the thumb drive on the seventeenth. Maybe she'd met with him and updated her files on her computer. If so, she hadn't backed up that information on her thumb drive. Because there was no mention of the meeting on the drives Russell or Abby had given her, Katie was left to wonder if Danny's version had been accurate. Could he have felt more threatened by Taylor's questions than he let on? Had he really been immune to Heather's taunting? If the meeting had been recorded on Taylor's computer, then it was out there somewhere. Probably with Taylor's murderer.

Katie went back to Hope's interview, trying to find the thing that had triggered Taylor's conviction that Eugene was innocent.

Officer James: What happened after the fight with Danny Lloyd?

Hope Frost: I'm not sure where Heather went at that point. I assumed she'd gone to the bathroom to take a minute after the fight, but then I didn't see her again.

James: And what did you do?

Frost: I stayed at the party until about midnight. It was still going on when I left. A couple of girls from my apartment building were leaving, so I decided to walk with them. I don't like to walk home alone in the dark.

James: What time did you get home?

Frost: Maybe twelve fifteen. Brad's door was closed, so I assumed he had already gone to bed. He hates parties and only goes if Heather and I beg him.

James: Was anyone else in the apartment when you got home?

Frost: Alicia and Nathan were there, too.

James: Full names, please.

Frost: Alicia Stewart and Nathan Nielsen.

James: Are they also roommates?

Frost: No. Alicia is . . . was a friend of Heather's. She was staying with us for a few days. Nathan knew Alicia from high school or something. But he and Heather had been dating until the end of September, when she broke up with him. Actually, I was surprised to see him there, but assumed he had walked Alicia home.

James: Anything else?

Frost: No. I went to bed and didn't find out about Heather until the next day.

"Katie, you might want to see this," Caleb said.

He turned his laptop toward her and pointed at the screen. "According to the case notes from Taylor's dad, Russell Hunt was the last person Heather called on her phone. He had a copy of the phone records. Russell said she wanted to talk to him, and he waited for her at his apartment for an hour. She never showed, and so he went out with his friends. That's the guy you said Gabrielle is dating, right?"

Katie nodded. "Right. Matt said he saw Russell at the party that night."

"Matt was at the party?"

"From the way it sounds, the whole campus was there. Russell was a grad student at the time and a TA. I'm not sure why he'd be at an undergrad party, but he was."

"Hmm," Caleb said. "He sounds sketchy."

"You think every guy who dates Gabrielle is sketchy," Katie said.

"And your point is?"

"Just because you don't like him doesn't mean he's a murderer. Plus, you've never met him. Maybe you guys would hit it off."

Caleb muttered to himself and typed something into his computer. He continued to scroll. "Why would she have called him that night?" Caleb asked. "I mean, she's at a party, and she calls her TA? That sounds like something else was going on. Isn't there some rule about dating your students?"

"Maybe," Katie said. "And you're right, he told Matt and me that they dated briefly."

Caleb grinned in a triumphant way.

She hated to think that Gabrielle was dating someone who had been involved in Heather's death. Of course, Katie was dating someone who had been there that night as well. And maybe that was all it was. Russell had been at the party, even though that was a little weird, and she had called him. Caleb was right, Russell was a little sketchy. But that didn't mean he'd murdered Heather.

"Here's something," Caleb said. "She had a fight with one of her exes at the party." He scrolled some more. "His name was Danny Lloyd. Sounds like it got physical and his friends made him leave the party. Oh, that's the guy you just asked about. Did you read his statement yet?"

"Yeah, I spoke to him the day I went to see Abby. He says Heather had broken things off that spring. Plus, he had an alibi. He left the party with his friends and they all went home."

"That doesn't sound like the strongest alibi," Caleb said. "Could he have circled back to the party?'

Katie sighed and pulled her notebook closer. This was not going to be as straightforward as she'd thought. She had imagined that Taylor's thumb drive would contain a nicely thought out paper with references, and instead she was plowing through notes and documents with no guidelines. Taylor's personal notes were so cryptic as to be almost useless. The files on each person included police summaries, and Taylor had made a few cross-referencing notes to try to tie the people together.

"Based on what she said to me the night she went missing, she suspected someone of a crime," Katie said. "I just wish I knew who it was. I wish I had stayed and talked to her."

"Katie, this isn't your fault," Caleb said. "You can't control everything, no matter how hard you try."

"At this point, all I can do is try to get justice for Taylor. And maybe for Heather as well."

Katie took a big swig of coffee and began drawing her own map of relationships.

34

By six o'clock, Katie was only too happy to close her laptop. She stretched and closed her notebook as well. Caleb glanced at her and shook his head.

"You have no stamina," he said.

"We've been at this for three hours," Katie said. "I feel like I'm only skimming the words but not really reading them. I never thought I'd be looking forward to a Halloween festival meeting."

Caleb snorted and turned back to his laptop. "I'm not finding much else here, either. It's like once they had Eugene in custody, they just went through the motions."

"We'll regroup after the meeting," Katie said. "Why don't you take a break too, and we'll start fresh this evening."

Caleb shut his computer. "If you insist . . ."

"Want to come to the meeting with me?"

"Nope. Not even a little bit." Caleb grinned at her. "You have to learn to say no."

Katie grabbed her bag and headed out the back door to

her car. She did need to say no more often. The word just always got stuck on the way out of her mouth, and before she knew it, she was volunteering for something else. She steered her Subaru in the direction of her clinic.

When she arrived in the lot, she texted Matt that she was outside.

"Hey," he said as he climbed in beside her.

"Hi, how was it?"

"Not too bad," he said. "The afternoon was slow. I got caught up on dictations, though."

"That's better than I did today," Katie said. "The dictation police are going to come after me soon if I don't get over there to finish up some discharge notes for the hospital."

"You definitely don't want that," Matt said. "I've met Edna, and she is no softie like your buddy Carlson."

"Edna?"

"She's in charge of patient records over there." Matt shook his head somberly. "You don't want a visit from her."

"Another thing to worry about," Katie said as she backed out of her parking spot.

"How did it go with Eugene?"

"As well as expected, I guess." Katie turned onto Main Street. "I convinced him to turn himself in. I think it's the only way to keep him safe right now."

Matt nodded. "It was the talk of the clinic in the afternoon. Everyone had a theory, and most of them included Eugene."

"I hope I'm not wrong about him," Katie said.

"You think he might have killed Taylor?"

Katie glanced at him quickly. "Not really, but what do I

really know about him? He and his mother told me he was innocent. My gut tells me he's a good guy. But there's definitely something a little off about him. I just can't put my finger on it, and it makes me doubt everything."

"Well, I guess if you *are* wrong, at least he's in custody now."

"I suppose that's true." Katie pulled into the high school parking lot and found a spot.

She killed the engine and turned toward Matt. "Are you ready for this?"

He squared his shoulders and nodded. "As ready as I'll ever be."

They got out of the car, and Katie clicked the lock button on her key fob. She stood straight and took a deep breath.

"Okay, let's do this," she said.

They went straight to the gym, the multiple turns and staircases familiar in that same nostalgic way. The noise was even louder this time around. It seemed that more volunteers had been recruited. Delores actually needed her bullhorn to be heard over the melee.

Katie and Matt presented themselves at the parade table and were issued paintbrushes. They'd been assigned to work on the main float for the parade. It had definitely seen better days. Katie couldn't believe it would hold her weight, much less be able to travel the five blocks of the parade route.

"Huh," said Matt. "Do they think a new coat of paint will fix all this?"

Katie shrugged and dipped her brush in the paint can.

"Let's hope there's an engineering crew as well to make sure this thing will run."

They spent the next hour painting the float, and by the time they were done, Katie had to admit that it *looked* sturdier. She climbed up onto the platform and imagined trying to keep her balance while it was in motion and she was wearing a pumpkin suit. Her imagination was not that vivid.

"I should probably try on that pumpkin costume and maybe even try to climb up here and see how it will feel," she said. "I don't want to totally embarrass myself by falling off of the thing."

"I'll help you," Matt said. He tapped the lid back on the paint can and wrapped the brushes in a plastic bag. "Do you think it's still in the costume room?"

"Let's go see." Katie led the way across the gym and out the door headed to the costume room.

She pushed open the door and saw Nathan Nielsen and another man standing by the pumpkin costume. It was the same man that had been talking to Nathan when they unloaded the pumpkin.

"Oh, hello," she said. "I was just looking for that." She pointed to the pumpkin costume.

"Great. We were going to bring it to the gym," Nathan said. "We can take it from here, Mike." The other man rapidly exited the room, and Katie got the distinct impression he was grateful for the interruption.

"I'll just try it on, then," she said.

Matt stepped forward to help, and he and Nathan lifted it over her head.

Katie took a deep, musty breath and coughed. She'd have to breathe through her mouth to avoid the dank basementlike smell that permeated the pumpkin. There were shoulder straps on the inside, and she slid these over her shoulders and made sure she was standing on the floor in the space made by the bottom hole of the costume. The pumpkin was heavier than she had expected, and she lost her balance as she struggled to lift it off the ground. The foot hole was not very big, so she had to shuffle along only taking short strides.

She felt the men turn her in the right direction.

"You okay in there?" Matt couldn't keep the smile out of his voice, and Katie narrowed her eyes even though he couldn't see her face. There was a piece of fabric right in front of Katie that was semitransparent. She assumed it looked opaque from the outside, but she could make out the hazy outlines of objects in the room.

"I'm just great," she said in a monotone.

"You'll get used to it," Nathan said. "Plus you don't really have to move at all, just keep your balance when the float is in motion."

She sighed and ratcheted up her worry about her Halloween assignment. Why did Cecily hate her so much? Maybe if she accepted more cast-off cookies from Delores, she could switch duties with someone who got to wear normal clothes.

* * *

Later that evening, Katie pulled into her driveway and Matt parked his car in the street. They had escaped the festival meeting with minimal paint stains but more worries about their Halloween duties.

They met on the front porch, and Katie unlocked the door and pushed it open.

"Hey, Matt!" Caleb approached and shook Matt's hand like he was a long-lost brother. He turned to Katie and said, "Oh, hi." He couldn't hide his grin as he turned away. Katie shoved his shoulder and pretended to be hurt by his greeting.

They slung their jackets over the back of the couch and moved into the dining room.

"How's the app going?" Matt asked. He surveyed the table and its usual state of disarray.

"It would be going a lot better if I could figure out . . ."

"Wait," Katie said. She held up her hands. "Matt is here to help *me*. Our custody arrangement is very clear."

Matt and Caleb grinned at each other, and they all sat at the table. She settled Matt at the far end of the table from Caleb and opened her laptop.

Matt scrolled through the files and opened the police interview of Eugene. After a few minutes, he said, "He didn't help himself very much, did he?"

Katie shook her head. "No, he never had an explanation as to why he was in Ann Arbor that night. He claimed he didn't know anyone there."

Caleb looked up from his computer. "It's like he didn't get it. Everything he said, or failed to say, just made the police suspect him more."

"Have you ever asked him about that night?" Matt asked Katie.

She nodded. "He told me the same thing he always said. That he found Heather on the ground and was just getting ready to find help when he was discovered with her body."

They were silent for a moment.

Katie took a deep breath and let it out. "I don't believe Eugene killed Taylor any more than I believe he killed Heather. The whole case against him for Heather's death is circumstantial. It's like he was covering for someone, or covering up something."

"Look at this," Matt said. "Eugene says he saw a blonde girl in a witch costume walking alone. He claims he followed her to be sure she was safe. He lost her in the Law Quad—they were doing some landscaping and repairs, so there was a lot of equipment and supplies piled around."

Matt turned to Katie. "I remember that. The Quad was a mess that autumn. I used to cut through there to get to one of my classes, but that fall I had to go around because it took less time to go the long way than to take the shortcut."

"So you think Eugene could have lost sight of her for long enough for someone to kill her before he found her again?" Katie said.

"Maybe," Matt said. "But I just thought of something about that party. There were at least five blonde witches that night."

"How can you recall *that*?" Caleb asked.

"Remember I told you it was a big deal to wear a costume?" Matt asked Katie.

She nodded. "You said it wasn't worth it to dress up, because you had to have a movie-worthy get-up."

"Right, and I was sure Heather would have some amazing costume because that was just the way she was. Any opportunity to attract attention and she would grab it."

"But she was only wearing a witch costume?"

"Right. Some of the girls had gone all out with Disney princess costumes or other ball gown–type things. Others had amazing makeup done to look like vampires or zombies or whatever. But Heather came with her roommate—I can't remember her name right now—and Alicia, I think, and a couple of her sorority sisters, and they all dressed the same."

"Blonde witches?" Caleb asked.

"*That's* what Eugene meant," Katie said. "He said Alicia and Heather were dressed the same. It's why he thought it was Alicia who was laying on the ground."

"Right. And these weren't fancy. They were like costumes you could buy at any of those pop-up Halloween stores. Just a black cape and a pointy hat. And, to answer your question, Caleb, I remember because I was surprised the costumes were so lame and also because they all came to the party together."

"Did you tell the police when you talked to them?" Katie asked. She was already scrolling to Matt's interview.

"I don't know if I did. The truth is, it just struck me now that the costumes were weird. At the time, I was so freaked out that Heather had been killed, I'm not sure I gave a second thought to the costume she was wearing."

Katie scanned the interview. "It doesn't look like you mentioned it."

"What difference does it make?" Caleb asked.

"I'm not sure it makes a difference in Eugene's favor," Katie said. "In fact, it might make things worse. If he was following the witch costume and knew that Alicia was wearing it, that would almost give him a stronger motive—at least in the eyes of the police. He had already been accused of stalking Alicia. If the police had put together the costume confusion, then that would actually give them a motive, which was the one thing they were missing in the whole case. They could have claimed it was mistaken identity."

Matt and Caleb exchanged a glance, and both of them watched Katie.

She noticed the two of them staring.

"What?"

"It's just that you've now identified a motive, which was one reason why you thought Eugene was innocent," Caleb said. He held his hands out, palms up. "Maybe he did do it and you just figured out why."

* * *

They continued into the evening discussing various small points and dissecting the interviews. Nothing else emerged that was quite as devastating to Katie as the realization that maybe Eugene *had* killed Heather—by accident, certainly— because he was trying to kill Alicia.

Katie needed to put that theory aside for the moment and focus on figuring out who else could have killed Heather. One person Katie kept coming back to was Heather's roommate. Heather had lived with two other students: Brad Humphreys and Hope Frost. Caleb had been able to track them both by using his "research skills." Katie suspected he'd just typed the names into a search engine and gotten lucky.

From Hope's social media pages, Caleb had learned that she still lived in Ann Arbor and was a teacher at one of the elementary schools. Hope and Brad had gotten married and had two very cute kids and had taken a trip to Disney World last spring. They also had a new puppy. Katie felt weird prying into a stranger's life. She had the feeling, though, that Hope would be open to talking to her. She looked friendly.

Brad Humphreys, on the other hand, had almost no social media presence. He was an engineer and had joined a small consulting firm. The only information Caleb could find was a brief bio on his new company's ABOUT Us page that said he was married and liked to hike.

Caleb handed her phone numbers for both of them. Hope's was her home number and Brad's was his work number. Katie took Hope's number and gave Matt the other one.

"Divide and conquer?" Matt said.

35

Wednesday afternoon, Katie pulled into the small neighborhood of bungalows and ranches about a mile outside campus. She had lucked out when she arranged the meeting. Hope had the day off due to parent-teacher conferences. Two young children played in the yard and stopped their game of kicking a ball back and forth in a lackluster fashion.

They stood and stared at her as she got out of the car. The older one, who was maybe about seven, grabbed the ball and ran inside yelling, "Mom! Someone's here!"

The younger one slid a thumb in her mouth as she watched Katie approach. "Hi," Katie said. "How are you?"

The little girl ran up the steps and into the house, slamming the door behind her. Katie convinced herself the girl had been trained in "stranger danger" protocol and wasn't just frightened because Katie seemed threatening. She straightened her shoulders and faced the house. She couldn't be that scary. All of her pediatric patients loved her. The nurses gave the shots, allowing Katie to be untainted by the trauma. She noticed movement in the window and glanced over to see both kids watching her climb the steps to the porch. She didn't have a chance to knock before the door swung open.

"Hi, you must be Dr. LeClair," the woman said. She was taller than Katie by an inch or so and had long golden hair pulled up into a ponytail. Katie recognized her from all the photos she had seen online. She smiled warmly at Katie and opened the door wider to allow her to enter.

Katie put her hand out once she was in the entryway. "Call me Katie, please. You're Hope?"

The woman nodded. "Please come in. Welcome to the chaos!"

Hope gestured to a family room cluttered with trucks, dolls, board games, and DVD cases. It looked like a hurricane had been through. Hope rolled her eyes at Katie. "It's okay; you can be shocked. It's the reason they were outside playing. I went upstairs for about two minutes, and this is what they did. Normally, I'd make them clean up, but I promised them a movie to watch when you came."

Hope turned to her son. "Okay, you can start the movie, but keep the volume low."

The kids plunked down in front of the TV and ignored the two adults.

"Let's go into the kitchen. They should be good for at least fifteen minutes."

Katie followed her down the hallway to the kitchen, which was bright and cheerful. The walls were painted a soft yellow, complementing the blue countertops and white tile backsplash. A red table with colorful mismatched chairs sat against one wall, and large windows looked into the backyard. The effect was one of homey comfort.

Hope offered Katie coffee and used one of those fancy machines with the little plastic cups of coffee grounds. She put the mug in front of Katie and sat across the kitchen table with her own drink.

"You said on the phone that you wanted to talk about Heather?" Hope said.

Katie nodded, grateful for Hope's straightforward manner. She had decided to lead with Eugene's situation in case Hope hadn't yet connected the dots that Taylor was the missing girl. Katie knew from Taylor's notes that they had met.

"I met Eugene Lowe recently, and I wanted to find out more about the events surrounding Heather's death."

"You're a doctor, though, not a lawyer, right?"

Katie nodded. "I am, but you see, Eugene has had a tough reentry into society, and I'm trying to figure out how best to help him."

Hope shook her head. "I'm not sure I can help you. And honestly, I'm not sure I would want to if I could." Hope turned and looked out the window. When she looked back at Katie, there were tears in her eyes. "Heather was my best friend. Losing her was devastating. Not only because we were so close, but also because the campus that I'd grown to love was suddenly dangerous and scary."

"I'm so sorry for your loss," Katie said. "I'm sure it was a very difficult time."

Hope pulled a tissue out of the box that sat on the table

and dabbed her eyes. "What's been happening to Eugene Lowe?" she asked.

"There have been some threats, some damage to his property, and some violence."

"Oh, I see. Baxter doesn't want him back?"

"You could say that."

"Like I said, I'm the last person who would want to help him, Dr. LeClair. I never thought ten years was enough."

"What if he was innocent?"

Hope sniffled. "What?"

"What if he was just in the wrong place at the wrong time and he never touched Heather?"

"Is that what he claims?"

"I think it's what he has always claimed."

Hope nodded. "I guess I do remember that."

"I'm trying to piece together Heather's life leading up to that Halloween party to see if anything got missed before," Katie said. "The truth is, I'm worried someone has gotten away with murder all these years."

"Mama?" the little girl stood in the doorway, her thumb in her mouth again. "Why you crying?"

"I'm fine, sweetheart," Hope said. "Do you need something?"

"Go potty."

"Excuse me," Hope said. "I'll be right back."

She hustled her daughter out of the room. Katie wondered if this had been a waste of time. Maybe this whole thing was a waste of time. But *if* Eugene was innocent, that meant a murderer had been free all this time. And she was convinced that whoever had killed Taylor had also killed

Heather. She felt a shiver of dread as she followed her line of thought. If Taylor had been killed because she had learned something about Heather's death, what would that mean for Katie? And Caleb. Even Matt might be in danger just for helping. It was too late now to back away from this investigation, but she'd better figure things out quickly.

Hope came back into the room. "Sorry about that." She sat down again.

Katie could sense she had come to a decision. She braced herself for Hope telling her there was nothing she could do to help.

"I do have a couple of things I remember that always bothered me. To be honest, I tried not to think about them at all, but maybe it will help."

Katie waited and nodded to encourage her.

"Heather always had boyfriends. She was the sort of girl who collected admirers but never really committed, you know?"

Katie took a sip of coffee and, thinking of Gabrielle, nodded again.

"That fall, she had met someone who really turned things around on her. Instead of her being chased, she was doing the chasing. My sense was that she had just met her match in the manipulation game." Hope stopped and blushed. "I know that sounds terrible to say. She really was my best friend, but I never liked the way she treated the guys in her life. Partly because I was always the one picking up the pieces when she moved on to the next one. I don't know why Brad stayed in the apartment after the way she treated him. Even after she broke up with him, he still followed her every move. It wasn't until after she died that we got together. Anyway, she met this older guy, and they were having a pretty intense thing for a while. She'd been dating another student, Nate, who seemed like a nice guy and gorgeous. I could never figure out why she ended it with him. But I guess this older guy swept her off her feet. I know it sounds awful, but I was almost glad to see the tables turned on her."

"Do you remember his name?" Katie had leaned forward in her chair.

"Russ something. He was her TA in a psych or sociology course she was taking."

Katie swallowed. It couldn't be. "Russell Hunt?"

"That's it!" Hope said. "But how did you know that?"

"I think I saw it in one of the newspaper articles from the time," Katie lied.

"Well, anyway, I think the police did talk to him, because he was the last person she had called and she was found not far from his apartment."

"Really? I didn't realize that." Katie didn't need to tell Hope she had access to the phone records from Taylor's files. She wanted to keep her talking and feeling like she was being helpful. Katie had found that the more excited she seemed at the information a patient gave, the more likely they were to offer more. And she had gotten some new information. She hadn't realized that Russell had lived close to the Law Quad where Heather had been found. Or that they were much more serious than he had claimed.

Hope nodded. "I always wondered why she was found where she was. She never would have cut through the Law

Quad on her own. She thought it was creepy at night. And, of course, it was a mess at that time. But she must have been desperate to see him. I know they had some kind of argument at the party, because she followed him outside, and when I saw her come back in she looked upset. I asked her what was wrong, and she said Russ was being a jerk but it was nothing a few shots of vodka couldn't cure."

Katie thought back to the file about Russell. She wondered if Taylor had known all of this, or if she had known only what was in the police report.

"Hope, this might seem like a weird question, but has anyone else contacted you to talk about Heather's death?"

"No, not recently."

"But at some point?"

Hope looked down at her coffee mug. "About two years ago we were at a block party—we had just moved in—and I got talking to one of our neighbors. They lived just down the street. He was an ex–police officer and he said he recognized me from that time. We got talking, and I told him the same thing I just told you." She hesitated and took a deep breath. "He got irritated with me, claiming I should have come forward with the information about Heather and her TA. I said I assumed they knew, since I knew he'd been interviewed."

"Did anything ever come of it?"

Hope shook her head. "Not really. The family moved out about a year ago. He had died from a heart attack, and the wife and kids moved across town. I think I heard they had moved in with the wife's mother, who was in poor health but had a bigger house. Anyway, I did hear from

Taylor, the daughter, a week or so ago. She said she was going through her dad's things and doing a project for school and just wanted to verify some things about Heather's death."

"And you told her what you just told me?"

Hope nodded. "It seemed like she already knew everything. She said her dad had kept notes for years trying to figure out what might have happened because he never believed it was Eugene."

Katie struggled with herself. Should she tell Hope about Taylor? Should she leave it for now? She wondered if Taylor had known this part about Russell Hunt. It wasn't in her notes. Was it possible that Taylor had died because she knew? And, if so, was Hope now in danger?

"Hope, I have some bad news for you. Have you heard about the young woman who was found strangled in Baxter?"

Hope nodded, her eyes wide. "I just heard a snippet on the news this morning but switched it off right away. I don't like the kids hearing about every bad thing that happens."

"The young woman was Taylor Knox."

Hope's eyes filled with tears again. Her hand went to her mouth, and she just stared at Katie for a long moment. "Oh that poor girl. And her poor mother. Oh my God." Hope stood up and paced around the kitchen.

"Mom?" a small voice said from the hallway. The boy came into the room and looked at his mother, then cast an angry look at Katie. Probably assuming—rightly so—that Katie had distressed his mom.

Hope spun around and tried to smile at her son. "What do you need, honey?"

"Just a drink for me and Lizzie."

Hope went to the fridge and pulled out two juice boxes. The boy's eyes went wide. This must be a special treat. "Thanks, Mom." He ran out of the room with no further concerns about his mother's emotional state.

"I don't want to scare you, Hope," Katie began. "But it's possible that Taylor was killed because she was looking into Eugene's case." Katie held up her hands at Hope's surprised expression. "I can't be sure, and I don't know if the police are pursuing this line of questioning, but just be careful."

"Be careful?" Hope said. "What does that even mean? I have two little kids. I don't know anything." Hope sat and put her head in her hands. "I knew it would be a bad idea to talk about this again. I remember Nate telling us to all keep quiet and only answer direct questions."

"Heather's ex-boyfriend said that?"

Hope nodded. "His dad was a lawyer, and Nate said we should just lie low."

Katie paused, wondering how to proceed with her next question.

"But *did* you know anything that would help the police?"

"No! I don't think so." Hope stood and dumped her coffee in the sink. "We had all been drinking a lot that night. I don't remember what time I got home, or what time I went to bed. Nate said we should all alibi each other and then we'd be out of it."

"So you lied?" Katie asked quietly.

"Not really. I told them I didn't really remember anything, and by the time they questioned us, they already had Eugene in custody. It didn't seem to matter if I came home at ten thirty or midnight." Hope turned to face Katie. "I was clear that I didn't really remember, which I didn't, but I told them the story that we had all agreed to."

"That you were all back to the apartment before Heather was killed?"

Hope nodded and sat across the table from Katie. "I thought I was doing the right thing. In fact, I don't even remember now which one of us came up with the time and the story. It could have been Brad or even Alicia."

Katie didn't know what to make of Hope's story. She had definitely noticed the discrepancy in their statements to the police, but what did it mean? Were they just kids trying to keep their heads down? Or did one of them know more than they had said?

"Mom! Lizzie spilled her juice box!"

"Did not! You did!" Lizzie yelled at her brother.

"I'll be right there," Hope called into the other room.

"Thank you for talking to me, Hope," Katie said. She stood and held out her hand. "I won't take up any more of your time."

Hope followed her to the door.

"Dr. LeClair, will you let me know what you find out?"

"Of course," Katie said. She pulled open the door and stepped outside, shutting it on the juice box catastrophe.

36

Katie drove back to Baxter on autopilot. Thoughts were flying through her mind so quickly, she could barely acknowledge one before the next shoved its way to the forefront. It was like trying to keep track of a multicar accident. Which victim was the most hurt? Which one could wait to be treated? Her fingers itched to write in her notebook and to compare her new and unwelcome theory to the rest of her information. She had to tell Caleb and Matt to see what they thought.

She also had to tell Gabrielle.

Katie took the exit to Baxter a little too quickly and had to focus to make the turn without driving into the ditch. Apparently, distracted driving didn't apply only to people looking at their phones. Contemplating the possibility that your best friend was dating a double murderer could throw off your driving skills as well.

That's what this all came down to. Gabrielle might be in love with a murderer. And how was Katie going to tell her?

Should she wait and be sure that he was a likely suspect or tell her right away? Was Gabrielle in danger?

Katie argued with herself all the way home and was still arguing when she pulled into her driveway. She got out and went inside.

Caleb was in the living room, laptop open but staring into space.

"Hey," Katie said. "What's up?"

"It's finished," Caleb said.

"What is?"

"My app. I just worked out the last bug and I've got a beta tester running it through its paces, but I think it's done with only two days to spare before Halloween."

"Caleb, that's awesome!" Katie said. She held up her hand for a high five, and Caleb tapped her hand with his. "How come you don't seem very excited?"

"I am, but now I'm also nervous. I'm going to send it out into the world and wait to see how many stars it gets."

"I see," Katie said. And she did understand, sort of. He'd been working so hard on the app that she had forgotten about the judgy aspect of releasing something you care about into the great unknown. It might be like putting your kid on the school bus for the first time. You had to let it fend for itself. "You're about to give up control of where it goes and what it does."

"Yeah. I'll be a terrible parent. I can't imagine handing over my car keys to some teenager."

Katie laughed. "That's what I was just thinking. At least your app won't crash your car."

"No, just my reputation," Caleb said. He took a breath

and smiled. "I think we should celebrate with one of those girly drinks you made the other night."

Katie suppressed a self-satisfied smile and went into the kitchen for the ingredients. When she came back, the laptop was closed and Caleb looked a little less bereft.

"Want something to take your mind off the nervousness?" She handed him a martini glass.

"Always," Caleb said, and took a big swig of his drink.

"Not the drink, a puzzle," Katie said.

Caleb's face lit up. "Of course," he said. He leaned forward and put the drink on the table.

"Matt is on his way; let's wait for him, and then I have an interesting story for you."

Right on cue, the doorbell rang.

"I'll get it," Caleb said, and hopped up to answer the door.

Katie heard mumbled voices and a bit of backslapping from the front hall. Matt and Caleb came into the room grinning.

"Did you hear?" Matt said. "The app is ready to go."

"Yes, I heard," Katie said. "Want a drink?"

"Sure." Matt frowned at Katie's martini. "But maybe not one of those."

Matt wandered into the kitchen, and Katie heard him rummaging in the cupboard. He came back with his usual shot of whisky.

"You said you had news about Heather's murder?"

Katie nodded and pulled out her notebook so she could write down her thoughts as she told the story again. The story about Russell dating Heather and how she had been killed not far from his apartment after calling him and asking to meet. Katie told them that according to Hope, it had been a volatile relationship. And Abby had said she thought Russell made a habit of dating students. Had there been a relationship with Taylor?

When she was finished, Caleb and Matt just stared at her.

Caleb spoke first. "Gabrielle is dating a killer?"

Katie shrugged. "I'm not sure, but it sounds suspicious. At the very least, she's dating someone who doesn't balk at dating a student. I don't know how much she knows about this guy."

"I don't understand why he would assign this project if he was the killer," Matt said. "Why would he take the risk?"

"Maybe he didn't think there was a risk. He got away with it," Katie said. "Plus, remember when he said he thought the students would pick a bigger case? One that had a lot of media coverage? Maybe it never occurred to him that anyone would even remember Eugene Lowe or Heather Stone."

"But wouldn't he have put a stop to it once he realized?" Caleb asked.

"Maybe he thought *that* would look suspicious," Katie said. "He could have just been hoping that Taylor wouldn't uncover anything new."

"I don't know, Katie," Matt said. "Are you sure about this?"

Katie shook her head. "No, of course I'm not sure. I'm not even sure if I should tell Gabrielle or wait until I know more. But what if he *is* the killer, and what if he also killed Taylor?"

"We need to find out what he was doing the other night. If he has an alibi, at least we'll know he didn't kill Taylor," Matt said.

"Right, and then we can continue to look into the old case and see what we find." Katie made some more notes in her book. "How did it go with Brad Humphreys?"

Matt sipped his drink and set it down. "It was a bust. Nothing like what Hope told you. I got the impression there was some tension in the apartment between Brad and Heather."

"What kind of tension?" Caleb asked.

"I remember from the brief time I dated Heather . . ."

"Wait, you dated Heather?" Caleb said.

"Yes, just a couple of times, and it was over way before she died," Matt said. "Anyway, I just remember this general animosity from Brad when I was at the apartment. Sort of like a big brother or an ex-boyfriend. But I'm pretty sure they never dated."

"According to Hope, she broke his heart," Katie said.

"That explains it, then."

"What did he tell you?"

"Not much. He said that he came back that night and passed out in bed. He wasn't even sure what time he got back. Hope woke him up in the morning to say that Heather had never returned from the party. They were getting ready to go look for her when the police arrived."

Caleb flipped his computer open. Katie frowned. He had his "aha" face on.

"What is it, Caleb?"

"I wanted to check the statement from Brad. I thought I

remembered him saying he saw Alicia and Nathan that evening when they came back from the party." Caleb scrolled his mouse. "Here it is. Brad said they got back around midnight."

Matt shook his head. "Today he said he got back at ten and passed out."

"Hmm," Katie said. "Hope told me that none of them really paid attention to when they got home. They just agreed on a story."

"So he lied," Caleb said. "Either today or back then."

Katie tried to fit this new piece of information into her developing timeline. She wasn't sure it would make a difference, but it was interesting.

She realized she was only putting off the one thing she had to do. No matter how much or how little she knew about Russell, she had to at least warn Gabrielle. She'd never forgive herself if something happened to her. She pulled out her phone and called Gabrielle.

After the initial small talk was over and before any gushing about Russell could ensue, Katie said, "Gabrielle, there's something I need to tell you."

Gabrielle lowered her voice. "Please tell me you and Matt are still together. You didn't break up?"

Katie sat back in surprise. "No. It's not about me."

"Okay, good. Shoot," Gabrielle said.

"It's about Russell . . ." Katie began.

"Isn't he awesome?"

"He seemed . . . very nice," Katie said. "Remember how Matt said he'd seen Russell at the party on the night Heather died?"

"He explained that. He crashed the party with some of his grad school buddies. They didn't stay long after they realized it was all a bunch of undergrads getting drunk."

Katie hesitated. "I talked to Heather's roommate today, and she said that Heather had been having a pretty intense affair with Russell just before she died."

"But . . ." Gabrielle hesitated. "That doesn't make sense. He said she was just a student."

"I think it was more than that," Katie said. "Russell may not have realized how extensive Taylor's research had been. She had transcripts of the police interviews. Russell admitted that Heather called him that night and wanted to meet him at his apartment. He said she never showed. But she was found not far from where he lived at the time."

Gabrielle's voice sounded sharp. "Are you accusing him of something?"

"I think it's worth being careful. I'm convinced that Taylor died because she was getting too close to the real killer."

"You know you're a doctor, not a police officer or private detective, right?" Gabrielle's voice shook.

Katie blurted, "What was Russell doing Monday night?"

Gabrielle sounded confused. "Monday?"

There was no coming back from it now. "The night Taylor's body was dumped in the woods."

"He was supposed to meet me after work," Gabrielle said. Her voice became very quiet. "He called to cancel. Some sort of work emergency."

"What kind of emergency does a sociology professor have?" Katie asked.

"I don't know. I didn't even ask," Gabrielle said. "I guess I'm so used to work emergencies, it didn't occur to me to ask."

"You didn't see him the whole night?"

"No, but that's not unusual. We don't live together."

Katie heard Gabrielle's doorbell ring.

"I'd better go," Gabrielle said. "Russell's here."

Before Katie could stop her, she had hung up the phone.

Katie pushed redial on her phone, but it went right to voicemail. What was Gabrielle up to? And was she safe with Russell? Katie worried that she had put Gabrielle in danger by making her suspicious of Russell.

She texted: Just let me know everything is ok.

Five long minutes later, Gabrielle texted back: I'm fine, don't be so dramatic.

37

Carlson put his cruiser in gear and pulled slowly into the street. His passenger was quiet. He didn't blame him. Eugene Lowe was being released from jail into what could be a dangerous life outside prison. Carlson knew that there were people in town who were convinced Eugene had killed Taylor Knox. Carlson was not one of those people.

Eugene had cooperated completely with the police, and nothing he said indicated he had harmed Taylor. Carlson wished he had a better alibi than his mother, Gretchen, but still. She said he had been home all night.

Carlson now knew that Taylor had been strangled a week ago, around the time she disappeared. The fact that she had not been found in all that time indicated her body had been hidden elsewhere. The pathologist said that insect activity was minimal, so it had to have been kept somewhere inside.

"I'll have an officer watching your house around the clock, Eugene," Carlson said.

"Thank you," was Eugene's mumbled reply.

"I don't know what else to do," Carlson said. He flicked his blinker and turned onto Eugene's street. "Call me if anything seems suspicious or if you feel threatened." Carlson handed a card to Eugene, who slipped it into his shirt pocket without looking at it.

Carlson pulled into the driveway, and Eugene barely waited for him to stop before he opened the door and climbed out. He held up a hand in a half-hearted wave and went in through the front door.

Carlson debated with himself over whether to get out of the car and talk to Gretchen. He decided to leave it alone for now. Eugene was a grown man; he could tell his mother what the plan was. But there was something about Eugene that *felt* young. Carlson understood why Gretchen was so protective. It was like he hadn't yet grown a tough enough skin to survive on his own. Carlson had no idea how this kid had survived prison.

Debate over. He reversed out of the driveway and headed home, not seeing the figure slip out the back door and disappear into the trees.

38

Thursday morning, Katie pulled open the door to stop the frantic knocking. She had staggered to the front door, pulling on a long cardigan over her sleep shirt.

Gretchen Lowe stood on her front porch looking like she had just escaped from a wolf pack. Her hair stood on end, her shirt was on inside out, and her shoes didn't match. But the wild look in her eyes was the most worrying.

"Mrs. Lowe, what's happened?" Katie opened the door wider and gestured her inside.

"I'm sorry to barge in on you like this, but Eugene is gone again!"

"Okay, come sit down and tell me what happened." Katie sighed inwardly. She wished Eugene would at least let her know when he was going to take off like this.

"I got up this morning and went to feed the cat. He's usually very pushy about getting his breakfast. Well, any of his meals, really . . ." Gretchen seemed to catch herself. She continued, "Anyway, I couldn't find the cat, and so I went up to Eugene's room. I thought maybe Eugene had closed the door with the cat inside. But when I went up there, he was gone. Eugene, not the cat. The cat *had* gotten trapped in his room, but Eugene was nowhere to be found. Most of his things are still there, but he did take his duffel and his bathroom stuff." Gretchen reached for a tissue from the box on the table. She scrubbed at her eyes.

"There was no note? He didn't tell you anything last night?"

Gretchen shook her head. "No, he seemed happy to be home after his stay at the jail. I'll have something to say to John Carlson next time I see him. Arresting Eugene for no good reason!"

Katie put her hand on Gretchen's arm. "Don't be too hard on him. I asked him to take Eugene into custody to keep him safe. I was very worried about how people would react when they heard about Taylor Knox's death."

Gretchen's tears started up again. "Oh, that poor young woman. She was so lovely. I could tell that Eugene liked her, too. I heard them laughing together when she came to the house. I hadn't heard him laugh in years." She gave Katie a watery smile. "It was good to hear. I'll never believe he had anything to do with her death."

"I understand, but there are people in town who aren't as convinced of Eugene's innocence as you are."

Gretchen sniffled. "I know. Eugene has always been just different enough to draw attention, and usually the wrong kind of attention."

"Mrs. Lowe, Gretchen, you have to go to the police with your concerns. I'm only Eugene's doctor. If I hear from him,

I'll do my best to convince him to contact you, but that's really all I can do."

"Okay, I just thought he might have said something to you about where he might have gone, or why."

Katie shook her head, but she did try to run the conversation through her mind. *Had* Eugene told her anything that day that would help her find him? She couldn't remember. She had been so surprised that he had come to her house, she wasn't sure she had paid much attention to where he'd said he had been. He'd likely just gone back to whatever place he thought was safe. Katie could hardly blame him for wanting to get out of town. She suspected that he had gotten as far from Baxter as he could. Katie wondered if that meant he would be in trouble with the police. If Carlson had told him to be available for questions and now he'd disappeared, did that mean he was guilty? Would it make it *look* like he was guilty? Why did he have to leave now? Katie was more irritated with Eugene than worried about him.

"Did he say anything to you last night? Did anything happen? Any more threats or vandalism?"

"No, nothing happened last night. I was kind of surprised, to be honest. They've been coming a few times a week since he got home. I don't know why it was so quiet last night."

Gretchen seemed more in control now.

"Why don't you go home, have some tea, and get cleaned up. Then, go to the police station to report that he's missing. He'll likely turn up again, just like last time."

Gretchen nodded. "Okay. You're right. I have to trust

the police to do their jobs. I have to trust that Eugene is making the right choices." She smiled ruefully at Katie. "Both of those things are hard to do."

Katie walked her to the door and waved as Gretchen drove off down the street. She closed the door and pulled out her phone.

39

Nathan Nielsen paced again in John Carlson's office. He had been pacing for the past fifteen minutes, and nothing Carlson said could get him to sit.

"Okay, let's go over this again, Mr. Nielsen."

Nathan stopped walking and turned toward Carlson.

"What else do you need to know? My wife is missing. My daughter is missing. You let a killer back onto the streets yesterday." Nathan threw his hands up. "It doesn't take a genius to figure it out. But just in case you need some help, I'll spell it out for you. That little freak has my wife and child. If anything happens to them, I'm going to make it my mission to make your life miserable. You should have kept him locked up. You should have given my *wife* protection instead of protecting that murderer!"

Carlson clenched his jaw and took deep breaths. Linda had told him to focus on his breathing when he felt stressed. It only made him dizzy. Or maybe it was his soaring blood pressure that made him dizzy.

"Mr. Nielsen, I will file a missing persons report. But I don't expect that nearby police departments will give it much credence until she's been gone for at least twenty-four hours. And there's no proof she's with Eugene Lowe. As far as I know, he's still at home with his mother."

"My daughter is missing, too. Don't you start searching immediately for children?"

"Yes, but she's presumably with her mother. Her mother is an adult and is allowed to roam freely. How do you know she didn't just go to her parents' house for the day? Maybe she's out with a friend."

"She's not answering her phone, and Olivia's things are gone. She took her travel bed and a suitcase full of—" Nathan stopped abruptly.

"So, it looks as if she planned to be away?"

"No." Carlson could see Nathan backtracking. "I can't be sure."

"If she packed her things and went away, I can't even call her a missing person. There is no sign of foul play. Have you two been having trouble lately?"

Nathan wheeled on Carlson. "Don't start your counseling crap on me. She's gone and I need you to find her." Nathan sank into the visitor chair and put his head in his hands. "I just want my family back."

At least we're finally getting somewhere, Carlson thought. It would have been helpful if he'd mentioned the suitcase up front.

"I'll put out a notice to local law enforcement to be on the lookout," Carlson said. "In the meantime, go home and call anyone you can think of to see if she's just gone to visit someone."

"Yup, okay," Nathan stood. "I'll just go home and wait. That sounds like a great idea."

He stormed out of the office for the second time that week.

40

Katie stepped quickly out of the way as Nathan Nielsen stomped out of the police station. She watched him stalk down the street and felt her stomach knot up. What was he doing here and why was he so mad?

She went inside and asked to see Carlson. The young woman gestured to the door and told her to go on back. Katie walked down the hallway to Carlson's office and peeked around the corner.

He sat with his head resting in his hands, breathing deeply and loudly. Katie had a moment of alarm thinking that he was unwell, but he must have sensed her there in the doorway and he looked up suddenly.

"Hi, Doc," he said with none of his usual enthusiasm. "I hope your day is going better than mine." He waved in the direction of the chair Nathan had just vacated. "Have a seat."

"Are you okay?" Katie said as she sat.

"Fine. Let me guess why you're here. Eugene was beat

up again." Carlson pulled Eugene's file toward him and flipped it open, ready to take notes. "Is he okay?"

Katie shook her head. "No. I mean, yes. Well, I don't know."

Carlson put down his pen and met her gaze.

"According to Gretchen, he's missing. Again."

"What do you mean, missing?"

"She says she went to find him this morning and he wasn't in his room. Some of his things are gone and his truck is gone."

"Why does she go to *you* with these things?" Carlson asked. "She should come to me."

Katie shrugged. "They seem to have adopted me as their general advocate. Eugene and I have a rapport, and I guess Gretchen thinks I'm the one to go to."

Carlson closed his eyes and rubbed them with the pads of his fingers.

"I wonder if she mentioned this to the officer sitting outside her house, theoretically guarding her son?"

Katie held her hands out, palms up. "I did tell her to come here and make a report."

Carlson sighed heavily and picked up his pen. "Okay, tell me what you know."

"That's really it. She said he got home last night, they had dinner together, and then he went up to his room. She hasn't seen him since."

"I dropped him off in the afternoon," Carlson said. "I saw him go inside. Where was he all afternoon and why did my officer not report it?"

Katie waited. She didn't think he was really looking for an answer from her.

"Doc, I'm going to tell you something in confidence." Carlson leaned forward.

Katie sat up straighter in the chair. "What is it?"

"Alicia Nielsen and her daughter are missing as well."

"What?" Katie sat back to distance herself from this new piece of information.

"Nathan was just in here yelling at me for not protecting his wife. I told him he should check with all of her friends and relatives to be sure she isn't visiting someone. I didn't know Eugene was missing, too."

"You don't think Eugene could hurt Alicia, do you?"

Carlson held his hands out, palms up, echoing Katie's gesture. "I have no idea. I hardly know the kid. I only know that he spent time in prison for manslaughter. A month after he gets out, another girl is dead not even a quarter mile from his house, and now a third young woman goes missing. It doesn't look good."

41

Carlson set the phone down gently, carefully, in its cradle. What he wanted to do was slam it down over and over again until the damn thing shattered.

How could two adults and a baby just disappear? Alicia was memorable. With her light-blonde hair and open, lovely face, she got noticed. For that matter, Eugene was memorable. Big ears and even bigger glasses.

When Katie had told him that Eugene's truck was gone, he had hoped they would be able to find it easily. And they had. Parked along a side street near Alicia's house. Unfortunately, if Eugene and Alicia were together, they had taken Alicia's car, a nondescript tan Ford sedan. There were only thousands of those in the area.

Regardless, there had not been one sighting of them together or apart. No stops at restaurants or drive-throughs or gas stations. He'd had his whole department calling every place they could think of all morning. He'd really thought it would be easy to track them.

It was the last thing he needed right now in the middle of a murder inquiry. He couldn't spare the manpower any longer on a fruitless search for people who had every right to go off together, regardless of what Nathan Nielsen thought.

Carlson got up slowly from his desk chair, feeling old. He walked down the hall to the staff room to organize his team for the rest of the day.

He entered the team room where they all had their desks. Sean Gallagher spun his chair around to face Carlson. He was a good cop. He'd have been excellent if he'd been able to keep a secret from his wife.

Molly Hart continued to type on her computer, but Carlson knew she had one eye on him to be sure he divvied up the duties fairly. She was a great cop, but her moods could rub Carlson the wrong way.

Rounding out the team was Henry Crabbe. A brand-new officer who barely knew how to write a speeding ticket, Crabbe was eager to prove himself. Carlson worried that that was how mistakes got made. At least he'd have some help from the Ann Arbor police.

"Any new information on Taylor Knox or Eugene and Alicia?" he asked.

Sean shook his head.

Molly stopped typing. "The preliminary results are back on the autopsy." She pulled a sheaf of papers off the printer and handed them to Carlson. "She'd been dead for at least a week, according to the pathologist. He says she was killed and the body was stored somewhere inside. There was minimal insect activity."

Carlson noticed Henry's face go white. He looked like he might pass out.

"Sit down, Crabbe," Carlson said. "Put your head down. If you have to puke, make sure you make it to the bathroom. Thanks, Molly; I saw the report earlier. So, we're looking for a place where the body might have been stored this past week."

Crabbe sat down and breathed heavily into his lap. Carlson just caught the amused expression that passed between Molly and Sean.

"You're all right, Henry," Carlson said, quietly. "It's hard to hear all the details sometimes."

He watched his officer for another few seconds, then, reassured that he was not going to pass out, looked at his other two officers.

"We'll need to interview the people she was last in contact with again. Find out who might have access to a place to hide a body for a week. You can't just hide a body anywhere, and this one was protected from the elements until just before it was found. I assume there's still no sign of the car?"

Sean, who had been given the unwelcome job of tracking down Taylor's car, shook his head. "No one has reported an abandoned car. I checked parking garages in Ann Arbor just in case she met her murderer there. I thought maybe she'd just been dumped in Baxter to throw us off." Sean flipped a page in his notebook. "I've checked parking lots here in Baxter and I drove around to all the places kids tend to like to park, and still no sign."

"I like the idea of the murderer coming from Ann Arbor, Gallagher. Good thinking."

, with only a few people sitting in
r of the room.

arade team leader is here, we can get
h. She looked down her nose at Katie.
ad done something wrong, but had

the man in charge of food asked. Katie
man who had been talking to Nathan
e thought Nathan had called him Mike.
was absent on Monday during our
ting of the season. I had to ask him to
't have semicommitted team leaders,"
Besides, he needs to be focused on his
e moment. He did promise to be at the
e float."

ispers traveled around the group. Katie
Nathan had been. He'd seemed pretty
e parade. He even stored the equipment
It sounded like everyone else was wonder-
d been and how he would react to a new-
ver his role. Katie looked down at her lap.
n pulled her bullhorn out of her purse and
und near her chair. The whispering stopped.
our troubleshooting reports," she said. "We'll
orations."
s glazed over as the team leaders recited their
troubles. She wondered if the royal wedding
ite so involved. Delores Munch graciously—it
cused Katie from giving a report since she had
n the role.

Sean smiled and flipped his notebook closed in a self-satisfied way.

"Chief, wouldn't there be a . . . smell if the body was stored somewhere?" Molly asked.

"Good point, Molly," Carlson said.

She nodded and ducked her head to hide her smile.

"I'll need you and Sean to call storage facilities here and in Ann Arbor and see if anyone connected to Taylor has a rental. Some of those places have minimal supervision. I suppose a decomposing body could be hidden in a place like that without being discovered right away."

"Yes, sir," Molly said.

Sean nodded and spun his chair back to his desk to get to work.

"Henry, you come with me," Carlson said. "No one has seen Alicia or Eugene, which means they're probably holed up somewhere. No idea if they are together or apart."

"Do you think he kidnapped them?" Henry asked.

"I'm not sure what to think," Carlson said. "It sounds like Alicia may have left willingly, and we have no way of knowing whether she's with Eugene or if she's just gone off to stay with a friend. I need you to look into it. Call around local hotels and motels with their description. And try to think of any place in the area that two adults and a baby could go to hide."

"I'm on it, Chief," Henry said.

42

atie had been going over her notes until her head hurt and her eyes blurred. She had come to no conclusions. She had no idea if Eugene was innocent. Had Alicia left with him willingly, or was he really the strange, obsessed stalker so many people in town thought he was?

But why would he take the baby too? Katie didn't know and wondered if she ever would. She had been working from the mind-set of doing the best she could in the moment and trying very hard not to second-guess herself. In medicine, doctors were often put in the position of making a snap decision. They ran the possibilities through their decision tree and tried to choose the option that would be most helpful and least harmful.

Sometimes they didn't succeed. Every single doctor Katie had ever known carried a burden of guilt for those few wrong decisions. The faces of the healthy, successfully treated patients didn't follow them around saying, "Way to go!" It was only the failures that came out in those moments

much quieter than usua
folding chairs in a corne
"Well, now that the
started," said Mrs. Mund
Katie felt like she h
no idea what.
"Where is Nathan?"
recognized him as the
in the drama room. Sł
"You'll recall he
most important me
step down. We can
Mrs. Munch said.
family issues at th
parade to drive th
A swell of wh
wondered where
committed to th
during the year.
ing where he h
comer taking o
Mrs. Munc
set it on the gr
"Let's hear
start with dec
Katie's ey
concerns an
had been qu
seemed—ex
just taken o

t
on
Son
each
balan
Sh
Alicia a
Her
"Hello
"Dr. Lo
Katie fo
even before
"Yes, Mrs
"I'm prom
Mrs. Munch sa
minutes. We me
"Team leade
about the parade.
"I am aware of
take over, I would, I
"Everything is alrea
Katie glanced at t
bles and notes. Sudder
get out of her house.
"Okay, I'll see you in
"Twenty-nine minute.
dead.
Twenty-five minutes lat

DAW

"Since Nathan is gone, you'll have to do one last check on the costumes before tomorrow."

Delores clapped her hands, and that seemed to be the signal that the meeting was over. Katie ruminated on her inability to say no and its repercussions on her life as the rest of the people milled around and compared notes.

Katie slipped out of the noisy gym and walked down the hallway to the drama department. She might as well check on the costumes now, while she was already here. Her footsteps echoed as she moved further away from the gym. The lights were dim, and she cast foggy shadows on the lockers and walls.

The door to the drama department was closed. Katie tried the handle, and it clicked open easily. Inside, it was dark and the shrouded stage sets and racks of costumes hulked in the shadows. She felt along the wall for the light switch. When she couldn't find it, she pulled out her phone and turned on its flashlight. She shone the light along the wall on both sides of the door and finally found the panel of controls.

The third switch flicked the lights on. She wondered what else she had triggered while flipping switches. She saw the rack of costumes for the parade in the middle of the room. The pumpkin costume sat jauntily at its side. Katie glared at it and would have given it a kick if she'd thought she could do so without damaging it.

There was a box tucked under the rack. Katie pulled it out and saw the label: NEW COSTUMES. Great, now she'd have to track Nathan down and find out whom he had assigned to wear them. She flipped the lid back to see what kinds of costumes they were and let out a shriek.

There, curled on top of a pirate costume, was a large

snake. It seemed just as surprised to see her as she was to see it. It hissed lazily at her and began to uncurl.

She saw the note taped to the inside of the lid. Addressed to *Dr Laclare*. Whoever had sent the package clearly didn't know Katie. Not only did they not know how to spell her name, but they didn't know she had an affinity for snakes. Her best friend from grades three to five had owned a snake and had carried it around draped over her shoulders. This guy was a boa constrictor and must have been a pet. He gently flicked his tongue out to her hand as she lifted him out of the box.

She was about to open the envelope when Mrs. Munch burst into the room, red faced and out of breath. Several other people from the meeting stood behind her.

"Dr. LeClair!" Mrs. Munch said. "We thought we heard you scream. Where did you get that snake?"

Katie gestured toward the box, but Delores wasn't finished.

"We do not allow live animals in the parade. I'll get you a copy of our regulations."

One of the men pushed forward. He was tall and thin with dark receding hair, heavy rimmed glasses, and the rounded shoulders of someone who wished he were shorter.

He held his hand out for the snake. "I think that's Lester," he said. "He belongs in the science lab. I hope he didn't scare you."

Katie shook her head. "He seemed friendly enough."

Excitement over, the crowd dispersed, led by Delores. After the door swung closed again, Katie opened the envelope.

Mind your own business was scrawled in thick black marker and underlined in red.

Sean smiled and flipped his notebook closed in a self-satisfied way.

"Chief, wouldn't there be a . . . smell if the body was stored somewhere?" Molly asked.

"Good point, Molly," Carlson said.

She nodded and ducked her head to hide her smile.

"I'll need you and Sean to call storage facilities here and in Ann Arbor and see if anyone connected to Taylor has a rental. Some of those places have minimal supervision. I suppose a decomposing body could be hidden in a place like that without being discovered right away."

"Yes, sir," Molly said.

Sean nodded and spun his chair back to his desk to get to work.

"Henry, you come with me," Carlson said. "No one has seen Alicia or Eugene, which means they're probably holed up somewhere. No idea if they are together or apart."

"Do you think he kidnapped them?" Henry asked.

"I'm not sure what to think," Carlson said. "It sounds like Alicia may have left willingly, and we have no way of knowing whether she's with Eugene or if she's just gone off to stay with a friend. I need you to look into it. Call around local hotels and motels with their description. And try to think of any place in the area that two adults and a baby could go to hide."

"I'm on it, Chief," Henry said.

42

Katie had been going over her notes until her head hurt and her eyes blurred. She had come to no conclusions. She had no idea if Eugene was innocent. Had Alicia left with him willingly, or was he really the strange, obsessed stalker so many people in town thought he was?

But why would he take the baby too? Katie didn't know and wondered if she ever would. She had been working from the mind-set of doing the best she could in the moment and trying very hard not to second-guess herself. In medicine, doctors were often put in the position of making a snap decision. They ran the possibilities through their decision tree and tried to choose the option that would be most helpful and least harmful.

Sometimes they didn't succeed. Every single doctor Katie had ever known carried a burden of guilt for those few wrong decisions. The faces of the healthy, successfully treated patients didn't follow them around saying, "Way to go!" It was only the failures that came out in those moments of silence. The ones who didn't get better, the ones who had to live with health problems, the ones who died.

Katie had decided long ago that she would choose which ones followed her. She had been only moderately successful. Some of the bad outcomes refused to be left behind, but for each one of those, Katie chose a good outcome to counterbalance it.

She just wasn't sure how she would balance the lives of Alicia and Olivia if she had misjudged Eugene.

Her phone rang, and she snatched it up like a lifeline. "Hello?"

"Dr. LeClair, this is Delores Munch."

Katie felt her brows draw together. They had reacted even before she was able to think *uh-oh*.

"Yes, Mrs. Munch?"

"I'm promoting you to team leader of the parade team," Mrs. Munch said. "I'll expect you at the meeting in thirty minutes. We meet in the gym as usual."

"Team leader?" Katie said. "I don't know anything about the parade."

"I am aware of that, and if I could find anyone else to take over, I would, but you are my last resort," Delores said. "Everything is already planned; you just have to supervise."

Katie glanced at the table filled with charts and timetables and notes. Suddenly, she wanted nothing more than to get out of her house.

"Okay, I'll see you in half an hour," Katie said.

"Twenty-nine minutes," said Mrs. Munch. The line went dead.

Twenty-five minutes later, Katie entered the gym. It was

much quieter than usual, with only a few people sitting in folding chairs in a corner of the room.

"Well, now that the parade team leader is here, we can get started," said Mrs. Munch. She looked down her nose at Katie.

Katie felt like she had done something wrong, but had no idea what.

"Where is Nathan?" the man in charge of food asked. Katie recognized him as the man who had been talking to Nathan in the drama room. She thought Nathan had called him Mike.

"You'll recall he was absent on Monday during our most important meeting of the season. I had to ask him to step down. We can't have semicommitted team leaders," Mrs. Munch said. "Besides, he needs to be focused on his family issues at the moment. He did promise to be at the parade to drive the float."

A swell of whispers traveled around the group. Katie wondered where Nathan had been. He'd seemed pretty committed to the parade. He even stored the equipment during the year. It sounded like everyone else was wondering where he had been and how he would react to a newcomer taking over his role. Katie looked down at her lap.

Mrs. Munch pulled her bullhorn out of her purse and set it on the ground near her chair. The whispering stopped.

"Let's hear our troubleshooting reports," she said. "We'll start with decorations."

Katie's eyes glazed over as the team leaders recited their concerns and troubles. She wondered if the royal wedding had been quite so involved. Delores Munch graciously—it seemed—excused Katie from giving a report since she had just taken on the role.

"Since Nathan is gone, you'll have to do one last check on the costumes before tomorrow."

Delores clapped her hands, and that seemed to be the signal that the meeting was over. Katie ruminated on her inability to say no and its repercussions on her life as the rest of the people milled around and compared notes.

Katie slipped out of the noisy gym and walked down the hallway to the drama department. She might as well check on the costumes now, while she was already here. Her footsteps echoed as she moved further away from the gym. The lights were dim, and she cast foggy shadows on the lockers and walls.

The door to the drama department was closed. Katie tried the handle, and it clicked open easily. Inside, it was dark and the shrouded stage sets and racks of costumes hulked in the shadows. She felt along the wall for the light switch. When she couldn't find it, she pulled out her phone and turned on its flashlight. She shone the light along the wall on both sides of the door and finally found the panel of controls.

The third switch flicked the lights on. She wondered what else she had triggered while flipping switches. She saw the rack of costumes for the parade in the middle of the room. The pumpkin costume sat jauntily at its side. Katie glared at it and would have given it a kick if she'd thought she could do so without damaging it.

There was a box tucked under the rack. Katie pulled it out and saw the label: NEW COSTUMES. Great, now she'd have to track Nathan down and find out whom he had assigned to wear them. She flipped the lid back to see what kinds of costumes they were and let out a shriek.

There, curled on top of a pirate costume, was a large

snake. It seemed just as surprised to see her as she was to see it. It hissed lazily at her and began to uncurl.

She saw the note taped to the inside of the lid. Addressed to *Dr Laclare*. Whoever had sent the package clearly didn't know Katie. Not only did they not know how to spell her name, but they didn't know she had an affinity for snakes. Her best friend from grades three to five had owned a snake and had carried it around draped over her shoulders. This guy was a boa constrictor and must have been a pet. He gently flicked his tongue out to her hand as she lifted him out of the box.

She was about to open the envelope when Mrs. Munch burst into the room, red faced and out of breath. Several other people from the meeting stood behind her.

"Dr. LeClair!" Mrs. Munch said. "We thought we heard you scream. Where did you get that snake?"

Katie gestured toward the box, but Delores wasn't finished.

"We do not allow live animals in the parade. I'll get you a copy of our regulations."

One of the men pushed forward. He was tall and thin with dark receding hair, heavy rimmed glasses, and the rounded shoulders of someone who wished he were shorter.

He held his hand out for the snake. "I think that's Lester," he said. "He belongs in the science lab. I hope he didn't scare you."

Katie shook her head. "He seemed friendly enough."

Excitement over, the crowd dispersed, led by Delores. After the door swung closed again, Katie opened the envelope.

Mind your own business was scrawled in thick black marker and underlined in red.

43

Friday morning, Katie's phone rang as she was clearing up her breakfast dishes. She was relieved to see Gabrielle's name pop up on the screen. Katie had texted and left voice messages since Wednesday evening after Gabrielle had texted she was fine, and she'd not heard back from her.

"Gabrielle, hi," Katie said.

There was silence on the line. Then Katie heard Gabrielle sniffle.

"What's the matter? Are you okay?"

"I have the alibi you were looking for. Russell says he had a date on the night that Heather Stone was killed and they were together all evening."

That wasn't what he had told the police, but Katie didn't want to argue with Gabrielle.

"Oh, good," Katie said. "Thank you."

"He also has an alibi for Monday night," Gabrielle said. "He was with one of his grad students. All night. After he canceled plans with me." Gabrielle's voice cracked.

"Gabrielle, I'm so sorry," Katie said. She wished she were with her in person. Gabrielle dated a lot of guys, and she almost never got upset when they moved on. Usually it was Gabrielle doing the breaking up.

"No, it's fine. I'm glad I found out now. It's better this way."

Katie wondered if that was true. No matter when you found out, betrayal was betrayal. And she felt responsible on some level. She had pushed Gabrielle to question Russell. But would it have been better for Gabrielle to get even more attached? Katie didn't know. Maybe Gabrielle would have gotten bored and none of this heartache would have happened.

While she was sorry that Gabrielle was so miserable, she didn't think she would believe Russell's alibi until he produced this mysterious grad student. And she had passed a lie detector test. Russell had chosen a good story. Just shocking enough to sound true, hoping that Gabrielle and Katie would not try to follow up on it.

"I know what will cheer you up," Katie said.

Gabrielle sniffled. "What's that?"

"Watching me try to stay on the Halloween float while dressed as a pumpkin."

"Oh my God. Yes. That will go a long way toward making the world right again."

"Parade starts at six o'clock."

"I'll be there."

44

Halloween had ushered in cooler weather, and there was even a threat of snow. Katie was not looking forward to her parade duties, but she was afraid of Delores and knew she'd have to go.

Katie and Matt drove together to the high school to don their costumes and receive their final instructions. The now familiar walk to the gym was louder as all of the different teams spilled into the hallways to spread out and move their equipment to Main Street. They dodged coolers, hot dog carts, pumpkins, ghosts, skeletons, and streamers to get to their section of the gym.

Katie's pumpkin costume sat on the float, ready for action. It looked perfectly fine just as it was; why did someone need to be inside? True, the tiny green hands hung limply at its sides, but how much could Katie really wave with only her wrist and hand sticking out of the pumpkin? She was just glad that she didn't have to wear a green hat and smile for the whole thing. The suit was big enough to cover everything but her feet and hands. She had worn her comfortable fleece boots and now slipped green covers over them.

"Are you ready for this?" Matt asked.

"I suppose," Katie said. Matt had already changed into his pirate costume, and the young pirates had spotted him. They ran at him, yelling, "Pirate King! Pirate King!"

Miss Simms and Mrs. Peabody followed them across the gym. Miss Simms had a whistle, which she used to no effect. Mrs. Peabody had an air horn that stopped the marauding pirates in midchant.

"All pirates come with us—we have to line up," said Miss Simms. She adjusted her eye patch. She held a Jolly Roger flag aloft and the pirates fell in line.

Mrs. Peabody took a position at the back to corral the stragglers. "We'll see you outside in two minutes," she said to Matt, then turned to Katie. "By the way, I wouldn't get into the pumpkin quite yet. We still have a half hour before the parade starts," she grinned. "Keep your freedom as long as you can."

Delores Munch approached at that moment. Her helmet of hair had glitter in it, her lipstick was smeared, and she had orange and black streamers wrapped around her neck. "This is a disaster!" she exclaimed.

"What's wrong, Delores?" asked Mrs. Peabody. She rolled her eyes at Katie as if to say, "This happens every year."

"I can't get in touch with Nathan Nielsen. He's supposed to drive the float. No one else knows how."

Katie felt a weight lift off her shoulders. Maybe she wouldn't have to be the pumpkin after all.

"I can drive it," Matt said.

Delores looked at him as if her were insane. "Who would lead the pirates if you are driving the float? No, no, that won't do."

"I guess we'll have to have the parade without it," Katie said hopefully.

Delores wheeled on her. "Of course we can't have the parade without it. It's the centerpiece! It won't be Halloween without the pumpkin float." Delores put her hands on her hips. "I guess I'll have to drive it. It's been a while, but we can manage."

Katie tried to hide the horror she felt at this development. She said, "I know someone who can step in. Let me just give him a call."

Katie pulled out her phone and called Caleb.

"Hello? I thought you would be a pumpkin by now," he said. "Are you calling from inside the pumpkin?"

"No, we have an emergency," Katie said.

"A pumpkin emergency?"

Katie rolled her eyes, even though Caleb couldn't see her. "We need someone to drive the float."

There was a long silence. "You know I've always wanted to drive a float."

"Yes, I remember," Katie said.

"Where are you?"

"In the high school gym."

"Be there in ten minutes," Caleb said, and ended the call.

"I have someone coming in just a few minutes," Katie said.

"Thank you, Doctor," Delores said. She turned to Matt

and said, "You should go catch up to your pirate crew. They get restless without a leader."

Matt waved to Katie and headed off in the direction of the pirates.

"When your driver gets here, have him take the float out through those doors and loop around the parking lot to the front of the line. As long as we're only a couple of minutes late, the crowd will be fine. I don't let the beer truck start serving until the parade is over, so everyone likes the parade to run on time."

Delores bustled off toward the double doors that led outside. Katie saw her pull her bullhorn out of her bag, and the yelling began a moment later.

Katie sat on the float and waited for Caleb. She didn't have to wait long. He rushed in through the back door.

"That woman with the bullhorn told me to come in here," he said.

"Help me get this costume on," Katie said.

Caleb lifted the pumpkin up so that Katie could crawl inside. He started giggling as soon as she put her hands in the gloves. "This is the best thing ever!" Caleb said. "I would have volunteered if I'd known." Katie heard the camera-clicking sound of his phone and knew she'd be showing up on social media somewhere. At least no one could tell it was her.

"Just help me onto the float," Katie said.

Caleb steered her toward the float, but it became obvious that she wouldn't be able to climb on board while wearing the costume. Caleb was zero help. He could barely breathe, he was laughing so hard. Katie started giggling too.

A loud siren sounded throughout the gym, and they

stopped laughing and turned toward the sound. Katie looked through the small area of thin fabric that served as her only view out of the suit. She could just make out Delores striding toward them with her bullhorn.

"Control yourselves!" she said. "This is not a game. The parade must go on!"

Caleb lifted the pumpkin again so Katie could climb out. They had decided she would have to suit up while on the float.

Delores handed Caleb a face mask that also looked like a pumpkin. "I forgot to give you this. The driver always wears it," she said.

Caleb's face fell, and he slipped the mask over his head. "I can hardly see out of this thing."

"Don't worry, I'm the parade leader," Delores said. "You just follow me and only go about two miles an hour. The whole parade is only five blocks long—you just drive in a straight line."

Katie climbed onto the float, and Caleb helped her into the costume once again.

"See that X on the float?" Delores asked.

Katie looked down and saw a masking tape X to her right. "I see it."

"You stand there," said Delores. "If you move too far to the left, the driver's view will be blocked by the costume."

Katie stood where she was told, and she assumed Caleb had gotten into the driver's seat because she heard the engine start up. She almost fell backward when the float started to move forward, but caught herself and remained standing on her X.

She watched through her small peephole as Delores directed the float out to the parking lot. The parade people cheered as the float passed by the ranks of fairies, pirates, ghosts, skeletons, and zombies. Finally, they were at the front of the line, and Delores announced through the bullhorn that they were ready to start.

The float lurched again, and Katie struggled to stay upright. She took her hands out of the gloves and pulled her phone out of her pocket. She texted Caleb to take it easy on the acceleration. The float began to veer toward the right and then adjusted course. Caleb must have checked his message.

It was just beginning to get dark as the float pulled onto Main Street. The high school band was right behind the float, so all Katie could hear were the drums. She kept her eye on the end of the street, waiting for it all to be over. She kept waving, in the sense that she flapped her hands up and down, and stood with her feet as far apart as possible to give herself a solid base.

Things were going quite well, and she relaxed a little bit. She turned to look at the crowd, recognizing many of her patients. She saw a familiar face in the crowd that she didn't expect.

Eugene Lowe stood at the corner of Main and Second, hands on hips. As they approached, he stepped forward and went to the door of the float. She heard him yelling but couldn't hear what he was saying. The float veered to the right, and the crowd gasped and moved back away from the slow-moving threat. It then jerked back to the left, and Katie lost her footing. She fell over and landed faceup, legs kicking in the air.

She pulled her hands out of the gloves and wrestled with her shoulder straps to disentangle herself. The float had stopped moving and she felt someone pulling at her legs.

"Katie, are you okay?" Gabrielle asked.

"I'm fine, but I need help lifting this thing over my head."

Katie and Gabrielle finally got her free from the costume. The band had stopped playing, and she heard Eugene's voice shouting.

"Ten years, you bastard!"

The crowd surged forward to help Caleb. Eugene had him by the throat and he was screaming at him.

Katie ran up to them. "Eugene, that's Caleb! What are you doing?"

Eugene turned to Katie. "What?"

"That's my brother," Katie said.

Eugene let go of Caleb, who pulled his mask off. He was red in the face and breathing hard.

"I'm so sorry, Caleb," Eugene said. "I thought you were Nathan. Alicia said Nathan was driving the float."

"Alicia is okay?" Katie asked.

"Of course she's okay. She's been with me."

John Carlson appeared out of the crowd. "What is going on?"

"Eugene thought that Caleb was Nathan."

"Oh, that makes assault and ruining the parade okay, then." Carlson said.

"Where is Nathan?" Eugene asked. His eyes were wild and he looked around desperately.

"No one has seen him today," Katie said.

Eugene swore. "Alicia went home to get some things for the baby. She thought it would be safe during the parade because Nathan wouldn't be there." Eugene ran into the crowd.

"Wait!" Carlson said. "I need to talk to you!"

Without stopping to think, Katie ran after Eugene.

45

Eugene had cut through the alley behind the Purple Parrot. Katie caught up with him on the next street over.

"Eugene, wait!" she called.

He slowed and then stopped. "Dr. LeClair, I think Alicia is in danger. We have to find out if Nathan is home."

"Why?" Katie asked. But as she said it, everything clicked into place. Nathan had been the ex-boyfriend who was jealous. Nathan had been absent from the planning meeting the night before Taylor's body was found. And Nathan didn't want Eugene in town bringing up the past.

"I don't have time to explain, but Alicia thinks Nathan may have killed Heather Stone and Taylor Knox," Eugene said. "Come on!"

Katie followed him through a backyard into another street and then through a side yard until she saw that they were in the backyard of a two-story yellow house.

"That's her house," Eugene said. "Nathan's car is in the driveway. We have to get inside."

"Why can't we just ring the bell?" Katie asked.

Eugene gave her an incredulous look. "We can't let him know that we're on to him."

They sneaked through the backyard to the back door. From this close, they could hear an argument emanating from inside.

Eugene started lifting up the potted plants that sat on the back deck.

"Found it!" He held up a key.

"Wait, we can't go in there. It's breaking and entering. Or maybe just entering . . ."

A loud crash sounded from inside, and they heard Olivia crying.

"I'm going in," Eugene said.

Katie looked at this skinny guy with his big ears and ridiculous glasses and wondered what he thought he was going to be able to do against a big guy like Nathan. But she saw the determination in his eyes and nodded.

"Okay, I'll come with you," Katie said.

Eugene put the key in the lock and turned it. He quietly opened the door and stepped inside. Katie followed, and they stood silently by the door. The argument was louder now that they were inside. They stood in the kitchen, listening. It sounded like Alicia and Nathan were upstairs.

Eugene and Katie cautiously peeked in the living room. Empty. They made their way up the stairs. At the landing, Eugene hesitated.

"Don't hurt her, please, Nathan," Alicia cried.

"Stay back, Alicia, or I'll do it. I swear I will."

Eugene and Katie exchanged a look. What was going on?

"They're in the baby's room," Eugene whispered.

They moved warily down the hallway to the nursery. The door was open and they heard Alicia crying.

Sirens sounded in the distance.

Katie stepped into the doorway with Eugene right behind her. Nathan stood on the far side of the room with the crib between him and the door. The window was open wide and cold air gusted in from outside. He held the baby, and his hand circled her throat. One twist and he could break her neck. She continued to cry, but in an exhausted rather than outraged way. Nathan seemed to be ignoring it, as if it were just background noise.

Alicia rushed to Katie as she came through the door. "He walked in when I was packing up more of Olivia's things. He grabbed her and threatened to hurt her if I refused to stay with him."

"Nathan, give me the baby," Katie said. Her voice shook with concern for the child.

Nathan shook his head. "This is between me and my wife. What's *he* doing here?"

"He was worried about Alicia," Katie said. "Eugene, maybe you and Alicia should go downstairs."

Someone began pounding on the front door.

Alicia stepped across the room to join Eugene, but she refused to leave without Olivia.

"It's over, Nathan; the police are here now," Katie said. "You don't want to hurt your daughter."

"How do you know what I want?" Nathan sneered. "I have nothing left now. Alicia is just like all the other girls. She got tired of me and decided to leave." He clutched the baby tighter and she cried louder. "Now she can feel what it's like to lose someone you love."

"Who did you lose, Nathan?" Katie asked in a calm, quiet voice.

Nathan looked bereft. "Heather," he said. "I lost Heather."

"What happened?"

Nathan's shoulders slumped and Katie worried he would drop the baby, but he seemed to catch himself and he readjusted his grip.

"She just broke it off." Nathan shook his head. "For no reason. Said she'd met someone else. But I loved her."

Nathan's eyes pleaded with Katie to understand.

"I'm sure that was very difficult. I've heard she could be cruel to her ex-boyfriends."

A bark of laughter escaped Nathan. "You could put it that way. But I showed her, didn't I?"

"Did you?"

Nathan nodded. "I caught up to her after she left the party. She laughed at me and said she was dating a real man, not a little boy." Nathan stopped. Remembering. "I don't know what came over me, but I grabbed her neck and squeezed. She actually laughed. Looked me right in the eye, while I had her life in my hands, and laughed. I pushed her away, hard."

Alicia gasped, and Nathan looked past Katie to his wife.

"I didn't mean to hurt her. She just made me so mad. She hit her head on a rock, and I couldn't wake her up. I heard someone coming and I ran back to the party."

Out of the corner of her eye, Katie saw Eugene slip out

of the room. She hoped he was going to let the police in—she assumed that was who was pounding on the door.

"What about Taylor?" Katie asked.

"She had to go. She had figured everything out. She'd been talking to people. Picking apart their stories until she realized I was the one." Nathan took a shaky breath. "I didn't want to lose Alicia and Olivia."

Katie took a step forward. "I'm sure you don't want to hurt your baby."

Nathan adjusted his grip on the infant, and she seemed to settle a little bit. Her little eyes were red and swollen and her face was flushed and wet.

They all heard footsteps on the stairs.

Nathan's eyes went wide, and he looked frantically around the room.

Sean Gallagher and a young woman officer stood in the doorway with guns drawn and pointed at Nathan.

"Put the guns away!" Katie said. "You can't shoot him without endangering the baby."

Carlson came into the room and gestured at his officers to stand down. The small nursery had gotten crowded in the past several minutes.

Carlson put his hands out in a calming gesture. "Nathan, you don't want to hurt the baby. Just give her to Dr. LeClair and we can talk this out."

"I'm done talking to you," Nathan said. He stepped closer to the window. He put one foot on the sill.

"Nathan, please, give me the baby," Katie said. "Whatever is going on here, she is innocent. Look at her. She hasn't had a chance to even experience life yet. She's your daughter.

Don't you want to see her walk and ride a bike? Don't you want to hear all the things she'll have to say?"

Nathan kept his eyes on Katie, and one tear escaped as he stared at her. He looked at Olivia and smiled sadly.

"Okay, just Dr. LeClair can come take the baby."

Katie stepped forward, her arms out. She knew the second she had the baby that Carlson and his officers would move on Nathan. She prepared to grab the child and step out of the way.

Nathan waited until Katie was just on the other side of the crib, and then he slowly handed Olivia to her. Katie felt the warm weight of the little girl in her arms and turned away from Nathan, but not before she saw the flash of a gun in his hand. He'd been holding it in the same hand as the baby.

Katie instinctively curled her body around the child and ran away from Nathan. She heard Alicia scream. Then the shot.

And the rest was chaos.

46

The light fixture shattered and rained shards of glass down on Katie and the baby. She kept her head down and ran for the door. As soon as she turned the corner into the hallway, she stopped and was almost run down by Alicia.

Alicia reached for the baby and in her haste ended up hugging Katie and Olivia at the same time. There was another shot inside the room, and Eugene staggered out into the hall clutching his shoulder. Blood seeped between his fingers. He leaned against the wall and slid slowly to the floor, leaving a bloody streak on the robin's egg–blue paint.

Katie made sure Alicia had a good hold of the baby, and then she rushed to Eugene's side. He was awake, but his breathing was shallow and fast. Alicia had appeared at his other side.

"Don't you die on me, Gene," she said. "I just got you back. I'll need my best friend more than ever now."

Eugene smiled weakly and reached a hand out to Alicia.

Katie heard scuffling and banging from inside the room, and then Nathan was being frog-marched out by a none-too-kindly-looking Carlson. Nathan's hands were cuffed behind his back, but that didn't stop him from glowering at Eugene.

"I knew you'd be trouble the minute you stepped foot back in Baxter," he said.

"Gallagher, get the EMTs up here," Carlson barked as he passed the trio on the floor. "How's he doing, Doc?"

"I think the bullet missed anything important, but he needs to get to the hospital as soon as possible. I don't like the way he's breathing."

Carlson nodded and continued down the stairs with Nathan.

Molly Hart came out of the room and bent to help Alicia stand while still clutching Olivia. Olivia's bawling had drowned out the sound of the sirens outside.

Katie, still crouched by Eugene, turned to be sure they were heading downstairs, and when she turned back to Eugene, he had stopped breathing.

"Eugene!" Katie yelled and shook his good shoulder.

She checked for a pulse. There wasn't one. She lowered his head gently onto the floor. She got into position and began chest compressions.

Alicia handed the baby to Molly Hart and came back up the stairs. "Is he going to be all right? What can I do?" Alicia cried.

Olivia cried.

Katie almost cried. Then she heard the heavy boots of the EMTs clomping up the stairs. One of them came and knelt next to Katie and asked for a report.

Between compressions, she told him that Eugene had seemed fine and then stopped breathing. "I think he might have a collapsed lung. I thought he got hit in the shoulder, but it's more central than that. We need to bag him." Katie hoped they had brought their defibrillator.

"You're a doc?" he asked.

Katie nodded.

The other EMT pulled out an oxygen mask, placed it firmly over Eugene's mouth and nose, and began squeezing. He handed a large-bore needle and syringe to Katie.

She inserted the needle over the top of his rib high up on his chest and pulled on the syringe. As the air entered the syringe, Eugene's lung expanded. The EMT nodded at her.

Katie backed away and let the EMTs prepare to defibrillate.

Olivia was only whimpering now, and Alicia was quietly crying and shushing the baby at the same time. Katie gestured that they should all move back as the whine of the machine charging up filled the hallway.

After the thump of the electric shock, Katie checked for a pulse.

"Okay, he's back," she said. The taller EMT put away the paddles. The other put a stethoscope on Eugene's chest and nodded. He strapped an oxygen mask over Eugene's face, and they gently but rapidly moved him onto their stretcher and carried him down the stairs.

Katie and Alicia followed right behind. When Alicia tried to climb into the ambulance, the EMT held up his hand.

"You can't bring the baby," he said.

Katie put her arm around Alicia's shoulders. "We'll

meet him there. They won't let you see him until he's stable anyway."

Molly Hart had followed them out to the street and offered to take them to the hospital. Alicia gratefully accepted and climbed into the back seat with Olivia. Katie was about to slide in after them when she heard a shout.

"Katie, over here!"

Katie turned to see Matt, Caleb, and Gabrielle running in her direction.

She was engulfed by the three of them as they hugged her, scolded her, and told her how brave she was all at the same time.

She extricated herself from her friends and climbed into the police cruiser. Eugene was still her patient and he needed her now more than ever.

47

Thanksgiving morning dawned cold and clear. Katie woke up early and couldn't go back to sleep. She slipped out of bed and padded into the kitchen to make a cup of tea and watch the sunrise. They were planning on a full house later in the day.

She thought about the group that was gathering at her place. Caleb and his new girlfriend, Bella. Gabrielle and her new man, Joseph (a radiologist—Gabrielle was back to dating doctors). Eugene and Alicia and Olivia, John and Linda Carlson. And Miss Simms and Mrs. Peabody had promised to stop by for dessert. Actually, they had demanded that they be allowed to stop by and *bring* dessert.

It was an interesting group. Some were her people and always would be. Others were passing through her life on their way somewhere else.

After Nathan's confession on Halloween, Chief Carlson had interviewed everyone who was there and managed to get the rest of the story from Nathan. The night Heather died, he had run back to the party and convinced Alicia that it was earlier than it actually was. She gave an alibi based on the time he had told her it was when they got home. She had always figured she was just drunk and didn't remember things clearly. But when Eugene returned to Baxter, she had started thinking about it all again. She wondered if Nathan had lied to her about that long-ago party. He'd been so insistent that everyone in the apartment agree on the time they had returned home.

Taylor Knox had been getting too close to figuring things out. She had talked to Alicia and was putting all the pieces together. When he met with her to talk about her "project," he realized she was only carrying out the last wishes of her father, who had failed to find the real murderer all those years ago.

Nathan had been watching Eugene's house as part of his campaign to scare him into leaving town. When he saw Taylor leave Eugene's place, he saw his opportunity to implicate Eugene in another murder. He followed her and convinced her he had information for her project. She still hadn't figured out it was him. They drove to his office, where he strangled her. In a panic, he hid her body in the unplugged freezer he kept in his rented storage unit and drove her car out to an abandoned building in the woods. He thought he would have time to get rid of all the evidence, but then the search moved to Baxter. He dumped her body near Eugene's house in the hope that it would give him some time to get rid of her car.

Later, when Alicia confronted him and said she wouldn't lie for him again, even though she hadn't realized she'd lied the first time, Nathan knew it was all over. Alicia was gone the next day, and Nathan had become desperate to find her in case she was planning to turn him in to the police.

He was facing charges of obstruction of justice, perjury, murder, and manslaughter. Lawyers were circling Eugene, trying to convince him to sue for wrongful imprisonment.

Once Nathan had been arrested, his buddy Mike Sherman had confessed to harassing Eugene and leaving the snake for Katie to find. He denied all knowledge of Taylor Knox, and so far Chief Carlson hadn't found anything to tie him to that crime. Katie wasn't pressing charges, but Eugene and his mother were still considering.

And finally, the one piece of the puzzle that continued to nag at Katie was the question of why the pathology report that was released to the police had only given part of the findings. With Caleb's help, she'd tracked the retired doctor down and confronted him. She'd been disgusted to learn that the answer was simple. Alicia's father and the pathologist had been old frat buddies, and he had done a favor for a friend. He'd left out the part about the strangulation and lack of defensive wounds, knowing that would likely expand the search beyond Eugene. Franklin Stewart had been determined to keep Eugene away from his daughter, even if it meant sending an innocent man to prison. Alicia's father had died five years ago, and Katie was leaning toward keeping the information to herself. It would help no one and would only cause more heartache.

Katie wasn't sure what was going on with Alicia and Eugene, but they had been spending a lot of time together, if gossip was to be believed. And Katie had some good sources.

Katie had just finished her tea when Matt tapped on the back door. She opened it, and he brought some of the cold in with him. He took off his coat, revealing his scrubs underneath. He'd pulled an overnight shift in the ER.

"Why are you up so early?" he asked.

"Couldn't sleep," Katie said. "Too much to think about."

"Like potatoes and turkey and stuffing?"

"Mostly." She kissed him and then said, "And other things, too."

Matt hugged her close. "I'd like to hear about the other things."

Katie laughed. "You go get some sleep. People will be here before you know it." Katie had offered him a place to crash, both so he wouldn't have to drive to Ann Arbor after an overnight shift and to be sure he woke up in time for the Thanksgiving festivities.

Matt yawned. "Okay, just a couple of hours. I promised I'd help cook."

"Oh, I remember," Katie said. "And I'm going to hold you to it."

* * *

Hours and loads of turkey, potatoes, stuffing, gravy, and a few carrots later, Katie's house was full of people sitting around complaining about how much they'd eaten. The doorbell rang and no one moved. Katie hoisted herself out of the armchair and went to the door.

Miss Simms and Mrs. Peabody stood on the porch holding four pies. Miss Simms had a cooler bag hooked over one arm.

"Hope you saved some room; we have dessert!" Miss Simms exclaimed.

Katie heard a muffled groan from the living room.

"Come in. We were just recovering from dinner."

The ladies entered and set the pies down on the dining room table. Mrs. Peabody stood in the doorway to the living room with her arms crossed. She *tsk*ed.

"What this group needs is a brisk walk," Mrs. Peabody said.

There were faint protests.

Mrs. Peabody held up her hand. "No excuses; nothing gets a body ready for dessert like a good walk. I'm sure the doctor will back me up on this."

Mrs. Peabody gave Katie a beady-eyed stare that dared her to contradict.

"Guys, there are four pies here and ice cream," Katie said. "We can do this if we put our minds to it."

Gabrielle stood up and pulled Joseph up with her. Bella tugged on Caleb's hand. Carlson glowered at Mrs. Peabody but stood up as well. Linda took his arm. Soon the whole crew was outside in the crisp evening air.

They walked through the streets, exclaiming at the holiday lights that were shining for the first time of the season. Delores Munch felt that holiday decorations were acceptable only after Thanksgiving and took it upon herself to have a discussion with any early adopters.

Katie took Matt's hand and spied unrepentantly into the other houses with their inside lights on and curtains open. It was like browsing a bookshelf. What stories lay within those rooms?

They returned to Katie's house, invigorated and ready to tackle the pies. Just as they were about to go inside, it started to snow. Large fluffy flakes fell slowly through the tree branches, coating the ground in a blanket of white.

Baby Olivia spoke for everyone when she held her hands out and said, "Oooh."

Katie looked at the group gathered on her front lawn and realized that, whether they were with her for years or days, these were *all* her people.

ACKNOWLEDGMENTS

First, thank you to my editor, Jenny Chen. Her attention to detail, insightful comments, kindness and enthusiasm made working on this book a pleasure.

Thank you to the Crooked Lane team for all their hard work to bring the finished product to readers.

To my partners in crime: Wendy Delsol, Kimberly Stuart, Kali VanBaale, and Carol Spaulding-Kruse. As always, you make the writing journey more fun than it should be.

To my street team: Ann and Robert Eastman, Brent and Nancy Eastman, Alyce and James Mooradian, Kristin and Tom Morton, Barb and Pete Laughlin. Yes, they are related to me. And yes, they will foist my books upon you.

Finally, thank you to Steve, Jake, and Ellie who inspire and support this writer every day.